DRAGON PROPHECY

Sea Dragons Trilogy Book Three

AVA RICHARDSON

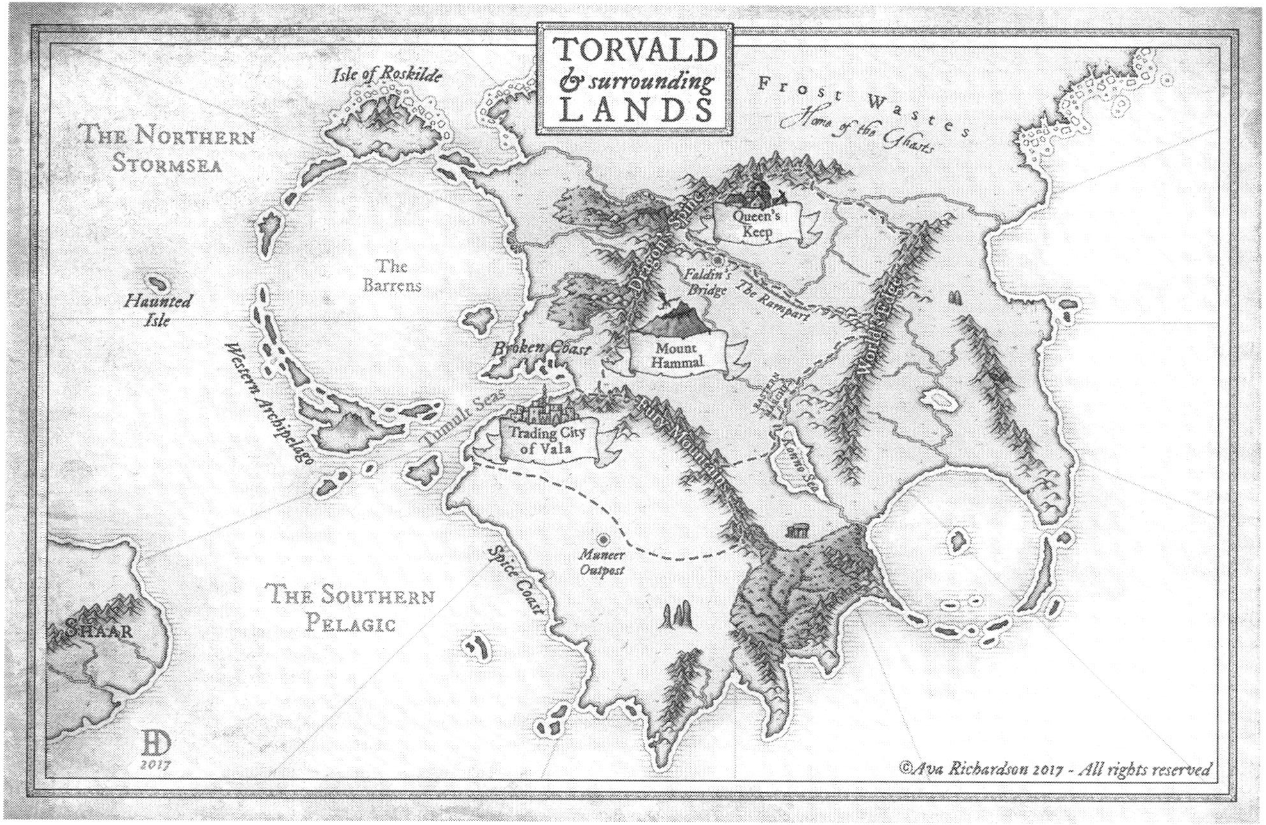
TORVALD
& surrounding
LANDS
Isle of Roskilde
Frost Wastes
Home of the Ghasts
The Northern
Stormsea
The
Barrens
Queen's
Keep
Dragon's Spine
Faldin's
Bridge
The Rampart
Haunted
Isle
Broken Coast
Mount
Hammal
World's Edge
Western Archipelago
Tumult Seas
Trading City
of Vala
Fury Mountains
Konno Sea
Muneer
Outpost
Spice Coast
The Southern
Pelagic
Shaar
HD
2017
©Ava Richardson 2017 - All rights reserved

CONTENTS

Sea Dragons Trilogy	vii
Copyright	ix
Mailing List	xiii
Blurb	xv

PART I
SURVIVAL

1. Lila and the Dead	3
2. Danu, Conflicted	17
3. Lila, Spear or Net	23
4. Danu's Sorceries	32
5. Lila and the Blockade	51
6. Lila, Reunited	62
7. Danu and the Dragon Riders	68
8. Lila, Shush Wyrm	79
9. Lila, Choices	91

PART II
MAINLAND

10. Lila, Desertion	105
11. Danu, the Western Track	117
12. Lila and the Locket	127
13. Lila and the Fearful Dragon	143
14. Danu and the Guardian Dragons	147
15. Lila and Torvald	159
16. Lila and Saffron	174
17. Danu and the King	191
18. Lila, What A Queen Names You	203

PART III
REVENGE

19. Lila, Leader, Captain, Commander	213
20. Danu, Would it be Enough?	231
21. Lila, a Dragon Raider's Mercy	238
22. Danu, a Queen's Offer	249
23. Lila, the un-Free Islands	256
24. Lila and the Storm	259
25. Danu's Sight	267
26. Lila, My People	277
27. Danu, Battle-magic	285
28. Lila and the Witch	290
29. Danu, War Council	301
30. Lila, the Attack	309
31. Danu, the Locket	316
32. Lila, Family	319
Epilogue	328
End of Dragon Prophecy	333
Thank you!	335
More Books by Ava	337

SEA DRAGONS TRILOGY

Dragon Raider

Dragon Crown

Dragon Prophecy

This is a work of fiction. Names, characters, places and incidents either are the product of imagination or are used fictitiously. Any resemblance to actual persons, living or dead, events or locales, is entirely coincidental.

RELAY PUBLISHING EDITION, MAY 2018
Copyright © 2018 Relay Publishing Ltd.

All rights reserved. Published in the United Kingdom by Relay Publishing. This book or any portion thereof may not be reproduced or used in any manner whatsoever without the express written permission of the publisher except for the use of brief quotations in a book review.

Cover Design by Joemel Requeza

www.relaypub.com

Dragon Prophecy

MAILING LIST

**Thank you for purchasing 'Dragon Prophecy'
(Sea Dragons Trilogy Book Three)**

I would like to thank you for purchasing this book. If you would like to hear more about what I am up to, or continue to follow the stories set in this world with these characters—then please take a look at:

AvaRichardsonBooks.com

You can also find me on me on
www.facebook.com/AvaRichardsonBooks

Or sign up to my mailing list:
AvaRichardsonBooks.com/mailing-list/

BLURB

From humble beginnings, a heroine will be forged in fire.

Forced to retreat from the Army of the Dead with her remaining force of Raiders and their dragons, Lila begins to despair that her people will ever be anything but a ragtag band. Even wielding the fabled crown of Roskilde, she cannot unite the Raiders—it seems she is not the one to fulfill Danu's cherished prophecy.

But Danu isn't giving up yet. Though he suspects the evil Havick has obtained an ancient book that will allow him unspeakable power, help may come from an unlikely source: the Dragon Riders of Torvald. These brave warriors could be their last chance to defeat the evil of Lars and Havick—but they are also the Raiders' sworn enemies. Now, Lila, Danu,

Crux, and their friends have no choice but to make a perilous journey into hostile territory to seek allies against the darkness threatening to consume them all. To save her friends, Lila must become the legendary leader she was born to be.

PART I
SURVIVAL

CHAPTER 1
LILA AND THE DEAD

"Lila – wake up!"

I awoke in a snarl of blankets, disoriented, to the sound of Danu hissing at me urgently.

"Wha-?" *Where am I? This isn't home.* My mind scrabbled into wakefulness, noticing the stretched sails of the roof, the smell of wood smoke still hanging in the tent.

Oh yeah. We don't have a home anymore. I almost forgot – or maybe I *wanted* to forget. I was a part of the refugee group that had fled to the southern mainland – the last of the Sea Raiders of the Western Archipelago and what was left of the Free Islanders. We were encamped just under the bluffs that allowed us to look out into the western storm seas, as we regrouped after our last battle with Lord Havick.

"Lila!" This time Danu, with his messy thatch of hair, shook me.

"Ger' off!" I told him angrily, swinging my legs out from the small cot bed and planting them on the floor. *Cold.* This wasn't the colonial mansion of my family home on Malata, either. "I'm awake and I'm sitting up – what more do you want?" I groaned. My father had always said that I was "a joy" to be around in the mornings. I don't think that he was talking descriptively.

Kasian. My heart lurched at the memory. *Dad.* My Sea Raider foster-father who had fallen trying to defend our home of Malata. I gritted my teeth. It's funny how you can almost convince yourself that you have forgotten how much loss hurts, until one little memory brings grief racing back to hit you in the stomach.

"What is it?" I groan wearily, my morning grumbles replaced with the sensation of despair.

"The dragon scouts are back, and something is moving against the encampment," Danu breathed, and in a rush, my mind caught up with what my eyes had been trying to tell me. Danu was dressed in his torn and threadbare black cloak, and underneath it I could see his leather jerkin that the Raiders had loaned him. His heavy canvas trousers had a sturdy sword belted to their side, and on his feet were heavy boots. Danu was dressed for war.

"Damnit!" I seized my own things to struggle them on under my blanket, as the witch's apprentice made an embarrassed noise and turned on his heel. Whatever. You don't grow up as I did, spending most of your life close-quarters on raiding ships and still have that much modesty, I guess. In a trice, I had my breeches on and my tunic wrapped and tucked into my broad Raider's belt, already jangling with hooks and knives and the many other small implements a life at sea requires.

"Throw me the boots, will you, Danu?" I say as I try to tame my hair back into its braid. "And tell me—what is going on?"

"Some of your mother's scouts have just come back – but not all of them. They say they were attacked about a league up the coast from here." Danu chucked first one, then the next of my calf-high boots. I listened as I strapped them on and pulled them tight.

"It was the dead, or so the survivors say. Your mother wanted to head out to meet with them, but I suggested the dragons." Danu looked tense with energy, and my heart thumped with the same. Despite our dire situation, every time I thought about flying on Crux, it gave me the same sense of excitement.

"We hunt?" Crux said in my mind, barreling into my thoughts with all of the strength and fire that he usually did.

Morning, wyrm, I thought as I stood up. *Yes, we are going hunting.* But first, there was one last thing that I knew that I couldn't leave unguarded here. Turning back to my small sea-chest, I opened it to pull out the heavy linen wrap that hid our great prize: The Sea Crown of Roskilde itself. For a chance moment, the linens fell away, revealing an edge of the strange green-gold treasure; its rim crafted into fluting and leaping waveforms.

Strange to think that this sat on the head of my real kin, all the way back into ancient times, I thought, as that same old shiver of unease at seeing it juddered through me. I don't know why I felt squeamish around it. It was mine by right. I was the last heir of Roskilde, Havick was my uncle, and he had killed my blood-parents to get it. But it was also the same object that had sat on my Uncle Havick's head – under whose authority the Black Fleet of the dead had been raised, and under whose direction so many of the Free Islanders had been attacked and purged.

And it is the crown I was prophesized to wear. It was the prophecy that had spurred Danu on his original mission to find me in the first place. It foretold that I would one day wear the Sea Crown again, that I would rise from the waters, and that I would bring in my wake blood, fire, and the dead.

Well, it seemed that I was already fulfilling at least one part of that prophecy, wasn't I? I thought grimly. I had retrieved the Sea Crown, and here the dead are.

"Lila? What are you waiting for?" Danu said, as behind him there was the distant banging of a pot, and a muffled shout of alarm.

"Nothing. I'm coming," I said as I stuffed the Sea Crown

into my backpack, slung it over my shoulder and followed Danu out into the gloom.

※

The camp was still in its predawn dark and the assembled tents and huts were little more than deeper pools of shadow against the greying sky, as Danu and I snaked our way towards the headland where the dragons were roosting. The clouds scudded low across the horizon this morning, and I cursed under my breath. That might mean rain, which would make it harder for me to shoot my bow accurately.

"Where's Mother?" I hissed to Danu, before my question was answered by the sudden clang of a pot from up ahead.

"Up and at 'em, boys and girls!" my mother bellowed from one of the small guard fires as we rounded the last tented avenue. "Up! Up and to your posts – never let it be said that the Raiders were caught in their beds by their enemy!"

Around her was gathered a motley of Raiders and Free Islanders, hurriedly buckling on armor and lacing boots. The Raiders did so with a calm efficiency, and even the Free Islanders I saw now had that air of casual competence around swords and spears. A lot had changed since the last battle. Ever since, the Free Islanders had really started to think of themselves as a fighting force, as opposed to fishermen and traders who happened to be fighting for their lives.

Fighting for their very survival, I reminded myself.

"Ah, Lila – you're here, good." My mother Pela was handing out unlit torches to everyone, and she threw one to me.

I looked at it in confusion. It was a simple wooden stake, with wrappings of linen and old shirts, bound tight and soaked with precious ship oil.

"The dead don't succumb to our weapons, remember?" my mother said. "You'll need flame to kill them."

"I'll be on a dragon, Ma,'" I said dryly.

"Never can be too careful. Put it in your belt and give me some peace of mind, okay?" she said to me sharply, and I heard an echo of the chieftain that she had been back on Malata, *Pela, Thunder of the Seas,* I could almost hear my father's words call her.

"What is it, Lila?" My mother paused as she looked at me with worry. She must have noticed the look of misery that crossed my features every time that I thought about my foster-father, and her husband.

"Just. You remind me of dad," I told her – which I knew wasn't strictly true, but I also knew how she would take it: as a compliment. I recognized an echo in her of that same fierce spirit, seeing the light of the watch fire illuminating my mother's warrior braid and her stern face.

"Funny. I have always thought the same thing about you," my mother said. "Now. The scouts came back not half an hour ago, and they say that they were attacked inland, straight up the coastal track to the northeast of here," my mother said.

"On land?" I paused. "That means that Havick is pushing his invasion." We had already known that Havick had sent the Black Fleet of the Dead ahead of him to reach the southern mainland, but with our success in the last battle, I had somehow naturally assumed Havick would pull them back. How stupid I had been!

"Aye – and more importantly, it means that Havick – or his dead allies, at least – are right on our doorstop!" Pela nodded. "Go. I still need another hour to rouse this ungrateful lot."

"We'll buy you that time," I promised her, crossing the space to fold the fierce little woman into a hug. "And one more thing," I suddenly thought, loosening my shoulder bag and pulling out the wrapped linen bundle with its priceless prize inside. "Take this. Keep it safe," I told her.

"No!" My mother instantly pulled back. "That's yours. You should keep it with you, look after it…"

"No, Mother." I was adamant. "I'm going to be flying and fighting. If anything happens – I need to know that this is safe, I can't risk it being captured by enemy hands again…"

If anything happens. My own words hung in the air between me and my mother as showy as if they were one of Danu's magic tricks.

"I understand," my mother nodded, accepting the heavy burden and instantly turning to put it in her own backpack of belongings. "I'll stay with the fleet, so it will be surrounded by fighting Raider guards," she promised me. And then we had no time left at all, and with a nod at my mother, Danu and I turned, and raced past the last watchfires, climbing to the headland where the dragons were already hooting and whistling.

"You have a plan?" Danu said, wheezing as we jogged up the incline to the land of rocks above.

"Burn them until they stop moving?" I hazarded, earning an eye roll from Danu. I knew what he meant. "We keep most of the dragons back to guard the camp for now, until we know we need them. For the moment it'll be us, Senga and Adair if they're ready," I said. "This is a scout and subdue mission first and foremost."

"Subdue?" Danu echoed. "It's hard enough to kill the dead anyway – let alone 'subdue them'." We crested the rise and saw our dragons were already awake and waiting for us.

"Don't worry, Danu, with these guys as friends, we can do anything," I said, my heart lifting at the mere sight of the great beasts.

"Wave-rider," Crux greeted with his usual name for me, padding forward on claws that I could easily sit inside. Crux was a giant, but still only a young bull dragon – and a rare Phoenix one at that, too. Most of the scales on his body were a midnight black to blue, that would gleam unexpectedly in any light with greens and purples. A fiery line of orange scales edged his paler belly, and his eyes were a lambent green as he lowered his snout to nudge me gently against the chest.

"Hello, you," I said, allowing myself to feel the warmth of his breath and the strength of his heart for a moment. Any anxiety I had about fighting the dead vanished in this simple act. It wasn't just knowing that I would be backed up by several tons of fire-breathing muscle, it was that Crux completed my heart in a way I could not explain. He was a constant, warming flame in the center of my being, and just being in contact with him again reaffirmed our bond.

"We go hunt now?" he chirruped at me, stamping on the ground a little with his forepaws.

"Yes, Wyrm," I teased him, dragging myself away from that shared moment and back to the chill of the predawn, and to Danu's animated discussion with the two young Dragon Raiders Senga and Adair beyond. They were almost of an age with me, and we had grown up together on my father's flagship the *Ariel*. They were also the first two Raiders to take to the dragons I had brought to Malata, and they rode Kim, a long Sinuous Blue dragon that I could see lashing her tail expectantly.

"All right, listen up!" I called, as I made a quick headcount of the dragons we had here. Kim and her brother Thiel, Retax and Lucalia, and of course Crux with me. But so far Senga and Adair were the only riders who had made it up to what I was thinking of as 'the dragon grounds' up here on the bluff. It joined with the rocky cliffs that swept back down to the bay where the smaller Savage Orange dragons nested – who were right now chirruping and calling as they took flight in great billowing clouds.

Only four Raiders on two dragons? I thought for a

moment, before pushing my alarm away. *It would be enough. Scout and subdue, remember?*

I opened my mouth. "We're going to try and slow the march of Havick's dead, but we don't know how many we will face, nor what capabilities they will have." The last time we had met them, they had been surrounded by the strange spectral clouds Danu called the Darkening – some kind of living cloud of fear, from what I could make out.

"But we have dragon fire," I said, patting Crux's leg, who belched a great flare of the stuff at my words. "We'll set lines of fire between us and them, to buy time for my mother to ready the other fighters, and the other Dragon Raiders to get up in the air."

"We're not going for a full assault?" Senga was always the fiercest between her and her brother Adair. She looked at me like she didn't think much of my plan.

"No," I said stubbornly. "Two dragons. Crux and Kim with us. We're going to disrupt and wait for backup, okay?"

Senga shrugged like it was no big deal to her – but I could tell that she didn't agree. I gritted my teeth in frustration. I liked Senga. I didn't want to have to get into an argument with her over this, and especially not in front of the other dragons, who were now stamping and hissing in their frustration at not being asked to join the fight.

"They want to hunt with you, wave-rider. You are First Daughter. You lead us on the hunt," Crux informed me as tact-

fully as a dragon can do (which meant that he barged into my mind and hissed at me).

But no, I couldn't allow them to leave the camp yet. "I need all the other dragons protecting the refugees," I stated again firmly, and I could feel Crux's confusion at this human concern.

"We all fight. Human, dragon, young, old," he stated sullenly – but he was a dragon, and he did not have the same qualms and worries that I had.

"Scout, subdue, and disrupt – for now," I repeated firmly, nodding to Danu, who pulled himself up Crux's far shoulder to slide into his position between the Phoenix dragon's great wings. I joined him, settling onto the leather saddle that we had fashioned, and attaching the guides to my belt clips. Even though I was tired, and I had only ridden Crux just yesterday, it still felt like a return to normal to be here again.

"Are you ready?" I whispered, knowing that both Danu and Crux would hear me.

"I'm ready," Danu said.

"Always," Crux informed me. I turned in my saddle to see Senga and Adair finishing their pre-flight adjustments to their own belts and saddles, before Adair looked up with a broad grin, and gave me a big thumb's up sign.

"Okay, take us up, Crux," I said, leaning forward and placing my hands on his neck. In an instant I felt the surge of powerful draconian muscles, and Crux bounded forward towards the edge of the bluffs. Kim watched the Phoenix dragon with pinpoint attention, starting her own run a few moments after.

There was another jolt as Crux started leaping, once, twice, and—

Up! His claws pushed out from the edge of the rocks and his wings snapped out in a wide fan on either side of us as he jumped into the predawn murk. I felt my stomach drop as it always did, and that coil of terror-excitement that I always felt just before the winds caught us with a strong push.

And we were flying, gliding down the landscape in a short swoop as Crux gathered the momentum for the first big beat of his wings, executed at exactly the bottom-most point of his arc so that we shot into the sky like a speeding arrow.

"Skreach!" A call of joy resounded from behind us as the Sinuous Blue caught the wake of our air currents, and followed us, a little behind and to our right. These great beasts didn't need to be taught how to fly in formation, I marveled, remembering the picture books that I had of the ancient Dragon Riders of distant Torvald. They were always pictured in flying diamonds, or arrows – but the wilder dragons of the Western Isles naturally fell into a wide V like a bow of migrating swans.

Below us the land shot away and I saw the dark blanket of the seas beyond the coast. The lights of our encampment were on our left, more lights kindling in the dark. My mother would be down there somewhere, waking the Raiders and Free Islanders up and pushing torches and sabers into sleepy hands.

As we circled higher over the land, the Phoenix dragon underneath me gaining altitude to speed our eventual swoop north, I could see that full extent of our camp.

We had grown over the last few weeks since the battle with Havick. Of course, I had known this already – as smaller flotillas and boats arrived on a nearly daily basis full of other Free Islanders seeking the only refuge they had from Havick and the Black Fleet – but now, to my surprise, I was looking at a shanty that was almost the size of a small town. Not quite as big as Malata harbor has been – but it was close. Upturned boat hulls (the ones that had been limping, leaking, or too damaged for us to repair with our limited resources) had become small huts and halls, and there were even clearly visible "streets" now. A couple of round timber barns had been erected from the local stands of trees, and now I could see lines of people racing back and forth, carrying equipment, and groups congregating at the shoreline where our lines of small boats were staked out, ready to cast off for the larger fighting ships we had moored in the bay.

It was for them that we fight, I felt a great comfort in admitting– which was odd, now that I thought about it. *Didn't I want revenge? Didn't I want to make my uncle's army pay for what they had done to Malata? For taking the only father I had known from me?*

Of course I did, my anger surged at the memories of everything that I had lost – only now they were also tinged with guilt, at not having thought of them first. *A Raider is supposed to take revenge,* I scolded myself. We live and die by our honor, and our swords.

But why did I feel like I was failing at being both a Raider and a leader?

"I smell them on the wind! Bleurgh!" Crux's thought broke into my mind as we turned northwards, and, for a brief moment, I think I too felt an echo of that dragon sense pass between us. Something foul and horrid, overripe like fruit gone bad, before it vanished again as soon as it had arrived. I reminded myself that I would have to beg Crux sometimes, could he *not* share his mind with me on everything?

Anyway. Our dragon had sensed the enemy, and he now angled his wings to fly towards them as silently as a gliding hawk.

CHAPTER 2
DANU, CONFLICTED

I couldn't understand for the life of me why Lila didn't scramble all the dragons, or at least *more* of the dragons. It was a thought that kept bugging me through our morning flight, and I worried at it like a pained tooth.

Just two? I kept on thinking. *It was almost like she didn't expect us to be able to defeat them? But why – when we had before?* I recalled that last great battle in the straits between the two islands. I had summoned the elementals of the water, and Havick had rushed his Black Fleet towards us, but not only them – but also the malefic cloud of the Darkening as well. The sea had started to freeze (which had, oddly enough, worked more in our favor than his), and the dragons had roared their flame against the enemy.

Admittedly, for a moment there I had been as worried as

Lila must have been that we would fail. When Crux's wings started freezing up, when the Captains of the Dead had claimed the watchtower that we had come to defend, and when the full psychic might of the Darkening had broken around us like a hurricane, it had seemed hopeless.

But we hadn't failed. We had won – that was something, right? *Hell, that was more than something – that was almost miraculous!* So why might Lila be feeling this way – hesitant to commit to battling the dead?

When Lila had instructed us to seize the Sea Crown – believing that breaking Havick's hold on it would be the only thing that stopped the Darkening— she had been right. Lila had raced across the flagship of the Dead Fleet, seizing the crown itself from Havick's head. That instant she grabbed it, the Darkening had seemed to dispel – or greatly diminish— allowing the greater body of Ysix's dragons to attack the fleet. *Then why was Lila worried? We had the Sea Crown now – what could stop us?*

I would have pointed all of this out to her then and there, had we not already been on a mission. Now was not the time to second-guess Lila's leadership. Instead, my eyes scanned the dark of the world beneath us. The dawn was getting closer, and the sky to the far east was paling to a light grey in anticipation. I could now make out much more clearly the lines of hills, streams, and forests below. On our right grew the foothills of the Fury Mountains, somewhere on the other side of which I knew would be the trading city of Vala. Did Vala know that we were here? How could they not?

At distant points here and there on the horizon I could make out the twinkling of lights. Campfires or houses, I realized. *So, there were people living on this side of the mountains!* So far, our scouts hadn't managed to make contact with any other humans, and I was rather starting to believe that this whole area of land had been given over to the 'Orange drakes' as they apparently had a reputation for being fierce and unruly. (Which wasn't now the case around the larger dragons, thankfully; I was even starting to think that they rather looked up to Crux and the others, in the same way that a brood might fondly regard an older sibling.)

But where were the Dead? I thought, peering ahead. The problem with fighting an army of dead people was, that they needed neither sleep, nor rest, nor food, nor light with which to see. They also did not appear to talk much. So, we were looking for a movement of people who had no torches that we would be able to see, that would make no noise, and who all moved with an uncanny connection that did not require them to march in columns.

Great, I thought sourly, before Crux slowed, angling his wings as they flapped, so that we almost hovered.

"Are they there?" I called.

There was a tension in the air, like the heavy feeling before a thunderstorm which I knew presaged dragon tongue. *"They are, Danu. Those prunes in the middle of your face you call eyes cannot see them, but I can,"* Crux informed us both, and my mind was suddenly filled with crystal-sharp images of lurching figures picking their way with surprising care around tree trunks and over boulders. The dragon had falcon-like sight and could share his sensations with those with whom he had bonded.

"But where?" Lila said, looking first over one side and then the other. I copied her example, but all I could make out were the dark humps of trees.

"They are down there, heading towards the stream," Crux informed us, and I swiveled in my saddle, leaning out to find where a small, silvered stream was meandering through the wood. I breathed, waiting.

There. A dark shape lurched into the waters, not stopping or crying out or taking any notice of the sudden cold. It took a step, and another, and then out the other side. Behind it, and further up the bank followed another, and another, and still more…

They were too far away for me to make them out clearly, but on several I saw the dull gleam of the weapons that they held, on others, the rounded shapes upon their back where they must have slung their bucklers.

"There's no bird sounds," I murmured, not really realizing it until I had heard myself say it. In fact, there was no sound *at all!* No bird calls of alarm, no fox shouts, boar snorts. That should have been the giveaway that we were flying directly overhead. *The dawn chorus should have started up by now,* I thought, seeing the grey light now reaching the foothills and turning their faces a washed-out silvery-grey.

"Crux?" Lila whispered. "Can you tell Kim something, but using your mind only – as I fear that I cannot be strong nor clear enough, and I don't want to alert them that we're up here."

"Of course," Crux informed us, and I listened as Lila outlined her plan. We were to backtrack, go back to the next stream of river crossing through the wood and – as much as I hated to hear it, set fire to the wood beyond it. It would be a terrible destruction of land and habitat, but at least the animals had all fled the approaching march of the dead, I hoped.

"That might hold them off for a while. If we make a fierce enough inferno, then they'll have to find another way around," Lila was saying. "It will add hours to their advance."

I nodded that I understood and felt once again that tension of thunder-air as Crux relayed the plan to Kim, as he wheeled silently past her. Lila raised a defiant fist to Senga and Adair, who raised theirs in return. I didn't know how much of Kim's thoughts that they had access to (Crux seemed able to barge into ours without any effort or provocation), but I knew that Senga and Adair were also now experienced enough to trust that their Kim would do the right thing.

We cut through the night air, heading for the patch of forest Lila had targeted, before the Phoenix dragon softly beat his wings to send him into a dive. An attack run.

"Steady, steady…" I heard Lila whispering. The dead were

already climbing up out of the creek to this hill. If we hit it right, just ahead of them—

"*Now!*" Lila shouted, and there was a roar from the Phoenix dragon and a surge of power. I felt a wave of heat pass through the dragon's entire body as suddenly burning light spilled from his mouth, and onto the ancient trees below.

CHAPTER 3
LILA, SPEAR OR NET

Flames swept over the land beneath us as Crux poured his ire onto the land. "Senga! Adair!" I signaled with my hand, indicating that they sweep the area diagonally. With a roar, the Sinuous Blue was in motion, diving downwards before rising up in a long sweep behind us. Orange and red blossomed on the dark land like angry flowers.

"Did we get them?" Danu was saying, his eyes wide as he looked this way and that behind us.

"I don't know," I called, as the Phoenix dragon carrying us turned for another attacking dive.

Pheet! Pheet! From the edges of the burning wood ascended small black darts – *the dead could use bows?* I thought in alarm, before realizing that they could pilot a ship – so maybe using a bow wasn't that difficult for them. I leaned to one side and Crux followed my direction, to avoid most of the terrible hail of arrows with only a few clattering on his thick hide.

"Crux – are you all right?" Worry swept through me.

"Of course. A few pin pricks won't hurt me, Lila!" He let out a roar of victory as I let him arc downwards once more, throwing his dragon-fire over the already burning forest. We barreled into the thick black plumes of smoke, and I just barely remembered to take a deep breath and close my eyes as suddenly I smelled soot and ash. My ears rang with the roar of the fire and the crash of falling trees, and once again I was amazed at the destructive power that even one of these dragons had within them.

It had to be enough to stop them, I thought, opening my eyes to look down when my nose had informed me that we were clear. Danu was coughing behind me, and when I turned to check if he was okay, I noted that his eyes were streaming, but he nodded that he was fine.

The land was now a bonfire of massive proportions, which hurt my heart to see, *but what else could I do?* The camp of Raiders and Free Islanders was only a little way ahead of us now and could probably see the conflagration on their horizon.

A high-pitched whistle alerted me to Senga and Adair, rising from their second attack run to join us. When I made a circling motion with my hand, Adair nodded that he understood. Crux beat his massive wings and we rose into an ever-widening circle around the fire site, out of reach of both the arrows of the dead and the smoke.

"Can you see them?" I called to Danu, who was blinking and peering down.

"I can't see anything. Maybe we got them? Maybe they're all burning?" he replied.

I hoped so, but I couldn't put my faith in hope. The fires had now spread and covered at least a fifty meters wide stretch of the forest. The dead would have to lurch and crawl through that inferno to reach the other side – surely not even they would survive that?

"*Urk!*" There was a funny noise from Danu behind me as I scanned the ground, and by the time I turned around, he was sagging in his place, his eyes scrunched up as he breathed fast and shallow.

Oh no.

"Danu? What it is! What's wrong?" I shouted at him. Had he been hit by one of the arrows? Was he hurt? Was it the smoke?

He growled, shaking his head like he was trying to throw off a cloud of mosquitos, before his eyes found mine. The stern look of concentration on his face made me stop. "It's not the Dead. It's something else. Something coming." He pointed out over the dawning waters, to a sight that I hadn't registered in all of the action.

The land below us was dark and bright – a land of contrasts as the fire blazed and the smoke obscured. But what was stranger still, was the sliver of coast we could see from our great height, which I knew should be a bright, shining metal glimmering with the rising sun – but most of it was obscured by an ugly grey cloud.

"Is that smoke?" I said, knowing already that it wasn't. Something in my heart recognized what it was before my mind wanted to.

It was the Darkening, come to save its children.

I watched as the heavy grey and purple cloud spread out along the coast, eating up the silvered water underneath it until it was all gone. The funny thing was, that I could still see the morning skies behind and above the Darkening cloud, and so it appeared as though a grey line was being smudged out of the world, with sky above, and land beneath. Above us, the silhouettes of Senga and Adair on their dragon were high over the land, circling and awaiting my orders.

"We have to go," I said quickly, my heart fluttering with a rise of anxiety. I knew that the Darkening brought with it panic and fear, but it was impossible for me to tell if this was an 'unnatural' reaction to this strange enemy, or a perfectly justifiable one. I could see the eldritch mist hitting the coast and filling up the space until it started boiling over into the land beyond. Fingers of the strange clouds stretched into the parts of the woods where the fire hadn't reached yet. They moved like tentacles, as if seeking something.

"But I thought we dispelled it?" Danu said, his tone aghast behind me. "The Sea Crown – you *have* the Sea Crown – that vanquished it, right?"

"I thought it had," I said, hearing my own voice sound frail and small in my ears. Isn't that what had happened before? As soon as I had seized the Sea Crown from my uncle's head, the Darkening cloud then had dissipated, losing its power (or so it had seemed to us at the time).

"Ohotto must have discovered other ways to summon it," Danu growled in anger. He had a special sort of anger reserved for Ohotto Zanna, the witch who had been one of the senior sisters where he had trained at the Haunted Isle. Every time that we talked about her and what she had done, it was like Danu felt that he was personally responsible for her actions.

"But it's not the same," I said, directing Crux with my knees to rise higher and further away from the encroaching strange clouds. It felt good to be moving away from that evil, like I could breathe again.

"No," Danu agreed. "It's *changed,*" he said with that same eerie faraway look that made me think he was utilizing not his human senses but his magical ones. Even with my perfectly normal eyes, I could see that something was different. Before, the Darkening had been ugly black and purple thunder clouds, flashing with strange internal lightning, and looking as though it was about to vortex into one hell of a hurricane.

This one though? It *crept*. It was like the *'Dank Colds'* as my father used to call them – patches of sea mist that occurred at the later and early ends of the year, a product of cold waters and only slightly warmer airs, which would cling a few feet above the stilled oceans like a blanket. My father had always said that they were a sign of bad luck – but then again, the chief of the Raiders, my father, had been a suspicious sort.

Imagine what he would say now, I tormented myself by thinking.

"It's not the same" Danu repeated. "It's lost some of its power, I think, but it's gained something instead…"

"Spear or net," I suddenly recalled.

"What?" Danu shook his head again.

"You either fish with a spear or net, and when one fails, you try the other," I said, thinking that this was exactly what my father would have said. "This is what we're seeing. Ohotto and Havick failed with the last Darkening – the spear – and now they're trying the net." Which meant that there would be different ways to fight it, and that it would fight *us* differently, too.

"Come on," I said, raising my voice so that nearby Senga and Adair could hear too. "We need to get back to camp and let them know what is happening."

"Wait – what?" Danu seemed confused at my perfectly reasonable plan. "You have the Sea Crown. The thing that controls it – can't you use it? Dispel it again, just like last time?"

How can he ask me that! I coughed in shock. The Sea Crown was what all this mess had been about. The prophecy. The rightful heir of Roskilde. All of the blood that had been spilled in its name – and after all of the times that I had seen Danu's magic backfire on him! *No. I wouldn't do it.* I was already shaking my head. "No."

"But Lila – the Sea Crown is your birth right!" he pleaded with me. "If anyone can control it, it will be *you* – you can turn its powers to good." His eyes were full of sincerity and desperate belief. He had so much faith in me, it made my heart want to break.

You can't put this all on me. It's not fair. I balked. And besides which – it was no good what he wanted me to try. "I don't have the Sea Crown on me. I didn't even bring it," I told him.

"What?" He looked aghast. "You left it back at camp? How could you?"

All right, buddy – that's far enough. I scowled. I was already feeling pretty powerless and scared at the moment anyway, but now his words just made me feel mean. "Hey! You keep telling me that *I'm* the only one who gets to wear the crown, so surely *I'm* also the only one who says what happens to it, right? And I left it in safe hands. I'm not an idiot, you know!"

"Oh, uh, yeah, I know…" Danu looked stunned by the vehemence of my response. "Of course, I only meant that…"

"Stop squabbling, both of you!" Crux snapped into our

minds, and his anger rushed through me like a stern gale. *"This is not like you. This evil is seeping into your minds. You must guard against it!"*

Really? I thought. It felt to me like it was really me who was angry – but now Crux was saying that I wasn't? Even that thought made me annoyed. Just how many more times tonight would someone else tell me that I don't know what I'm doing, what I'm *feeling?*

"Wave-rider, this is me talking to you. Your bond-friend. You are my heart, so listen to me – or I swear I will drop you in the ocean and let you swim back to camp!" Crux was fierce. *"The darkness seeps into us like poison. It does not make us angry, or hurt, or petty, but it feeds any hurt or neglect that we already feel. That is what is happening to you. Now – guard your thoughts!"*

That was when I felt a sensation like a shove against my mind, a strong reptilian breath and suddenly Crux had left me alone to my thoughts – only it seemed *much* quieter than before. Had he walled me out of his mind and heart? Or was he protecting me from the effects of the Darkening itself?

"Lila?" It was Danu, his voice hesitant now as if he was scared of angering me. "Look." He pointed below us, at where the Darkening had entered the forest and was starting to overwhelm the forest fires.

I didn't understand it. *How could a mist stand the heat of the raging dragon flame?* But somehow it did. It swept against the dully glowing, smoking inferno and built up around it, as if being poured. Then, following some invisible law that I did not understand, it overflowed and subdued the flames in hiss of steam, before repeating the procedure with the next tract of fire.

It was hard to see what was going on underneath those fires, but I scanned the ground anyway. When the steam finally started to clear, I could see scars of blackened waste ground where the stumps and bodies of trees smoked. It looked like we had done Havick's work for him here. It looked terrible.

Something moved amid the sludge and ash. A tiny form burst out of the ground, caked in mud and tree soot, great clods falling from its side as it reached back down to pick up a slagged piece of metal. Its blade was oddly out of shape, but it still had a handle. Other forms burst from under their cakes of soot, and I realized that I was looking at the blackened bodies of the dead, rising once more to continue their dreadful mission.

"We have to call the other dragons," Danu whispered in horror.

I couldn't agree more.

CHAPTER 4
DANU'S SORCERIES

Despite Crux's grumbling, we managed to convince him to fall back to the next line of hills, landing upon an outcrop of rock while we waited for Retax and Lucalia, Kim, and Thiel, to arrive, with Lila's plan that the rest of the dragons Porax, Holstag, Grithor, Ixyl and Viricalia would protect the camp. With a loud thump, Kim landed on the rocks beside us as we slid from Crux's shoulders to the ledge.

From our vantage point almost a league away from the edges of the forest fire and the shambling dead, the land was like a bowl before us – a bowl that was slowly filling up with the strange mist, which was busy extinguishing the fires we had lit.

"It's a good setup." Lila had already moved to crouch right

at the edge of the ledge, looking out over the battlefield. But she sounded worried. I didn't know whether she was trying to convince herself or me. "We've got the high lands around them, the coast on the far side – they'll have to march straight past us to get to the camp."

"Uh-huh," I murmured, but we both knew none of that made it any easier to kill them. Lila must have sensed my hesitance, as she turned around to snap.

"Have you got a better idea then?"

Yes. Actually, I did. "The Sea Crown," I said once more. "Use its powers to dispel the Darkening."

Lila's face once again sparked in anger, but her jaw clenched as if she was biting down on the wave of dark feelings that seemed to be battering at us like a storm wave. I heard Crux's low, warning grumble in his throat.

"I told you before, Danu. That is something that is not going to happen," she said carefully.

"Even to save the camp?" I pointed out, the severity of the situation making me stubborn. Lila shook her head.

"Lila?" It was wild-haired and wild-hearted Senga, skidding down the rocks to stand at Lila's side. She had no fear of heights at all– which I guessed came from spending half her life climbing up and down a mainsail, though Lila even now sidled back from the edge a little bit more. "She doesn't have to wear that silly thing if she doesn't want to, mage." Senga was defiant, turning to her friend. "You said it was a curse for everyone anyway, right? Who wants anything to do with *that!*"

What? "You told her it was cursed?" I said in shock. *Is that what Lila thought about the Sea Crown?*

"I said it was *a* curse." Lila said pointedly, her eyes sidling to the edge as she took another step towards the rocks once more. "Look what damage it has done to the world so far. To the Free Islands. To Malata. Even to Roskilde."

"Is that what all this is about?" I said in sudden comprehension. "You have no intention of taking up the Sea Crown, do you? Of becoming the Queen of Roskilde? You just want to lock the crown away and go on being a Raider!" Everything I had done, everything that I had put myself through, I thought in a flash of anger. Right then it was hard to care if it was an anger born from the dark enchantment ahead of us, as it swelled to fill my chest. *I left Sebol to find you,* the thoughts flared in my mind. *My home was almost torn apart by Ohotto and I wasn't even there to help them because of that crown!*

"Look at what the crown does, Danu!" Lila said fiercely. "Havick and Ohotto were using it to control that thing out there. To summon it or whatever. I don't want anything to do with that – and neither should you!"

"But Lila – they clearly have some other way of controlling the dead and the Darkening now, so the Sea Crown is safe to use, right?" I pointed out – but even a part of me knew that 'safe to use' was a bit of a stretch. The libraries of Sebol had many stories of strange cursed artefacts that could be found in the world. That awareness dug at my conscience like a splinter, only making me more annoyed. *But it wouldn't be cursed for Lila. She was the rightful heir. It was her destiny.* "And what about the prophecy?" I added. The prophecy that Lila would have the Sea Crown had been made by none other than the Matriarch of the West Witches themselves, Chabon. Surely the fact that she predicted it meant that it would be safe, right?

"The prophecy says that I bring fire, blood, and death when I have the Sea Crown!" Lila's voice rose, and she pointed back into the bowl of steam and strange, oddly-glowing mist. "Now take a look down there and tell me that isn't exactly what is happening!"

I opened my mouth to counter-argue, but Lila had already beaten me to it.

"No, I don't want to use the Sea Crown – even if it can control the Darkening, Danu. I don't want to be tainted with that. I don't want the Raiders to be tainted with that. I won't be anything like my Uncle Havick!" Her words ended on a shout, her bottom lip quivering just a little and her eyes wet with tears.

Oh. What an idiot I had been – my rage and bad temper evaporated from me as fast as it had built up, leaving me feeling weak and wobbly. *This is what it has all been about.* I realized then just how hurt Lila was. *She thinks that she'll turn out like Havick.* This girl had lost her foster-father, and the only people that she had ever cared for – the Sea Raiders –

weren't even related to her, and I've been banging on about her real family – who turn out to be tyrants, or worse.

"I, I'm so sorry, Lila, I didn't know that you felt so strongly," I apologized, feeling terrible. *How could I have pressed her to do something that she didn't want to?*

"No?" Lila looked at me reproachfully. "You should have asked."

"You're right, I should have." I muttered, looking down at my feet as the sky was split by more shrieks of trumpet-calls of the other dragons.

"Never mind." Lila waved her hand to indicate that the argument was over (but not forgotten, at least by me. *How could I have pressed her so hard like that?*) as Crux emitted a keening whistle, and Lila was turning to wave her hands at the incoming dragons.

Their great bodies glistened where the dawn-light hit them. Shining blues and insect-green. Porax, Holstag, and Ixyl, Grithor and the others soared through the skies and it felt like they were bringing the morning with them. Just seeing them lifted my heart a little and made me regret our argument all the more.

"Shark patrol!" Lila was shouting up at the Raiders who sat on their backs, turning one fist in a wide circle in the air.

"What's that?" I asked a little warily – not knowing if Lila would even talk to me right now.

"It's a Raider move," Adair said from his place on the rocks above me. He sounded annoyed, but not as angry as his sister was with me, clearly. He had wild black hair and an open tunic, with his sabre strapped to his belt. He had grown from the scrabbling lookout rope-rigger that I had first met last year to a capable young man. I wondered for a moment if *I* looked different now too.

"When sharks attack, they encircle their prey, driving them into a fish-ball, before each one dives in, one after the other until they frenzy." Adair mimed the movements with one hand encircling his other stationary fist. "We Raiders copy it, when we have enough small boats and we're facing a larger galleon or something," he said over his shoulder as he scrabbled back up to the Sinuous Blue Kim, who was already keening with eagerness to get into the air with her brothers and sisters.

"Oh." I saw what Lila meant to do – encircle the bowl of land with the dead and the Darkening in the middle, and then dive-attack it like the sharks did. We would be fighting. *With only five dragons?*

"And mage-boy!" Adair called out to me from the back of Kim's leg as he dangled for a moment. "Don't worry about Lila. She's a Raider. You've apologized, and when she's calmed down, she'll remember that. We shout loud, but we know who our friends are," he said seriously, before quickly clambering up to his seat.

"Bah. I wouldn't listen to *his* advice," Lila muttered heavily under her breath. She must have overheard.

I just had to hope that what Adair said was true, because I didn't want to be going into battle with bad blood between us.

"Danu?" I looked up in surprise to see that Lila was already striding towards me, her short council with Senga now broken. "Senga had an idea, which I think might work. We follow her lead on this one."

"Absolutely," I agreed, trying to search out her eyes to see if she was still mad, but she had already swung herself up Crux's far leg and I just had to do the same if I didn't want to get left behind.

The newly arrived dragons started to circle the bowl of hills that opened out to the coast, rising high into the sky at the seaward edge to avoid having to fly through the supernatural fog. We had a little time, it seemed, while the Darkening was still slowly overwhelming the forest fires below.

"That one!" Lila called to Crux, pointing to the rocky edge of a hill behind where Kim the Sinuous Blue had just landed. I was trying to puzzle out what Senga's plan had been, until I saw the Sinuous Blue seize a great lump of gargantuan rock in her claws from the hilltop and, with a kick of her back legs and a grunt of effort, she was in the air (albeit flying lower than before). The boulder was easily several times the size of her riders Senga and Adair. As Crux scanned the ground for his own boulder, Senga called, directing with her hands as the Sinuous Blue beneath her let the rock carry her downwards, adding speed to her dive along the slope of hills until it seemed that she was going to swoop straight into the Darkening itself.

"*Hai!*" Senga shouted, and in that moment, Kim released the great boulder with a roar, and snapped her wings to skim the top of the fog and soar upwards to join the encircling others.

Crash! I heard the dull boom as the boulder hit the hillside, skid through the skree and then jump – spinning in the air as it bounded into the forest, scattering burning trees on either side of it as it powered into a group of the burning, lurching dead.

With a joyous screech, Crux selected a fire larger boulder and was already heaving it out of the earth to follow Kim's example, only, selecting a different slope to bounce his own missile down. I didn't know if even this could kill the already-dead, but I was certain that smashing them to smithereens would at least slow them down, right?

I could only hope.

Whump! Our boulder smashed through the burning trees, spinning several of the dead into the undergrowth like figurines in a children's game, before disappearing into the mist like a rock into water. It was oddly unimpressive how the boulder was swallowed up by that malevolent evil without even a ripple or a reaction – even the sound of crashing through the trees was muffled by the strange fog.

"Come on, Crux – you can do it!" Lila called as he turned in his flight and rose up over the land and out, turning away from our enemy. Tiny black darts rose from the mist below to clatter uselessly against his hide.

"Now!" Lila called, and the second part of the Lila-Senga plan went into action. The other three dragons started their strafing attack runs, spilling fire into the mist like molten gold. Instantly, the air was filled with steams and smokes as the Darkening tried to contain and overwhelm the new attacks. I even started to believe that we were winning.

But I was wrong.

"Ach!" Pain swept through Crux's mind and washed into my own. What was happening? "Crux?" I called, "Have you been hit?"

"It's nothing. Just a scratch." He hissed in anger, joining the rear of the attacking flight to line up for his own dive.

But something was wrong. The tremor shivered through the dragon – physically this time, and not in my mind. "Lila?"

"I know." She turned, her face pale with worry. "Where is it – there's no wound ahead of me!" She was already unclipping herself from the belt, intending to search for the injury if she could, I imagine – but I wouldn't let her.

"No – I'm further back than you, I'll go," I called, detaching myself from the leather saddle. Instantly the fierce winds pushed and pulled at me.

"I told you I'm fine!" Crux growled, his pain lending anger to his words. But I wasn't so sure. I could feel the knot of angry pain in his mind, although he was trying to shield it from me.

Suddenly, I had a thought. If I could sense the dragon's pain – could I also sense *where* it was? As he had shared his senses with me before, could I not do the same, from within my own mind?

"Danu..." Crux growled warningly, but I knew that I was onto something. I was a dragon-friend, one of the rare people in the world with the innate ability to understand and sense the dragons of the world, to reach out to them with my mind and make contact. Why had I not thought of this before? I wondered stupidly. It had always been the dragons who had initiated contact with me, and now I wanted to reverse that power and be the one to use the dragon senses myself. Maybe it was because the West Witches hadn't taught me about my ability. Once again, I felt that slight tick of frustration at being treated like I was a danger and an unknown by that powerful mystic order. The first mage to be trained since Enric the Dark King. Had the West Witches kept these secrets from me because they were scared of what I could become?

But there was no time to worry about my own problems – Crux was hurt. Taking a deep breath, I tried my best to reach out with my mind to the dragon – only to feel Crux's angry wall of reptilian flame.

"No, Danu. This hurt is mine."

"You said yourself that we were one thing," I responded. "You, me, and Lila." Stubbornly, I found that place in my own heart that was forever given to this brave beast, and from there slipped easily into the dragon's own senses…

Power. And pain. I could feel the pull and drag of the powerful muscles, the tight-knit overlay of the hardened scales that could turn aside sword blows, the primal fire that was forever in his – *my* – heart.

A dragon's senses are exquisite, unlike any other creature on the face of the world, and instantly I was overwhelmed by the roar of the winds, the crackle of the flames below, the popping of wood and the rustle of the other Raiders in their seats. Elsewhere, there was also the roar of snow-melt in the Fury Mountains, and the clash of swords and shouts from a battle farther south from us – *the camp?*

And pain. Pain was radiating from the dragon's side, just below the line of green and orange scales that demarked his heavier back scales from the more flexible belly ones. It was spreading like a fungus under his hide, a few meters in front of his rear right leg.

"I've got it!" I shouted, snapping my senses back into my own body and reeling as I started to climb, hand over hand clutching to the barbs of the dragon's spine ridge, grateful to just be Danu, a human once more.

"*You shouldn't have done that. This is my pain!*" Crux growled, and a tremor passed through his scales in the same way that a cat would flare their fur. He was annoyed with me and hurt – but Crux was a young bull dragon, and probably thought he didn't need any help. He would have to come to understand that I was here to help, and that neither Lila nor I were going anywhere.

It was hazardous going, crabbing down the back of the dragon between his wings and heading further back. After I had passed the midpoint of his spine, echoes of that pain shivered through me with every handhold that I took. His skin was sensitive, and every movement I made only made him more aware of the pain.

"I don't like this, human," Crux hissed. *"I don't need help! Dragons are excellent healers!"* Did I detect a note of worry in his voice, or was it just hurt pride?

"This is for your own good – please, Crux, trust me," I whispered as I tried to move as gently as possible until I could see where his rear right leg was curled up beside his belly. *I know some healing magic,* I thought, *but would it be enough on such a vast creature?*

Using the leather straps attached to my saddle, I quickly tied one into a sailor's hitch, passed it over the nearest tine and leaned back.

"Woah!" I slipped a few feet straight away, the leather strap burning even through my glove as I caught it. *Okay, Danu. You can do this.* Not for the first time I wondered how on earth the Dragon Academy at Torvald performed their aerial routines, and why on earth we hadn't spent some time trying to figure them out.

"Worrying won't help you now. Just get on with it!" Crux screeched into my mind, which I took to be a good sign. At least he was talking to me.

Taking a breath, I recalled the calming incantation that Afar herself had taught me, picturing the simple circle with the rippling wave passing through it. My mentor had first used that on me when I had been young and newly arrived on the isle of the West Witches. I had still thought of it as The Haunted Isle then, not Sebol, and every strange-garbed, austere and uncanny woman I had met had filled me with panic. I had skinned my knee collecting mussels on the rocks of the isle, and Afar had found me, blood pouring down my shins, and said this simple spell:

"Ma Pui, ma pui,
take my hurt, give it away,
ma pui, ma pui,
give me peace this day."

I said the words as I imagined the symbol - not knowing which part had the power, or even if it would work – but I felt the calming blue sensation rise up in my heart and pass through my hands and into the side of Crux beneath me. Instantly, there was a shiver of the great wyrm's scales and a rattling sigh. The pain was still there, but my little cantrip was doing something to ease the hot and inflamed flesh and allow me to continue my task.

With gritted teeth, I released my hold on the leather strap

and let gravity take me. I slid down the curve of Crux's side, my boots hitting his rear hip.

"Skreyargh!" he roared in pain, as I settled and clung to his side.

"I'm sorry, almost there…" I said, turning my head to see the source of the problem. Just a few feet ahead of me was a place where the scales had buckled to either side around a black dart. An arrow, unlucky enough to hit the space between the scales just right to find purchase.

Fish-meat! I cursed the dead, leaning out over the leg to reach the arrow.

"Hssss!" As soon as my hands touched it the dragon shuddered once more, and I had to pull back to my crouching spot on his hip.

"*Ma pui, ma pui…*" I chanted, willing the healing energy into him. It seemed to be working, as Crux, with shuddering movements, pulled the leg that I was crouched over up a little to give me a better position to reach the arrow. I kept up my litany of magic as I slid my hands towards the offending item.

It was rising from the flesh of the dragon, I saw in wonder. My simple little healing charm, coupled with the dragon's innate power, was working to expel the arrow from his body, and reknit itself behind it. I marveled again at the magical might of the dragons of the world, and what we could achieve when humans worked in tandem with them. It was true that my magic felt ten times more powerful when I was in close contact with the dragon.

"That is why..." Crux's mind was tight through his pain. *"Why so many dark sorcerers want us dragons for their experiments. They see us as fuel."*

"Not to me, you're not," I said, sparing the words from my mouth before, with a final push of my mind, I said the words to conclude the healing. The arrow, looking horribly gnarled like it was made out of black thorn wood, drew itself out from between the scales, but seemed unwilling to release its final bite for a moment, before the dragon shook his side, expelling the arrow and sending it spinning to disappear into the maelstrom of fire and fog below.

"Thank you, Danu," Crux said, in a rare sign of gratitude from the Bull Phoenix.

"You're welcome," I said, feeling clear-headed and lighter hearted myself. Healing magic always works like that, helping the sender a little as well as the receiver. I climbed back up Crux's side, aware that he still felt some pain from his side, and that his body was tender from the injury, but happy with my work.

The thrill of magic was strong in my veins, and I felt even better about my argument. Lila wouldn't hold a grudge against me. We could overcome any obstacle.

In fact, I was certain that we could beat these dead, if I just used a little more. As I scrambled back to the dragon's central spine, instead of finding my way back to my seat, I stood carefully, each hand holding the adjacent tines of the dragon's back ridge as I stared out at the battle.

Or not so much of a battle, but rather a conflagration. The four dragons were doing strafing attack runs into the fog or seizing boulders to launch down the hillsides, and the destruction was a cataclysmic, awesome sight.

"Danu? Are you all right – thank you for healing Crux. I can tell he feels much more comfortable," Lila called to me, her face serious as I laughed.

"I'm fine!" I shouted, as the ripple and surge of magic and dragon power flooded up through the dragon and into me. How could we lose, when I had this great reservoir of might? I released one hand to stretch it out towards the nearest of the foothills, and concentrated.

"Danu – what are you doing!" I heard Lila call.

Silly Lila. She doesn't understand magic, I found myself thinking. *Magic makes you powerful.*

"Skreee!" A sharp whine of alarm pierced through the air, and I saw that the Stocky Green Retax had strayed too close to the Darkening fog. Thick pillars of the stuff was somehow flowing over his lower legs and tail, refusing to break apart with the dragon's frantic thrashing. *Silly dragon,* I thought. *But no matter. I had a plan.*

"Danu – we need to help Retax!" Lila's voice rose into an alarmed shout.

"In a moment, Lila!" I said happily, as I reached out with my magic, to feel the different plates and bumps of the rock underneath the hill I had targeted. Ah, so it was put together just like so, I could see. Meaning all I had to do was to shake that large one there…

"Danu, careful – this is a great act of magic…" Crux said in my mind.

"I can control it!" I grinned.

"No, Danu – you do not have the reserves of power! You cannot do this alone!" The dragon was insistent.

Another anguished shriek from Retax.

"Crux! I have to – look at Retax!" I shouted at him.

"Danu!" Lila called as I pulled with my hands savagely, hauling at the rocky insides of the hill, to see the grass suddenly tear, great gobbets of earth break apart, and the hill to start sliding downwards into the Darkening. If we couldn't burn them, then I would bury the dead!

Boulders the size of carts broke from their ancient moorings, rolling and shaking down the collapsing hill, knocking others from their beds along with great swathes of earth and stone. Dust billowed into the air, obscuring my handiwork as the hill collapsed into the fog, engulfing half the land.

"Danu – no!" *Slap.*

Lila hit me, hard across the face and my magic snapped out, making me reel and lose my last handhold on the tine.

With a grunt, Lila seized my shirt front to stop me from falling off Crux's back, dragging both of us into a crouching position on the dragon's back.

"What?" I said, confused.

Lila had unclipped herself from her saddle, and, without

re-attaching as I had done, she must have quickly climbed to where I was to hit me hard across the chops, and then save my life. Although, as I opened my eyes and felt a thud of a monumental headache, I could see through the rising pain that she didn't look happy about it.

"We almost dropped into the accursed Darkening, you idiot!" Lila snapped, seizing one of my cold hands and curling it around the nearest tine. "Hold on!" she shouted, returning to her saddle and leaning over against Crux's neck.

"What happened?" I said blurrily, and "Retax! Is Retax all right?"

"They escaped, fool of a mage. Lucalia helped him," Crux said, his voice weak in my mind.

"Crux? What's wrong!?" I whispered into the scales against my face. They didn't feel as warm as they usually did. Was it the injury?

I was met by dragon-silence for a moment. *"Partly. But it was your magic. You were too deeply entwined with my soul."* Crux grunted. *"It costs. It costs either you or it costs me, but still it costs."*

"What? I don't understand?" What had I done?

"Magic is power. And dragons have magic running through them. You were casting a powerful spell. How could I let you kill yourself by using up all your life-force in one act?" Crux groaned.

It wasn't only Lila who had saved my life, but now the Phoenix dragon had done so as well. He had freely given more of his life and strength to me, because I was too stupid and intoxicated to listen.

"Oh Crux, I am so sorry…"

More dragon silence, making me feel terrible.

But at least, maybe, that spell had managed to halt the dead for a while? I tried to tell myself. It would give us time to get back to camp.

Our camp in the south. I suddenly remembered what I had sensed through Crux's own hawk-like senses. Fighting from the south. The camp must be under attack!

CHAPTER 5
LILA AND THE BLOCKADE

I couldn't believe Danu. He spent half the battle trying to tell me that I needed to use the Sea Crown – that same, terrible object that my uncle used to summon the dead and the Darkening both – and then he went and almost sucked the life out of Crux!

"I gave my life freely, Lila," Crux murmured at the back of my mind. But even I could tell that his voice sounded weaker, hesitant even. Not his usual bluster full of fire and fury.

"But still…" I muttered under my breath, too low for the pained Danu to hear, but not that I cared overmuch if he did. "He had no right to ask that of you."

"He didn't ask me. I gave him my life-force to stop him draining all of his own," Crux pointed out, as his body wobbled in the air. Even connecting with me in his mind was

causing him difficulty and I gritted my teeth at Danu's foolishness as we rushed south over the dark land.

Had we done enough to halt the army of the dead? I didn't know. I didn't think so – but it was hard to denounce the act of terrible magic that Danu had wrought. *He had destroyed an entire hillside!* I thought, with a flush of panic. I had seen him throw magic about before now, of course, when he had summoned the elemental ships against Havick's forces, when he had 'disappeared' Crux and us both as we had sneaked into Roskilde, but nothing like that. That was the sort of stuff out of legends. Out of nightmares.

No wonder the Western Witches were wary of training him. My stomach fluttered once again with worry and nerves. It suddenly dawned on me just how much this whole situation could spiral out of control – and I didn't mean us Raiders camping on the southern lands (that was already pretty chaotic), or the Darkening and the dead's attacks. I meant Danu.

No one should have that much power. I knew it as solidly in my bones as I knew I loved Crux. It only made me want to throw that damn Sea Crown away all the more – apart from the fact that it would probably wash up on the shore and get used by some other unsuspecting human. That was what the Witch's Prophecy of Roskilde was all about, wasn't it? That this was the time that the Sea Crown would be found, and used, and that it would bring disaster to the Western Archipelago. As unhappy as I was to admit it, I was starting to feel almost powerless in the face of that destiny - and threatened by it.

I don't want it. I don't want that future. I don't even want the Sea Crown!

Behind me Danu was slumped in his saddle but at least he had managed to tell me what he had sensed through Crux.

Which was another thing. *Why hadn't Crux told me that he had heard fighting to the south?* Did the dragon just not know what it was that he was hearing – no, I couldn't believe that. Just how hurt was Crux, really– despite Danu assuring me that he had healed him?

"Crux?" I whispered as the lightening lands swept in a blur underneath us. I leaned forward to place my hands on his dark midnight-blue scales, feeling the ghost of warmth under my hands. Crux was usually a lot warmer than this. And a lot closer to my thoughts whenever I was in contact with him. Now, when I reached out I sensed that he was far away – just a sensation of warmth like a fire at the other end of a room. *Crux?* He didn't respond, but he continued to fly. Was he holding himself apart from me, so that I wouldn't be any more alarmed than I already was?

"Lila?" shouted Senga, falling back on her and Adair's dragon Kim to glide just above us and to our right. "You're falling behind!" she hollered over the whip and whistle of the winds, and I looked up to see that it was true. There was Retax and Thiel, already as small as crows on the wind, while Kim must have swooped back around to see what was holding us up. A quick look behind me revealed Danu's still groggy and swaying form and behind that, Crux's tail and the rising smoke and mists of the destruction we had caused. This was bad, I thought. Even knowing that we had to do it to stop the dead, the sight of so much land being torn up, burnt, and demolished filled me with foreboding. *What was happening to us?*

Turning back again however, I saw that there was trouble ahead of us as well. We were on the last leg before the coast jagged in to a curve of inlets and broken rocks. There, where a fairly substantial but meandering river flowed out into the bay was where the Raider and Free Islander camp was. Or should be.

But the sky there was filled with smoke as well – not coming from cookfires, but from the waters of the bay. There were Roskildean galleons blockading the bay, and already I could see the Raider boats racing out to meet them. With the Army of the Dead behind us, and Havick's navy in front of us, I suddenly realized what had happened.

This had been a trap, and we had fallen directly into it.

"Attack the galleons! Break the blockade!" I shouted, but the only other dragon to hear me was Kim at our side. Crux was too slow – we needed to move faster – but the Phoenix couldn't. The great dragon's body trembled beneath me as

Crux tried to push himself onward as fast as I wanted him to go – but it was a strain, even for him.

"I don't think we should leave you!" Senga called out to me as we started to circle the camp. She looked worriedly at Crux underneath us.

"Don't worry about us!" I waved them on. "Spread the message to the other dragons. You *must* break that blockade, or else we're doomed! Now go. Go!" I commanded her, using my father's authoritative bark to do so. With a final concerned look, Senga nodded, set her head forward, and Kim sprang like a released arrow towards the fight.

"Right, dear friend. This isn't getting us anywhere," I said, quickly changing my plans. Normally I would have asked Crux to fling us headlong into the center of the fight, but I couldn't now. Even if he wasn't talking to me, Crux must have sensed my hesitancy, as he was already swinging around in a wide arc around the near side of the camp – where there was no fighting. Almost as if he was avoiding the battle – which was not like Crux *at all*.

"It's going to be okay," I whispered at him, hoping that his super-sharp dragon hearing, at the very least, allowed him to hear me. On the other side of the bay stood the cliffs where the Orange drakes nested. They were high and looked out over the bay almost as high as a mountain. "If you can, I want you to set us down in the camp, and then I want you and Danu to get up there to those cliffs, with your friends, the drakes, you understand?"

"They're not my friends," a ghost of his old arrogance in a whisper at the back of my mind.

At least he could still argue. His wings trembled as he slowed our descent to the wide sand and shingle spit before landing awkwardly, hopping and stumbling.

Oh, Crux, my heart went out to him. Would he make it up to the cliffs? What other choice did I have? I couldn't risk bringing Danu into the battle with me at the moment, not after what had happened. His magic might make it worse. I turned to secure Danu a little tighter into the saddle, before I slipped down to land in a puff of sand, turning to embrace him on the snout as was our custom. He felt cool, dank. "You get out of the way. Rest. Wait for me." I turned to survey the camp.

It was in uproar – but thankfully a semi-organized one. There were teams of Raiders and Islanders running to the boats (three were already out on the water and plowing towards the wide circle of the blockade) and still more were hurriedly packing things into sea chests. I ran for the nearest collection of people.

"Just take essentials. Weapons, food, tools. We can find anything else!" I called to the surprised family of islanders as I made my way through the shores of the camp.

"Lila?" It was Costa the Quartermaster, organizing the teams of fighters into each boat. Beside him was Thin Jac, One-Eyed Dima, checking to make sure that every Free Islander had the appropriate weapons and armor. "Thank the seas you're here, Lila. It's madness out there," Costa said.

"What news from the north?" He cast a wary eye to the highlands and beyond, where there was still a pall of cloud and ash.

I didn't even know what to say. Good? Bad? We might have halted the dead for a bit – but we also had the Darkening to contend with now, as well. As it turned out, Costa read my grimace well.

"I see. Well – about time for a change anyway. We Raiders are better on the water, right?" He tried to smile.

"Where's Mother?" I looked around the camp.

"Already out, on the *Ariel*." Costa nodded to the edge of the bay, where I could see the *Ariel* and the *Fang* had already engaged with the nearest of the galleons. There was a *phoom!* of cannonade as both sides tried to ram into each other.

"We've got more boats than them," I said critically. "If we can get our entire fleet out, we can swamp them."

"Aye, but half of them are still undergoing repairs…" Costa shuddered at the memory of the unholy fight for the watchtower. "But you're right. I'm getting the Raiders out first, then Free Islanders who have some naval experience."

"Good." I nodded. "Two banks." I held up my hands slightly apart, like opening double doors. Costa knew immediately what I meant, nodding vigorously. Another simple Raider movement, used to separate a larger force. If we presented two 'walls' of boats, the enemy would have to split their forces to deal with us. With our boats being the lighter and quicker, having Havick's galleons in smaller clumps gave us the advantage. "Can the families fight?" I asked.

"Some." Costa shrugged. "But not all. Plenty of old folks and kids in the camp."

"Okay." I nodded. "The larger merchants' ships join the fight, put the vulnerable into the smaller fishing boats." I knew that these were also the fastest moving of all of our assembled craft. "Hold them back, in the bay here if you can – when we've created a wide enough opening, they get out to sea and —" *The families couldn't go west, back to the archipelago as that was all Roskildean territory now. They might be able to go south, towards the Spice Coasts – but would Vala accept them?*

That only left north –where the Darkening had made landfall.

"Dammit!" I hissed, calling a snap decision. "South it is. Tell them to head for the Spice Coasts, and the Raiders will follow if we can."

My decision annoyed Costa, I could tell from the sudden alarmed beetling of his eyebrows, but he was also a Raider's Raider. Rising up to be the Quartermaster of the *Ariel* (and thus the second in command, under my father or mother) he understood hierarchy, and when to take an order and when to argue. Right now, I was thankful he took the order and started barking commands to the others.

I rushed to help those I could to the fishing fleet, although I really wanted to be out there beside my mother, fighting

Havick. Was my uncle out there on those dark waters even now? Was he searching for me, to have his revenge?

No time. What I could do, right here and now, was to help those infirm and young into the boats. *Another reason why I didn't want to send all the dragons north either,* I reminded myself. These people were my responsibility now as well. They had come to us Raiders to ask us to shield them from *my* uncle – and what had happened? They were now fleeing their new home for a second time.

And Havick was my uncle. My blood. I felt partly responsible for their plight. That was the reason I had been hesitant to attack the Army of the Dead this morning – not only because I didn't want anything to do with the Sea Crown. But because of my debt to the Western Isles. The prophecy said I brought blood and fire and death to them, and I wanted to do what I could to save them from it. *How could I throw them into the fight against such a powerful and strange enemy? An enemy that was summoned by MY uncle?* No. This was *my* debt, not theirs.

But catching a glimpse of that heavy cloud of ash and smoke to the north, to the site of our previous battle this morning, – how could I not be aware of the danger I was already putting these good people in?

With a roaring sound, the encircling dragons began their attack of the Roskildean navy in a classic fighting pattern. The dragons dove, one after the other, spewing their fiery wrath on their chosen targets. *How many of Havick's galleons were out there?* It was hard to see at this level, and I missed the bird's eye view that I would have on Crux.

Did someone warn the Raider boats to hang back until they had completed their attack runs? Did Senga and Adair know to target the Roskildean galleons not surrounded by Raider fighting ships? The questions were excruciating, but all I could do was trust that our forces would remember their training.

I helped where I could—steadying an old Free Islander as he clambered into a small sailing yacht, then picking up a toddler to plonk into his lap. "Who here has sailing experience?" I asked.

"I do." It was the toddler's mother, hurrying to board the boat. I told her my plan to hang back until there was a clear channel to make a dash for the south, and the woman nodded grimly. "Pass the message on to the others. Travel as a flotilla, for as long as you can," I nodded, turning to help the others.

It was a long, grim, and tiring morning, and one whose backdrop was the dragon and ship combat further out in the bay. Almost immediately, the dragons drove a wedge between the Roskildean warships, and, as the battle commenced, the last fighting vessel, with Costa, Dima, and Jac aboard, joined the rest of the Raiders' ships to attack on the right-hand, northern-most arm of the battle while the dragons fended and fired the southern 'wing' of the Roskildeans. Already three of my uncle's boats were afire, with one hissing with steam as it capsized.

He couldn't have sent that many to us. Not after the last battle. How many boats could Havick possibly have? *I should be out there!* I thought, cursing my luck as the cannons boomed and screams echoed.

But, as the sun rose into the sky, revealing just how terrible the battle was, it seemed like we were starting to win. But at what cost? How many had died?

The bay was now clear, and the Roskildean battleships had been forced further out into the oceans, but they were still there. We couldn't afford to leave them, even to escape. They would just chase us. We had to rout them completely.

Now was the chance for the villager flotilla to escape. "Go. Head south!" I shouted, waving my hands at the collection of yachts, rowboats, and catamarans in the inlet, and the woman I had spoken with earlier waved back, before pulling on the sail as the others in the boats around her heaved on their oars. The cloud of vessels broke out into the wider waters of the bay, turning raggedly around the burning vessels, and circumnavigating the southern cliffs.

That was when I felt it on the back of my neck, like a cold breeze.

The Darkening had reached the camp behind us.

CHAPTER 6
LILA, REUNITED

The Darkening's creeping, dark-grey and purple fog washed down from the headlands to the north. It brought with it a sense of fear and anxiety that made my teeth chatter, even this far away from it.

Was there anyone left in the camp? I thought in alarm, looking for signs of any movement. There were still people on the sands getting into the last Raider boats, but no one in the camp. If they hurried, then they would get out to sea long before the Darkening managed to reach the shores. Drawing my sabre, I ran to stand at their back, moving to the edge of the overturned huts. When the dead came stalking out of that fog, at least I might be able to buy the raiders a little time.

"Lila, come on! Get in!" a Raider called, one of the cooks from the *Fang* I thought, Olsgrud, was it? I paced backwards slowly, watching as the fog consumed the tents that had been our home, sending tendrils into the larger huts, and dousing the watchfires.

"Yip!" There was a sudden, unexpected sound from the camp's edge. A dog? Some of the Raiders had brought their dogs when we had left Malata. They might have garnered confused looks from the Free Islanders, but the tradition of a sailing dog was a fine one to us Sea Raiders. We bred the smaller terrier-type dogs that were 'more than half rat themselves' as my mother would say (although my father always encouraged one or two on board the *Ariel,* as they were excellent ratters).

Would the Darkening or the dead attack a dog? Would it be kinder to let it free to find its own way?

In this coastline that has just been invaded and wrecked by the dead and foul magic? I couldn't do it. Cursing myself for my kind-heartedness and my stupidity, I raced back into the camp, following the sounds of the yipping.

The Raider terrier was whining from where it had made its den under one of the unfixed row boats. There were larger tent shapes all around me, and people's belongings strewn all about on the sand as I ran towards it. Just a couple of tents away, the heavy grey fog approached, probing the thin canvas material, recoiling obscenely.

"Come on, fella, come on." I crouched down to call into the darkness, seeing a pair of eyes staring back at me, rolling white at the edges. The tiny mutt was terrified. It could easily have scooted out from under the edge, but the strange goings on (and doubtless the scent of the dead) had it terrified.

"Come on, please!" I called, shoving a hand into the gap as far as it would go to feel the brush of wiry fur. "I'm trying to help you!" I begged it, pushing on its solid little bum as it strove to sit down in the sand.

Crunch. There was a sound from the other side of the boat. The fog was just a few meters away, swirling and boiling, almost like it could sense I was nearby.

And there was a shape lurching out of the fog – lurching, because it was horribly injured and disfigured. One of the dead, its body now a lamp-oil char, with bits of fur cloak burnt into its body, caked with earth and the patina of ash. This thing had managed to survive dragon fire and landslide – what was *I* going to do against it?

"*Rakh-akh-akh!*" It made a terrible clicking noise in its throat as it opened and closed its jaws, lifting up something – its broadsword was broken, and had melted with its hand to form one living weapon as it brought it down in an awkward swipe against the side of the boat with a heavy thump.

"Ai!" I screamed a little involuntarily, shoving myself out of the hole to grab my sabre as the thing stepped around the side of the boat that separated us, and loomed over me.

In a flash, there was a small brindle and orange form between us, snapping at the form as the Raider terrier ran out from under the boat to protect me. I stumbled back, readying my blade as the dead hissed at the terrier and kicked it savagely. With a pained whelp, the dog rolled across the sand and took off, tail between its legs.

I don't blame you, I thought after it, swinging my sabre to sever the things head from its burnt neck. The head came off in a clean blow, but the body kept on stumbling as it fell against the hull.

Enough. I don't need this horror, I thought, turning to run back to the boats. I just hoped the terrier also had the sense to bolt for the shore as well.

"Lila?" A voice like a moan in the wind made me stumble, as the fog caught up with me. Fear like a wave of sickness locked my knees and I fell to the ground. *Had I really just heard that?* No. It was the Darkening. It was playing tricks with my mind.

I pushed myself up, kicking at the sand in my desperate terror to get away.

"Lila..." This time the voice was stronger, and it was right behind me. I knew that I shouldn't, but I couldn't help myself as I turned to look over my shoulder, to see a barrel-like shape burst out of the fog.

It was my foster-father, Kasian the Chief of Malata.

"Father?" I whispered in horror, now crouching, hyperventilating. I couldn't even see the nearest tents any more, the fog was all around me. But I could see my father, or what he had become.

It was undoubtedly him. Not some trick of the light. Not another one of the strange dead looking like him. He was short, as he always had been, he was large and barrel-chested, like he had been in real life, but his skin was drawn and wrinkled, like he had been preserved in salt.

And his eyes were a snowy white that burned with a cold glow as he searched for me on the ground. *"Lila, my leg..."* he whispered. *"It doesn't hurt anymore."*

His gammy leg, earned saving people from the First Battle of Malata, against Havick's navy. He was no longer limping, but he seemed oddly confused by this fact, as if he couldn't remember *why* he was no longer limping.

I screamed and ran.

"Lila?" My father's voice followed me as I tried to remember which way the beach lay. The fog was having a strange effect on my mind, making it hard to concentrate. No longer did it inspire anger, but terror, like the Darkening knew at which moment just what emotion would cripple me the most.

Tents loomed out of the mist, and other forms too – walking, stumbling forms, oddly disassembled – the dead who had walked through hell to get here.

Which way? Which way?

Suddenly, the skies blossomed with plumes of yellow-crimson, and the fog recoiled from their glare. There was a jet of flames shooting overhead, coming from one standing

Sinuous Blue dragon that I didn't recognize, and in its flame-light, I could see that it stood on the water's edge. I was only meters away from the beach proper. Thanking the gods and the stars and everything else, I ran under its belly to find the last boat with Olsgrud the cook already reaching his large hands to seize my tunic and launch me over the side and into the boat.

More roaring from the guardian dragon as we pushed off and the last survivors of the camp hurriedly rowed with all their might.

"Are you okay? Are you hurt?" the chef said worriedly to me, and something small and furry was licking my face. The dog. It had found its way home, I thought gratefully as I sat up.

We had escaped the Darkening and the dead, and it seemed that the battle of the bay was ending now too, with nine dragons surrounding the remaining Roskildean galleon.

Nine dragons? I thought in alarm. We only had ten dragons altogether – and one of them was Crux, wounded and near-dead on top of the cliffs with Danu.

Then who was that other Sinuous Blue dragon, then? That would make eleven dragons in total! I reached for the edge of the boat, to see it already lifting off into the sky, screeching in triumph.

CHAPTER 7
DANU AND THE DRAGON RIDERS

I awoke to the smell of pungent herbs and incense, reminding me of home. *"Afar?"* I murmured, thinking that I must have been asleep, maybe after a long period of illness. Like that time I had been bitten by the Kether Frog, in the forests of Sebol. I had been feverish and ill for days, I recalled. Maybe that was what was happening now – but why all of these dreams of dragons?

"He's waking up," a gruff voice said, and I felt cool, rough hands on my brow. The voice was heavy, a man's voice, so not Afar and any other of the Witches of the West. *I was the only man on Sebol,* and the realization kindled in me like a candle, casting light into the darkness. I wasn't at home. I wasn't in Sebol. I was on the southern mainland, where I had recently been fighting the Darkening.

I groaned and mumbled, struggling to push myself up from under the weight of blankets that had been laid over me. It was sweltering hot, and I was shocked to see that under the blankets I only had on my small clothes.

"Easy now," that same speaker said to me, as I peered blearily into the gloom. I was in a small tent or hut. The walls were made of simple wicker-work rods, with canvas stretched over their frame, and a small iron stove glowed merrily to one side, more than enough to make this confined space steamy with heat, and on its flat top I could see a bowl of minerals smoking heavy scents into the air.

And there was a man leaning over me.

"Who are you?" I gasped, pulling back. He looked old, with hair that was pepper-grey and shorn close to his scalp, and deep wrinkles around his eyes and the sides of his mouth. His skin was tight over his vaguely hawkish features, but his eyes were bright and darting as they sought me out.

"It's okay, Danu. He's a friend," said another shape in the gloom. Lila, on the other side of me and wearing her Raider shift and simple leggings. Her hair was tied back but not in its warrior braids, and she looked worried too. "His name is Rigar, and he and his friend Veen have their own dragon. They helped save both our lives."

"Lila? But…where are we?" I muttered, pulling the blankets a little higher to my neck.

"The southern mainland, near the Spice Coast," she said. "We managed to catch up with the Free Island flotilla and together we made landfall a couple of days south of where we were before." I noted that she said the words gingerly, carefully around this strange fellow who had turned to throw some more of the dried ingredients onto the steaming bowl. Instantly, the fresh and bright spell of alpine spring filled the tent, almost bringing tears to my eyes.

Lila was wary around this man. She doesn't know him well, I thought. But she trusted him to nurse me back to health. What did that mean?

"Danu Geidt, you have been lucky." The man turned back to me, the smokes fragmenting around his face like he was a dragon breathing fire himself. I felt a shiver of – *something,* recognition? Power? There was definitely something strange about this old man, but I couldn't tell if it was magical might or not, or merely something *uncanny.*

"You overreached your abilities, tapping into the currents of the world around you to make a vast change." The man's voice was not altogether kind, I thought, but stern. "The human mind can only handle so much power, but the problem is, that it can *sense* the great reservoirs of magic out there. You committed a titanic act of magic, but in so doing, if it hadn't been for your dragon helping you, you would have shattered your soul and wasted away then and there."

My dragon helping me. "Crux? How is he – is he okay?" I remembered sensing the pain through him, both from the arrow of the dead and from what I had taken from him.

The strange man seemed to ignore my question. "You will

need to rest and restore your strength, Danu Geidt – both physically and spiritually."

He's hiding something from me. "But what about Crux? Is he okay?" I turned to look at Lila, who was frowning at both of us, as if unsure what she could say.

"These men helped you, Danu. At the end of the battle, they flew up to nurse and coax Crux to fly south with them, to us. But Crux…" she said, before I saw her open and close her mouth to add something, trying to find the right words to say. *Oh no. What have I done?*

"Tell me!" I said. "This is my doing. If I have hurt Crux, I should know about it!"

Lila nodded, holding my gaze. I could tell that there were still oceans of feeling between us, but I could see that she respected my honesty, at least. "Crux has been affected by the battle, but we don't know how much was from the wound, or the magic that he gave you," she said carefully.

Oh no. I pushed the blankets away, then hesitated when I remembered what state of undress I was in. "I have to see him. Can I see him?" I asked Lila, not this strange man – but it was he who answered me.

"No one will stop you, Danu, but please, take this before you do. You need your strength, and to be protected." He brought from the stove two wooden cups, one filled to the brim with a thin sort of broth, and the other half full with a greenish sort of tea that smelled like more of that fresh alpine scent.

"Protected from what?" I asked as I gulped at the broth and realized just how hungry I was. I finished it in just three draughts, and already I felt better. I looked at the tea a little more warily, though.

"Magewort and heather-flower," said the man. "As the food helps your body, this will help your spiritual injuries."

"Magewort?" I muttered. "I've never heard of it." I was hesitant to take it. Everyone knew that the Western Witches were the best herbalists in the entire world.

"I'm not surprised. The Dark King Enric expunged a lot of the old knowledge from the records during his reign." The man pulled a sour face. "He didn't want another mage rising to challenge him. But Bower has been encouraging it to regrow in the Dragon Spine Mountains again."

"Bower… You mean Lord High King Bower of Torvald?" I said. This man knew a *lot* of world politics, it seemed.

"Aye, the same." The man nodded to the drink. "It won't harm you, I promise. It may deaden your magical senses for a while, but that will be like the natural swelling around a wound. Your soul will seek to protect itself as it gets strong once again."

"Deaden my abilities? But…?" I started to pull away, until I saw Lila's sharp glance. *It was my magical abilities that had brought trouble onto our heads. I had hurt my good friend Crux because of those abilities.* Right in that moment, I didn't care if I never used magic again so long as I lived. I downed the warm drink in one long gulp and waited as I felt an oddly warming, slightly comforting glow suffuse through me.

"There. Better?" the man asked pointedly, taking both cups from me. I was surprised enough by the result to say yes. But did my magic feel any different? I recalled the image of the calming sea that the witches had taught me so long ago as a way to settle my mind and reach for my magic. The image still had that calming effect, and I could feel the magic inside of me, underneath me, around me – but it was muted and distant. Normally I would have been worried about this, but after the news of Crux's malady, I found that I didn't mind.

At least I won't be able to hurt anyone with it, I thought, turning my mind to other matters.

"How do you know so much about this?" I asked the strange man.

He gave a small smile. "I should introduce myself formally, I guess. My name is Rigar, and my friend outside is called Veen, and our dragon's name is Halex. We were trained by the second Dragon Academy."

The second Dragon Academy?

"You mean Lord Bower's Academy?" Everyone knew the story – even out in the Western Archipelago. With the island girl Saffron Zenema, he had overthrown the dark sorcerous King of Torvald Enric, who had reigned for five hundred years and stripped the land of its beauty, created all of the new iron-machinery such as cannons that we saw in use everywhere and filled the lands with war and monsters. During that time all dragons had been hunted and had even become myths to most of the mainland folks, but now High King Bower and Queen Saffron had reinstated the Dragon Academy and the just rule of the Torvald Empire.

"Saffron and Bower's Dragon Academy was the *third* such school to sit on Mount Hammal," Rigar said lightly.

What? But that didn't make any sense. "That means that the second academy was over five hundred years ago?" I shook my head.

"Danu, it's true," Lila said. "Lords Rigar and Veen here are, ah…"

"Old?" the man said with a short bark of a laugh. "And I am not a lord, I am afraid. Although my ancestral lands were once one of the Great Houses of the Middle Kingdom." A look passed his face, wistfulness or melancholy. "That was a very long time ago now."

"The Middle Kingdom?" I coughed. That was *really* ancient! No one thought of the mainland in terms of the old divisions of the North, Middle, and South anymore. I tried to recall the old history scrolls in the witch's library. What had the three kings called them back then? "Lander, Vincent, and Griffith," I recalled.

"Ah – you're going back even before *my* time, young mage." Rigar laughed a fuller laugh now. "But you are right. The Northern Kingdom was North*lander* after Prince Lander, Griffith the Valorous…"

"The Trading City of Vala?" I recalled the name of the most prominent city of the Southlands.

"Aye, and Vincent, well…" Rigar looked suspiciously upwards, even though there was nothing but the smokes of our tent. "He's best off forgotten, because it was Neill Torvald, and House Torvald, who took over the Middle Kingdom and thus the Kingdom took his name – and the unified empire of Torvald after it."

"So, if Bower and Saffron now run the third academy, that means that you…" I pointed out.

"I and my friend Veen were trained beside Seb Smith, King Sebastian of the Middle Kingdom of Torvald," Rigar said heavily, his voice cracking with emotion. "I remember the Darkening when it first returned to our lands out of prehistory. It was the force that Seb and Lady Thea battled, when we nearly lost everything." His words were grim. "Times were happier after that. Seb and Thea were good rulers and none of us ever believed that something like Enric Maddox could happen to us, until it did."

I listened, rapt.

"The Dragon Riders of Torvald fought back of course, but Enric managed to cast some great spell, making the people's hearts cold and fearful of their great and noble friends in the sky. The dragons grew weaker, and finally fled to the mountains and farthest places."

"And it was Saffron who brought them back," Lila said

proudly. I knew that she had a deep respect for Lady Saffron, herself an island girl like Lila was.

I still couldn't believe it. How could this man, older even than Chabon, and his fellow Dragon Rider Veen still be alive? It seemed that my confusion was plain on my face as Rigar shook his head and grinned. "You have still much to learn, Danu Geidt. You know that the witches' long lives come from their magic?"

"From their ancestral friendship with dragons," I stated. It was something that I had worked out the last time I had been on Sebol. My mentor Afar was herself over a hundred and had fled to the west during the reign of Enric herself - although she did not look past sixty to me.

"Aye. Well. Think of how great that bond is when you have your companion dragon at your side all those years?" He smiled, and there was a distant screech from outside, that I knew didn't sound like Crux. "Veen – who is outside right now, tending to your Crux – and I fled to the mountains with our friend the Sinuous Blue Halex, seeking the refuge of the old Dragon Monasteries. And then we travelled south, seeking lands free from Enric's reign." His voice grew mottled and thick. "We saw many strange things out in the world and fought many ancient beasts that I have no name for, but when Bower's call went out for the dragons to return to the north, we heard it and returned."

"He knows Saffron!" Lila hissed excitedly.

"You know Torvald," I echoed her sentiment. I had never

been to the capital city of the word, but I had read Chabon's recollections of it; a tiered city built out of the steppes of a mountain, walls that shone in the light, crowned with dragons…

"Yes. But more importantly, I know when there is something wrong in the airs of the world," Rigar whispered into the gloom of the tent, and I thought for a moment I saw his eyes shine with the gold-orange metallic sheen of a dragon's. "The Darkening has returned. This time, out of the west."

"Havick and Ohotto," Lila said in disgust. "I have already told them what we know, and Rigar and Veen have agreed to help us defeat Havick. They have fought the Darkening before."

"What about the dead?" I murmured, and for some reason I felt a chill pass through this little tent. I didn't know if Rigar sensed it, but he busied himself with packing away his herbs and handing me my clothes as he got ready to leave. Something was troubling the ancient Dragon Rider.

"We still have much to discuss, Lila and Danu, but yes – I have fought the dead before, but only recently. They seem to once have been a warrior tribe that came out of the northwest, near the dragon spine mountains, and have been moving out to the western seas."

"Ohotto is summoning them to her," I murmured, fitting it all together. "That's where the Black Fleet came from."

"We followed them for a little, attacked them when they were on the mainland, but almost nothing could kill them,"

Rigar confessed. "Their bodies must be totally destroyed and burnt with fire. We were going to report the news to Torvald, but Halex sensed a great evil to the south. When we investigated, we found you. Yes, I and Veen and Halex will help you fight this threat – but this time we do not intend to fight alone. We fled Torvald once, and we will not act without its support again."

I saw Lila stiffen and her jaw clench, and I could tell that this was an argument that the two must be in the process of having. Either way, they still put aside their concerns and told me to get dressed and ready, if I felt able to.

I did.

CHAPTER 8
LILA, SHUSH WYRM

Danu looked drawn and thinner when he emerged from Rigar and Veen's 'healing tent' as they had called the small dome structure they had made on the lee of the hills. He had lost some of his squarish frame during the last couple of days that they had tended him in there, and his clothes hung a little loose. I would have to find some different leather armor that would fit him better down at the camp.

The *new* camp, I thought, turning to look down the side of the hill to where the long, golden beach sat next to the warm southern seas, before rising inland to become dunes and tufts of spiky grasses. We were a day and a bit south of the bay where we had fought the dead and the Roskildean navy, and I was still aware that our dragon scouts – Senga and Adair on Kim, hadn't seen any sign of strange fog coming our way.

But this place wouldn't last forever. My earlier enthusiasm at meeting the two ancient Dragon Riders dimmed. Once again, the refugees had pulled the smaller boats up onto the beach, but this time in a long line so that we could launch them quickly and easily at the first sign of trouble. Out in the water were moored the *Ariel,* the *Fang,* and the *Orchard,* each looking a little more battered and worse for wear with every battle they managed to limp through.

We can't keep going on like this. I bit my lips.

"Lila?" It was Danu, meeting me at the side of the healing tent. "Thank you," he said awkwardly. "For looking after me, and for…" his shuffled his untied boots in the dusty earth. The sun was hot and bright in the clear blue skies overhead. "For putting up with what I did back there."

I haven't exactly forgiven you yet, I wanted to say, with a flash of my old annoyance. Not for the first time, I wondered if my time spent in that healing tent tending Danu had meant that *I* got affected by those soothing herbs. Now that I was out here in the brisk warm winds of the south, I found my old ire for him returning a little, though it was nowhere near the fury and hurt that I had felt before.

But he had been quick to recognize his mistakes. That was something that I could approve of. It was something that my father would always have approved of. *'Let a man slip a knot or two, if he is ready to admit it and learn to put it right'* my father would advise me in his lessons about how to handle a crew.

Kasian. A shudder almost drove me to my knees. My foster-father. The man I had last seen lurching through the camp, his eyes pale with an unholy glow…

What did Ohotto do to you? I could feel my lip trembling.

"Lila? I know, it was terrible. If you never want to ride with me again, then I understand…" Danu said quickly, miserably. He must have seen the look of torment on my face.

"No. I mean, it's okay." *Kinda.* "It's something else," I admitted, waving off his querying look. I wasn't ready to tell anyone what I had seen up there in those last few moments of the battle. *Maybe I had dreamed it. Maybe the Darkening had twisted my mind, played tricks on me, just as it had made me angry and fearful?*

My head was a mess right now. There was the sudden arrival of Rigar and Veen – out of a different time, apparently, and then there was what we were going to do with the Free Islanders and Raiders down below. We had travelled farther from the Western Isles than we ever had before. What were we going to do?

"Can I see Crux?" Danu asked, his voice small. His question caught me off guard in my turmoil, and despite my earlier reservations about keeping the two of them apart at least for now, I nodded. *He admitted his mistakes. Let him learn from them,* the words cut through me like a knife.

As it was, it was also the way that I was heading anyway,

following in the footsteps of Rigar as he now went to tend to Crux – although I wasn't sure that 'tending' was the right word.

We padded up the hill, the heat instantly making the climb feel like hard work, and by the time that we had reached the top both of our brows were already glistening with sweat. Not so for Rigar and Veen, apparently – as they didn't appear to be bothered by heat, cold, or anything else.

Maybe that comes with age.

Veen was similarly tall and rangy-looking, but he was taller and thinner than Rigar was, with long blond hair that had faded to an almost transparent white over his own half-a-millennia and more. He raised his long face to regard us as we got to the brow of the hill where Crux sat, but aside from a small nod, he did not smile or indicate a greeting.

Our eyes were on the Phoenix dragon, however. He was sitting on all fours, wings folded in, but with neck and head up like a watchful cat, his barbed tail curled carefully around his paws. He had noticed our presence, his tapering ears flicking and swiveling in our direction as his head turned the other way and his great lambent eyes scanned the horizon.

"Crux?" Danu whispered. "What's wrong with him?"

Nervous energy trembled through the Phoenix dragon's body, resulting in a quiver and anxious twitching of his tail. His nostrils flared and moved as he tried to take in every scent, every piece of information that he could.

But what was worse was what I could feel coming from

him in waves, through our bond. It was fear, confusion, hesitancy. I had known the Phoenix to be surprised in battle before, alarmed for sure – even worried when there was a chance that I or Danu was being hurt – but never *scared*.

When I reached towards him with my mind, I found once again that he drew his connection from me, as if I would burn him just with my touch. Danu must have sensed something like this too, for his frown deepened as he crossed the space to reach out to Crux's hide.

"Danu, wait!" I said, but I was too late. Danu rushed to soothe the great beast, but as soon as he did so, Crux's back twitched and his head swiveled round to bare one side of his mouth, revealing fangs. He didn't snap or growl, but it was clear that he didn't want to be touched. Danu staggered back in alarm, but what was even worse was the rolling whites of Crux's eyes as he stared at us for a moment in anxiety. This was not the look of anger or bad temper, but of worry. I would have even *welcomed* Crux's anger right now.

"It's okay, boy, it's okay…" I said softly, stepping around Danu to raise my hands in the air so that he could see them. I stepped closer, and carefully, very quietly, he lowered his snout to sniff at my hands, then gently bumped me on the chest with his face."

"I'm sorry. I was surprised. I was so busy looking for the danger, that I didn't sense you…" Crux said in a wavering voice inside my head. Not his usual fire-and-fury brash confidence.

"I know you were, Crux. It's okay," I murmured soothingly, even though his words alarmed me. *When has Crux ever been too distracted to notice someone approaching?* I rubbed his nose in the way that I knew that he liked.

"I'm sorry, Danu." Crux lowered his head to sniff at him.

"No, it's okay. It was my fault. It's all my fault." Danu looked devastated.

"No!" Crux was adamant. *"If anything, I was stupid. I should never have got hit by that dart. I have been too reckless. I need to be more careful. We all do."* His voice was insistent in my mind.

"Shush. You big wyrm," I chided him affectionately, eliciting a purring sound from the discomforted dragon. When he broke off our connection this time, he did so with a feeling of slightly more confidence, but not a lot.

"What's wrong with him?" Danu whispered again as I stepped back. It was Rigar who answered.

"It's the Darkening, I think. I have seen it affect the dragons strangely before – when we rode beside Seb, the Darkening managed to break the connection between dragons and their riders; very much like Enric managed to do between the everyday people and the dragons." He paused, looking at the Phoenix speculatively. "But this is different. Perhaps the Darkening is not as strong as it was before, perhaps this Ohotto hasn't managed to summon all its powers yet – the wound your dragon took must have been laced with some kind of Darkening-curse, perhaps?"

This statement did not particularly do anything to make my day any better. *What were we going to do?* I thought once again, taking in the sight of my anxious dragon, the immense expanse of the southern seas beyond, and our tiny camp below us.

"There are cures," said a new voice. I spun on my heel to see the watchful Veen. The thinner Dragon Rider was cleaning his saddle as he spoke, dressing it with a small pot of oil and rubbing it into the ancient leather until it shone like polished oak.

"What?" both I and Danu said quickly.

"Now that both of Crux's true dragon-friends are here, I can tell you – as it would not do to offer such important information to one of you alone. There are two cures, that I know of," Veen said casually. "Before, it was the magic of the Dragon Egg Stones – holy artifacts from an ancient time – coupled with Seb and his crimson dragon Kalex's bond that broke the curse."

Great. You mean that I have to use the Sea Crown? I thought of the Sea Crown, down there unworn and out of sight, safely in my foster-mother's keeping. Pela was a force of nature, as so many others said about her, and she had been instrumental not only in defeating the Roskildean naval blockade, but also keeping the rest of the Free Islanders and Raiders alive. I didn't know what I would do without her.

"And the other?" I said.

"The dragon mother," Veen stated. "Every den has a

dragon mother, and she is the strongest of all of the dragons nearby. They're like queens over a territory." Veen cast a critical eye over the Phoenix dragon. "I have never seen his type before, not even in the far reaches of the south, so I am not sure if we can find *his* den mother."

"Queen Ysix," I said. "She is a friend to us, and several of our Dragon Raiders are of her brood. Do you think that she will be able to heal Crux?"

"She may," Veen was noncommittal.

"Or, Lila…?" I knew what Danu was going to say, even before he said it.

"No, I won't use it." I shook my head violently and saw Rigar and Veen raise an eyebrow between them at our little argument.

"The Sea Crown has gemstones on it," Danu pointed out. "If what Veen and Rigar says is true, that these old gemstones could break the spell – maybe the gemstones on the Sea Crown could, too? I'm not talking about you *using* the crown, just letting me use it."

"Ah…" Rigar coughed. "Danu, have you forgotten what just happened to you? You shouldn't be attempting any magic at all for at least a little while."

"Not even to save my friend?" Danu hissed angrily. Strangely, I found myself approving of his enthusiasm, if not of his plan.

"The Sea Crown is what got us into this mess. We go to Ysix instead." I put my foot down.

"And then we go to Torvald?" Rigar said.

Not again. "No," I said, turning and stalking back down the hill towards the small encampment.

Back at the camp, it took longer than I had anticipated to pass the message to Kim and Thiel to call their ancient mother Ysix, for Crux's mind was too distracted and caught up with danger to send the message, saying that he 'would not bring Ysix here to her doom.' It was frightening and frustrating, to say the least. I was annoyed by the time I had finished relaying the message and snapped at Danu to stay with Rigar and Veen to recover. I had annoyed Danu, I think – not that he had any right to complain at the moment! I had to signal to Senga and Adair to return to camp, and then pass my news to the dragons. By the time that the sun was setting over the west, and the land was starting to lose its warmth, Kim and Thiel had retired to a nearby outcrop of hill, to begin their keening calls into the night winds. It sounded mournful and I couldn't shake the feeling that it was a requiem for the Raiders and Free Islanders both.

"Lila, come and eat. You look worn out." It was my mother, regarding me from the edge of a firepit where spits were turning. Unfortunately, on the spits were only fish and a few of the wild game birds that our hunters had managed to catch.

"The supplies are running out?" I said with a nod to what she was offering.

My mother grumbled. "Most of the salted and dried goods we managed to bring with us have gone now. I've been organizing hunting and fishing teams to go out."

It was my turn to grumble. The more we scattered our forces – whether in fishing boats or land hunters – the harder it would be to flee when we had to.

Flee. I curled my lip at my own suggestion. *When did Raiders ever get used to fleeing?* I answered my own question in the next breath: *when we were facing vast supernatural and physical forces...*

But still, I found a measure of comfort as my mother ladled out some type of meaty broth and I ate it with some thin but delicious pan bread she had made in batches by the fire. My mother chatted a little about the types of waves and the winds that we had down here, and it was, for a very small moment, good to feel like a Raider once again.

Eventually, however, she sighed as she finished her bowl and turned to give me *The Look.* I was in for a talking to, it seemed.

Was everyone thinking that I was making all the wrong choices?

"So, Lila my daughter. Vala or Torvald?" she said heavily.

"Huh?"

"You heard me. Are you going to head to the Trading City of Vala, or the capital of Torvald?" Her face was impassive.

"Uh...neither?" I hazarded, before instantly seeing that was *not* what she had wanted to hear from my lips.

"You think that these people are going to last another week out here like this?" She nodded to the sounds of the camp settling down for the night. There was the wail of babies, the soft, worried voices of men and women around their own campfires.

"Raiders don't need aid from anyone," I said stubbornly.

"Ha. You sound just like your father." My mother flicked a bit of wood into the fire.

Kasian with his drawn skin and glowing eyes... My heart skipped a beat. *No. It had been a phantasm. A trick.*

"But if he were here now, even he would see the sense of what I'm saying," my mother continued. "We've lost Malata, and these good people have lost their homes. As far as we know your uncle now has complete control over the entire Western Archipelago, so there's no going back there for us now. We need friends – and that means either Vala in the south, or Torvald in the north." She was pragmatic to a fault, was my mother.

"But Mother!" I hated the fact that I sounded like such a child in front of her. "Torvald has classed us as outlaws, and the south hunts us whenever they see our ships."

"Whenever they see *Raider* ships," Pela pointed out. "And look at us; not even half are Raider folk anymore. We're not Sea Raiders right now, Lila – we're refugees."

"No." I was stubborn, glaring into the fire until my eyes watered.

"Lila, it's no crime to ask for help," Pela said a tad gently. "Would you expect a Raider to crew a boat on their own? No. They need others to help them. And these people down here," she nodded at the other tents, "they need allies and friends. They need houses and food and boats."

She was right. I sighed, not wanting to admit it out loud. I didn't have to, as my mother had known me all my life. I was grateful for the fact that she didn't rub my nose in it and let me at least have my semblance of defiance as she changed the subject.

"I've set up watch fires, and we have the *Ariel* out on patrol through the night. At the first sign of anything, we'll get a call." She eased herself to her feet. "Go on and get some rest with you, Lila. I'll tend the fire tonight."

"Thank you, Mom," I said as I stood up, and slipped into the tent that she had set up for me.

CHAPTER 9
LILA, CHOICES

"*Lila, wake up!*" Crux snarled into my dreams of flying and swimming. For a moment I sat, blinking in the dark of my tiny tent and trying to remember where the dragon was, until everything came slamming back home to me. I was on a blanket on the ground of the Spice Coast, in a tent surrounded by a couple hundred or so other tents, the last of a fleeing people.

"*Lila, please, you have to wake up!*" His voice was insistent, and I realized that he was communicating with me from where he was resting on the high ground with Rigar, Veen, Halex and Danu.

"I'm awake, Crux, what is it?" I murmured, reaching for my clothes and my water bottle.

"*I have been seeing things,*" the dragon said alarmingly.

"What? What kind of things?"

"Spirits and shapes in the dark. The souls of the unquiet dead. Ghostly forms that move over the desert, sometimes investigating your camp, sometimes moving away..." Crux whispered in the recesses of my thoughts.

"The dead?" My fear peaked, and I dragged on clothes, eyes searching out where my sabre was.

"Yes. But not the same as before. These are shades, spirits..." Crux said.

Oh. Was my dragon seeing phantasms, now? Had the Darkening driven him mad?

"But that is not all, Lila. There is more..." the Phoenix Bull said with a note of panic in his voice.

"Have you slept at all, Crux?" I sighed, sitting back down on my blanket. What was I going to do with him? What were we going to do at all?

"How can I sleep, with the spirits and danger around us at every turn?" the once-fearless dragon confided in me. I groaned.

"Okay, I'm awake anyway. Do you want me to come up and tell you stories?" I offered. It broke my heart to hear Crux like this, troubled and fearful.

"No, Lila, you're not listening to me. I was watching the spirits in the dark, in case they ventured too close to the camp, and that was when I smelled something."

"You did, huh?" I sighed, slipping on my boots. I

wondered if I even needed to take my sabre with me at all tonight.

"Yes! Man-tracks. Someone has passed this way. Recently. Sneaking into your camp..."

How did he know that they weren't some of the Free Islanders? Or maybe he was anxious enough to forget the scent of some of our own Raider guards? "I am sure that it is nothing, Crux, but I'll take a look – where did you say it was?"

"No – you cannot go alone! I think they must be spies, sent to do mischief in your camp..." the dragon thought sagely.

"I'm sure I'll be all right, Crux," I said, looking at the sabre once more. Then, knowing it would only drive Crux frantic if I didn't take it, I picked it up and stepped out of my tent. "Which way did you say you smelled these tracks, Crux?" I murmured sleepily, just as a shape emerged from the darkness.

He made the mistake of growling as he drew back his sword, telegraphing his action to me, and jolting me to a sudden, total wakefulness. But even so, I still gave a surprised whelp as I threw myself back inside the tent, landing on my back.

There was an angered thrashing as my attacker got caught up in the flap of the tent for a moment, before pouncing forward, while I scrabbled backwards, trying to get my feet beneath me, grappling for my sabre—

They wore a lot of dun and ochre colors, wrappings over

padded leather armor and a scarf over the lower half of their face. But their moment of confusion had given me the upper hand, as I slid my sabre upwards, and into the assassin's belly. My attacker coughed in surprise, their eyes rolling as they thumped to the floor – and then shouts broke out all across camp.

"Lila? Lila, my daughter!" It was Pela, pushing aside the tent seconds after the assassin had hit the dirt. "I was just fetching more wood – I was gone for but a moment!" She looked mortified. "What happened? Who is that?"

"Never mind him." I nudged the body now revealed to be a man. "What's happening outside?"

Stepping over the attacker, we saw that the night had been lit up by the blossom of orange light from high, raging fires – and we could tell instantly that these weren't the fires of the camp, as they were all dulled to embers now through the night. These were tall, eight feet, ten feet infernos racing up to the sky.

"The boats!" I breathed in horror, taking off at a run towards the beach.

I and my mother ran through the camp, the sand sucking at our feet with every step as we headed for the destruction. Pela behind me was roaring into the night. "Attack! Up and at 'em, Raiders! Defend yourselves!" Pela shouted. I heard the grunts, shouts, and clashes of swordfights in the gloom. Who was it? Who was attacking us?

A moment later I got a chance to find out as we emerged

from the last of the tents and found a skirmish battle going on around the boats, with our own Free Islander and Raider watchmen now engaged in a desperate battle for their lives with more of these assassins.

I swung my blade at the nearest one, for it to be parried with a shockingly strong *clang!*

My attacker had only one sword and no shield, but a part of me registered that it was a fine longsword. The sort that Roskildean naval officers used? He lunged for me, but I turned it aside, stepping into his reach and backhanding him across the face, driving him back. Beside me I heard the shout and screams as my mother, a far deadlier swordsmaiden than I ever was, drew both of her short swords from her belt and attacked two of the saboteur-assassins at once.

Raiders have a very special hatred for anyone who harms their boats, and I felt that same rage now as I stepped forward, intent on skewering this person at the end of my blade, before they cried out "mercy!"

I stayed my hand just long enough to avoid killing him. "Drop your blade," I snarled instead. He did, while all around us the battle raged on. I had no time to tie him up, I pounced forward, hitting him over the side of the head with the pommel of my blade and moved onto the next fight.

It was desperate and fierce fighting, with my foster-mother always seeming to be in the very center of the worst of it, but after we had managed to hold off the largest of the attackers, there were other Raiders making their way to the beach to help us.

"Capture them!" I shouted as the Raiders fanned out around the assassins who had dared to attack us.

"What?" This was from Costa the Quartermaster, carrying two very large cleavers in each hand. "*Save* these lubbers who attacked our boats?"

"We need information, Costa!" I demanded, but I could see that most of the crowd were on his side.

"If you want to live," I hissed at the wary assassins that still lived, backing away towards the burning boats. "then you had better drop your weapons and get on your knees, or my men will slaughter every last one of you."

Right then, Costa and the other burliest Raiders already marched forward, rage clear on their faces and murder in their eyes. The assassins looked at their advancing doom, and then at me and my mother, before one by one they dropped all their weapons and fell to their knees with their hands up.

"Don't kill us! Mercy! We're only taking orders!"

"Yeah, orders to kill…" Costa sneered, reaching our semi-circle and raising his cleaver.

"Raider! No!" I barked at the big man. "You would strike an unarmed man?"

Costa visibly shuddered in anger. "He burnt out boats! Look!" the quartermaster gestured to where there was a good three of the larger merchant-come-fighting vessels fired, and easily another five or six of the smaller rowing boats burning.

"They're *unarmed*, quartermaster. Law of the sea," I

snapped at him. Raiders have a strange code of honor to anyone else – we might kill and raid with impunity in the thick of action, but if a boat surrenders or an enemy falls overboard, we're obliged to give them a chance to survive, because the sea is a harsh mistress to us all and one day it might be any of *us* who are stranded in the ocean.

"We're not *at* sea, Lila…" Costa kicked the sand under his feet.

"A Raider is *always* at sea," I quoted the old wisdom, knowing that I would be stretching credulity, but praying that Costa would back down. He had been a friend of Elash the captain who had taken off with a dozen or so other Raiders when we had fled Malata. But Costa had been a far closer friend to my foster-father Kasian than Elash had been, and so had placed his faith in me, at least for now. If we were to fight, or if I were to lose Costa's support as well – then I wasn't sure how many Raiders we would even have left in the camp.

"As you wish, captain," Costa stepped back, grumbling and glowering at the man he wanted to kill, but obeying my word – *just*.

Phew. "Get these men tied up, quartermaster. And I don't care how rough that happens, either," I said. They had destroyed some of our boats, after all. "But leave me this one to talk to," I indicated the assassin with the fine officer's sword, who had just woken up to see himself surrounded by some very annoyed Raiders.

"Are you okay?" I whispered to my mother as Costa and

the others did as I had ordered (with not a few yelps of broken noses and bruises on themselves, I think I heard).

"I'm fine." Pela nodded wearily, wiping the sweat from her brow. "But... what is that?" She looked up sharply over my shoulder.

Oh no. Not another thing. I turned and raised my blade, only to see Danu, walking out of the surf and surrounded by a corona of water, like his own personal flock of dragons.

"What?" I said. "I thought he couldn't do magic anymore?"

I was clearly wrong, as I watched as Danu trudged, stepped, and stumbled to the nearest edge of the burning boats and made an overhead throwing gesture with his hands. The cloud of water flew from over his head and engulfed three of the burning boats, putting them out with a rush of steam. There was a loud cheer from the crowds of Raiders, who were also starting to race to the sea to get buckets of water to put out the fires.

"He *shouldn't* be able to do magic anymore," hissed Rigar, emerging from the crowd to glare at the mage in the swells of water. "I guess he is far stronger than I had anticipated. This is *troubling* news."

I had no time to worry about what Rigar was saying, as I turned back to call to my friend. "Danu?" But he didn't hear me. He staggered to one side, lurched, and summoned another gobbet of water from the dark seas to arc overhead and hit another fire. That appeared to be all the magic that he had in him, as he slipped in the surf and collapsed.

"Danu!" I shouted, as both Rigar and I broke into a run to reach him.

Our friend was breathing, but appeared feverish once again, just like before. "If he has used any of Crux's power to do this…" I swore as I helped Rigar carry Danu up the beach.

"I don't think so. Your dragon probably couldn't give any of its power the state that he is in right now…" Rigar said grimly.

Wow, great. Way to cheer a girl up, I thought when we had finally settled Danu down on the sands. "Is he going to be all right?" I said. *Will he live?*

"Not if he keeps on performing elemental magic at this rate." Rigar shook his head. "We need to get the pair of you to Torvald. To somewhere you can rest, and where Danu can talk with other scholars about his powers."

I couldn't believe that the aged Dragon Rider was bringing this up, right now. I groaned in frustration, ignoring the question and leaving him to tend to Danu as I turned back to the ad-hoc jury on the beach. I had to make sure that no one got lynched tonight either, despite what terrible things they had done.

"Mother? Pela?" I called out, to find her and Costa and

half a dozen others surrounding the one assassin. He had a new bruise on the side of his mouth, and his face coverings had been torn away to reveal a middle-aged man with steely grey eyes and weathered skin.

"Speak," I said as I pushed myself to the front of the circle, looking down at the man on his knees. "Who sent you?"

"Your uncle," the man said desultorily. I guess he knew that he was very close to dying tonight.

But then it hit me. He had said my *uncle*. I wavered on the spot. "He knows?" I murmured under my breath. He knew that I was alive. That I had survived his attempt to kill my real parents – the rulers of Roskilde.

"Of course, Lord Havick knows." The assassin took it as a question. "He has had that poisonous witch whispering into his ears about this Prophecy of Roskilde for years now." the man seemed disheartened, and I could see why, from his position. "Things would have been so much better if she had never come to our shores."

"If my uncle had kept on pretending to everyone that I had died, you mean?" I said pointedly, but the man said nothing.

"So, you're Roskildean. You were sent to what, kill me?" I said.

A nod from the man. "That, and make sure your boats didn't pose a threat to his navy."

And if it hadn't been for Crux waking me up, and Danu

using his fool magic, they might have gotten away with it, I thought in alarm.

"So Havick is worried about us," I said with a grim smile.

"He has other plans. Bigger plans," the man corrected me with a sneer. "He just wanted you out of the way."

"What plans?" It had been a mistake for the man to let that information slip, but I wanted to see this assassin's face when he discovered that I knew them already. The maps and charts we had stolen from Roskilde. "You mean his plans to invade Torvald?"

The assassin sat up sharply, looking at me in alarm.

"We know." I said, victorious.

Costa burst into our questioning with a savage laugh. "I say Havick is welcome to the mainland! Good riddance to him!"

How can he say that? I looked at Costa in disbelief. *Doesn't he realize that Havick already controls the archipelago?* If we want our home back, we have to defeat him!

The assassin was looking between me, Costa, and Pela with alarm and fear. I bet he was wondering how we knew, and what we would now do to him and his fellows. "How did you get here?" I demanded.

"There's a cove, a day's trek to the north. We landed and walked over the desert."

Tough, then. I shook my head. I wasn't about to kill half a dozen unarmed men. "Strip them of their weapons, put them on a row boat, and send them out to sea," I said with a snort of disgust. I had enough of dealing with them.

"What? You can't let them go!" Costa was indignant. "They attacked us! They'll tell Havick where we are!"

As if it really mattered now, I thought, looking at the steaming and blackened boats. The sun was rising, and it brought with it the full awareness of just how dire everything looked. We had even fewer boats to attack Havick. We couldn't hold him off now if he wanted to come for us. We couldn't return to the archipelago, and we couldn't stay here.

"Then we'd better not be here if Havick comes a-looking, had we?" I said to Costa. I had made up my mind. "You're going to Vala," I said. "Me, Danu, and the new Dragon Riders will be going to Torvald."

PART II
MAINLAND

CHAPTER 10
LILA, DESERTION

I watched as Rigar and Veen worked to secure the litter carrying Danu to Crux's back, using what they said were 'old academy knots,' I didn't see why new leather straps had to be threaded under Crux's belly and looping the tops of his legs, but they echoed the ones that Rigar and Veen used on their own ancient dragon Halex, allowing the dragon to carry a greater amount of luggage and armor. I had never imagined burdening Crux in that way.

But still, it had worked to secure the mumbling, feverish Danu for the long flight north.

"Lila, it's time," Senga said from behind me, and I turned to see her fierce expression, her hair newly-bound into a severe warrior's braid. *She had grown up in this war,* I thought grimly. She was no longer the mischievous, wild Raider girl that I had known a few summers ago, but was now lithe and tall, her strong limbs browned from the sun.

I wonder if I've changed too, then? I thought as I pulled my hair into a braid, a little self-consciously. It wasn't something that I had time to consider at all, but I suppose I must have. As I returned to the scene below us, I realized that people responded to me differently now. Was it since that battle on the shore? When I had spared those assassins' lives? Or had their reactions to me changed before then?

"Senga – how can this be the right thing?" I asked, wincing as I did so. The Raiders had been through so much, losing their home, their chief, all those lives lost to the war. Now I was asking them to give up the sea.

"What are you talking about, Lila?" My friend looked at me, as direct as ever. "We have to do this. Your father would have agreed."

"Do you think?" I said quietly.

"I do," she nodded.

"Lila," the nearest guard stood up as I walked down the sandy headland with Senga at my side. His name was Doul, if I remembered, one of Malata's hometown Raiders. I gave him a nod and earned one in return. Had it always been like this or was it because I had a dragon, had won the Sea Crown and had fought beside them, that they were giving me such respect.

Not all of them, though, I thought as I surveyed our camp below; Elash, for one, hadn't liked my new position. And

Costa was only barely in agreement with Pela and me. Our camp mostly gone, now, packed away into luggage bags and sea chests, and stowed in the bellies of the few boats that we had left, now out in the bay.

Two of which were now pulling away from the others.

"Senga? Doul!? What's happening out there!?" I asked, pointing down at the bay. The makeshift village that we had created over the last couple of days was now completely gone, with the intention of getting everyone back into the boats and take the nearest inlet to Vala. But now two Raider boats were already sailing, leaving just the *Ariel* and the *Fang*. "It's not time to depart yet, we need to wait for everyone to board!" I shouted in alarm, waving my arms at them.

"Oh no." I realized those two boats were currently under the command of Costa, my father's old quartermaster.

"I don't know what's happening, but here's someone who *will*." Senga gestured to where my mother was striding across the dunes towards me, her own pack riding high on her back.

"Mother? What is Costa doing!" I pointed behind her in alarm.

"That Costa has as much sense as a whelk!" my mother shouted, her face a picture of grim dismay. It was clear to everyone here that Costa and his cronies had apparently decided that enough was enough and had decided his Raiders were better served by him and him alone, rather than mother and me. Just last night I had wondered if he would do something like this, but I had held my tongue, not trusting my gut. I should have done something about it then. Maybe it had been saving those assassins from execution which had been the last straw, but more likely it was insistence that they go seek aid at Vala – a landlubber city.

"I can get him back," my mother was saying. "Give me a fast boat, and I can make him see sense."

You probably can, I thought. Mother would have her famous 'hard words' with him, and those 'words' would be in the form of glares and perhaps a few fists as well. No one messed with Pela and I felt the shadow of a smile upon my lips at the idea.

But no, I couldn't let her do even that. "No, Mother. If this is his choice, then we should let him go. I'd rather have fewer people than to have those whispering mutiny," I quoted my father.

"But, Costa…" my mother's eyes turned back to the boats, squinting at them as if she could ferret out the large man even from here. "He might be *difficult,* but I can handle him. I will get this whole ungrateful lot to Vala, even if I have to drag each one by the ear to do it!'

"Our scouts have found an inlet that is deep enough for the boats to travel through, and we think it should be the main river tributary that leads to the trading city of Vala. Once we're on it, it won't be long before we meet up with Vala merchant boats and scouts, and the biggest challenge will be to stop Costa trying to attack them." It was good to see my mother's old spirit returned again, that fighting, stubborn defiance that I had thought she had lost when my father died.

But he wasn't dead, was he? a treacherous thought said. That figure that had lurched through the unnatural fogs. The barrel-chest now strangely deflated, the ghostly-white eyes... Should I tell her what I had seen? Didn't she have a right to know, of anyone?

"Lila, it will be all right. I'll scull after them in one of the faster Islander boats and make them see sense. Your plan will work, I promise." She stopped talking and gave me a hard look. "You look like you've seen a ghost!" my mother said suddenly, as my eyes must have betrayed the horror of what I had seen.

You have no idea what I have just seen, I thought. And I am not about to share it with you, either. Pela had fought hard to get out from under that veil of mourning, and I was sure that she was only so strong for her people now because she was doing what her husband and my father would have done. I couldn't take that away from her and tell her Father was now *one of them.*

"No...I was just worried about Costa," I said – which was true as well, so it was easy to tell this little white lie. I shook the thoughts of what I had seen—of Father—in that battle from my head. *It couldn't have been real. It just couldn't!* I wondered again (and not for the first time) if my nightmarish vision of my walking dead foster-father was part of the same thing as was happening to poor Crux. Nightmares and visions created by the Darkening. *It had to be. My father wouldn't come back.*

I raised my eyes to my mother's and said firmly, "Let him go, Mother. I don't want to be worrying about you facing a mutiny every day I am away." That, at least, was true. It gave me strength to know my mother would be here and protected, with dragons over her and our friends at her side. I could travel far to the treacherous north even on my own, as long as I knew that to be true.

"Oh, my daughter!" She reached out and ruffled my braid, just as she always had since I was a girl. "I won't ask you if you will be safe, because I already know the answer. So, I will say to you what I said to your foster-father and my husband every time he went out on a raid without me: Be smart. Be smarter than any of those that face you. Be smarter than you think you can be, because you are. Understood?"

I nodded and spoke past the lump in my throat. "Thank you, Mother." I couldn't stop myself from asking this next question: "Do you think that this is wise?"

"Wise?" My mother looked at me with her hard as flint eyes. "When have we Raiders ever been wise? But you said it right last night. We need allies. And that boy of yours needs to get to Torvald healers."

"You mean Danu? He's not a boy of mine!" I said, but my mother just laughed.

"Never mind. You get yourselves to Torvald and make them hear you. Make them understand what is going on down here," she said, and I smiled in agreement just as I had when I was a little girl and she was instructing me on the finer points of sword-fighting.

"Our scouts have found an inlet about half a day to the south, and it's wide enough that it'll probably have reliable boat traffic, which means it'll have connections to Vala," my mother said. "If I can get our people there, I'll be able to get them to Vala by boat."

"Okay," I said. I knew that my mother could do it. Even without Costa. *That pig,* I allowed myself to think vehemently after their retreating boats. Where were they going to go now, in the whole wide world? Havick had the archipelago, and Torvald's coasts were far to the north. Perhaps they were going out to become deep ocean Raiders, meaning a life on the open waves and ceaselessly searching for fresh water. *They will become crueler, and fiercer than even the Malata Sea Raiders were,* and in that brief moment I could see the future.

"Good riddance to them," I whispered.

"There. Nothing to do now but the doing," Pela said, crushing me in a fierce hug, and then holding me at arm's length. We didn't need to say anything, as we broke away.

"Lila? When are we off?" Senga said from where she had been waiting for me, a little way ahead on the path. Her words forced me to consider the next terrible part of today.

"Senga? Ah… Actually, there is something that I have to ask of you and the other Dragon Raiders."

Senga saw what I was about to say almost before I had opened my mouth.

"Oh no you don't, Lila Malata," she said resolutely, using my old, Raider-name, "I'm coming with you. You can ditch my brother Adair if you want, but not me!"

But I knew that I could be even more stubborn than her when I had to be. It was one of the things that had made us such good friends – neither of us backed down from a fight. "I need you here, Senga. I need you looking after the Raiders and the Free Islanders."

"Let the other Dragon Raiders do it." She nodded to the eight or so young dragons that circled the airs far above us. "You're our leader, and that means you need a bodyguard."

"Veen and Rigar will be with me," I pointed out. "They know more than the rest of us combined about dragon flight."

"And you trust *them* now, do you?" Senga said. *Ouch,* another thing about Senga, she was always really good at choosing the most cutting remark. She wasn't being malicious — well, she *was* being cruel – but it was like the way a shark just eats whatever is in its path.

"No, I don't trust them. Or rather, I trust them *to be them.* They're ancient Dragon Rides from Torvald, and they have Torvald's future and the dragons in mind, not us. That means that I know that they are worried about Havick and Crux and even Danu as much as we are," I said. "And that means I can be smart."

"Huh." Senga sulked. "What if you run into that fog again?"

"The Darkening," I said. That was what it was called. That was its name. "We're not going to fight, not like last time. This is a mission of mercy."

Senga frowned a little at that – a true Raider response, I thought. Raiders didn't ask for mercy. We were children of the storm seas, and a landlubber's worst nightmare. Or so I had thought, before Malata was taken by my uncle and he brought the Dead Fleet to the Western Archipelago.

But Senga and her brother Adair were no Costa and his cronies, I knew. I saw her pout, and then nod. "Okay then. You want us to protect the people."

What's left of them. "Yes," I agreed. "The assassins said that Havick wanted us to stay away from his land invasion, which we are– so I don't expect him to come after the fleet, but you never know…" Senga nodded sadly. We both knew that it was a risk that we had to take. "But the southlands have never been friends to the Islanders, and certainly not us Raiders. And now that Costa and his men and women have gone, and with mother here leading the last of us across the hot-lands to this inlet of hers? You Dragon Raiders will need to protect the people and our last few boats from any attacks – because it's those boats that we need to keep us alive."

"And then there's Vala," Senga said.

"Yeah." A deep sigh shook my shoulders. And then there was Vala. No one knew what the city would think about a bunch of Dragons, Islanders and Raiders suddenly arriving in their territory. *Did they have dragons down here themselves?* I didn't think so, not in the same way as Torvald did, anyway. But still. A lot of scary questions.

"And finally, Senga…" I said heavily. "There will be the war."

"War," Senga said the word carefully.

I had managed to keep myself from thinking about it as I worried about Crux and Danu – but it was still there, an unstoppable certainty, *if everything went according to our plans.* "If we manage to get Torvald on our side, then there will be a battle to defeat Havick and the witch Zanna. A battle that I am going to want to take part in, and probably a lot of Raiders and Free Islanders will, too."

"And I will be at your side when that happens," Senga said, straightening and putting her shoulders back bravely.

Of course, I knew that she would. "Well, we don't know when it will happen, or even if Torvald will agree to help us retake the islands – or what they might want in return if they do – but that is what we are working towards. So, I need the Dragon Raiders eating, resting, and staying sharp by training and practicing their flying. My call could come at any time."

"And we will be ready," Senga said, and I knew that she would. With a friendly slap on the shoulders, I took my leave of her and climbed back up the hill towards where Rigar and Veen were looking at me gnomically from the back of their similarly ancient dragon Halex.

"Are you ready, Lila of Roskilde?" *They used my proper name,* I noticed.

"I am." I checked the straps and the saddles on Crux to make sure none of them were neither too loose nor too tight. They were perfect, of course, as I had expected any work of the aged Dragon Riders to be. As my hands smoothed over Crux's scales, it seemed the dragon wasn't as warm as he usually was, and his spirit was still muted and far away in my mind as it had been every day since his injury. On his back, between his wings was the litter that Rigar and Veen had attached to form a kind of one-person platform, with the semi-conscious Danu lying there, wrapped in blankets and strapped to the boards to stop him from sliding off.

"Crux?" I reached for him, to feel his body flinch from me.

"I am sorry, Lila," a second later, his words came back to me. They were not his usual fiery self. *"I did not expect you to talk to me."*

"How can you say that? I love talking to you!" I said, feeling a little hurt by that. *It's not his fault, he is ill,* I had to remind myself.

"I mean, I did not expect it to be you talking to me. There are so many voices you see, all of the dead who have fallen here..." His voice in the back of my mind sounded floaty, and far away.

"Really?" I shivered, my heart hammering in panic for just a quick moment. The dead were here? I looked around for the bewitched fog, and their shambling forms, but there was nothing.

"Not those dead, the normal dead. Those that wander the world and never seek to harm the living. I do not trust them," Crux confided in me.

Had my dragon gone mad? Or could a dragon's magical sight also see the dead of the world? It was something I had never asked Crux, and I was afraid to do so now, in case it worsened his condition.

"Well, we're about to fly now, Crux. There'll be no dead up there to harm you," I pointed out.

"Only the shades of the dragons who have passed," Crux said, freaking me out even more.

Really? A sudden shiver went through me as I thought of the sky filled with the ghostly, furious bodies of all the dragons who had ever lived. *No.* I was letting Crux spook me, and I couldn't allow his fears to do that. We had to get to Torvald, to get both him and Danu healed.

"Chin up, Crux. We fly towards your kin!" I said, climbing his leg and settling myself into the saddle. When he jumped into the air, I couldn't help noticing it was with a limp on the side where the dead dart had struck him.

CHAPTER 11
DANU, THE WESTERN TRACK

"*Danu...? You have to listen to me, we have only limited time..."*

It was the words of my mentor, Afar, coming to me in the darkness, but I couldn't quite see her. Where was she? How did she get here?

The last I remembered Lila and the two ancient Dragon Riders were letting me sleep. They had made a bed for me, a stiff, uncomfortable bed in which I couldn't move. Why did they do that?

"Danu. You need to focus on my words, or you will break the connection..." said Afar once more. She was always giving me instructions and advice. For a brief moment, I felt a surge of annoyance. Wasn't I a fully-trained acolyte now? After all the magics I had been able to cast? After helping

Lila to recover the Sea Crown? After proving to everyone that the prophecy was real, and that I had found the rightful heir of Roskilde? Even the dragons referred to me as a 'mage'!

I turned my thoughts to where I was, and what was going on. I could feel the confines of the bed somewhere under my back – it felt a lot more like a series of flat wooden boards to be honest, not a bed of soft duvets and blankets.

Probably because I was on a dragon, the thought swam into my mind. Aha! That was it. My mind started to focus, gathering sharpness to itself. I was on a litter, on Crux's back, and we were flying towards the north, towards Torvald. Why? Because Crux was ill – I could sense his worry and anxiety, and the embers of his inner fire as if they had almost gone out completely.

The dead had done something to him, I knew. That, or the Darkening – or both.

"Danu Geidt! Listen to your mentor!" This time, Afar's voice was impossible to brush away. It blew into my mind like a strong gale, and with it came the ghostly image of the woman's stern face that could be both kind and inscrutable, huddled over the glow of a lantern. She was meditating, communing. She was reaching out to me.

But where was her circle of other witches helping her? The previous times that I had experienced this sort of mind-to-mind magic, it had taken an entire coven of the Western Witches to cast their thoughts as the dragons seemed able to. A circle of chanting and meditating seers was needed – but all I saw was Afar.

"It is costing me much, you are right," my mentor said, and I swear that in that moment I saw one of her hairs slowly fade to white, and the crow's feet around her eyes deepen.

"What are you doing! The cost is too much!" I tried to pull away, but Afar wrapped her mind around me almost as forcefully as Crux had once been able to do.

This was real. This was actually happening. I was asleep, on the back of a flying dragon, and my mentor was reaching through to me with the power of her mind alone. I was stunned at the power that my mentor had, lying hidden within her.

"No time for that!" she said fiercely. *"You are surrounded by troubles and enemies, and you need to listen to me."*

"Afar? What enemies?" Apart from the dead, and the Roskildean Navy, of course.

"The Western Isles have fallen." The finality in my mentor's words chilled me to the very bone. She said it as if she were reciting a fact of history. *"The Pretender Havick, now with the help of the dead, have swept over the archipelago, and all those who have died in the fog return as the undead soldiers of the enemy."*

"What?" I stammered. But that could be hundreds of sailors, including Raiders.

"Only the dragons at their atoll are holding out, but Ohotto has been battling them with dark curses and enchantments, keeping them away from you," Afar went on. *"And

most worrying to me is this last piece of news that I have to give you, Danu Geidt. Sebol will be abandoned by the new moon."

"What?" But that was unthinkable. As long as there had been a Haunted Island, there had been the coterie of the Western Witches living there.

"I know. But it was not my decision."

"Can you not reverse it?" I burst out. "You are a senior Matriarch! You have the authority."

"I am no Mother Chabon, and neither am I Ohotto Zanna," my mentor said. *"I cannot lead what is left of the witches without their support, and I will not seek to rule over them and bend them to my will as Ohotto would."* Afar's strange mental telepathy weighed heavy and sorrowful upon me, as she continued.

"The witches have had a vote, and it has been decided. We take the Western Track through the oceans, to find safer land."

It was like listening to a legend, to a fairy story. I knew of what she talked about, of course, what she called 'the Western Track'. But it was little more than a myth – that various Matriarchs, over the long generations, had decided near the end of their time to take a small skiff and set out across the western oceans, following the light of the moon on the water. Legend had it that there was another land beyond Sebol, where the witches could find peace.

"That's a children's story," I said.

"Is it? There is still much that even you have not studied in

the Libraries of Sebol," my mentor said mysteriously. *"What you have not been told, because you never fully completed your training, is that sometimes we get messages back from the Western Track. There is a colony out there, but a strange one, and it welcomes us witches – although the way is hard."*

"But you cannot flee! You cannot leave Sebol!" I was frantic. Everything we had worked for, every lesson that Afar had tried to instill into me – was this the final lesson that she wanted to impart?

"The Council of the Witches have decided, not I, and I go to protect them if I can," Afar said resolutely, although I could sense her sadness, and perhaps a little guilt there too. *"The witches have decreed that no witch will fall and rise again in Ohotto's Darkening. To have an unliving, undead witch at her disposal would quite simply be too great a threat for the world. So, we will remove ourselves and that threat from the Western Archipelago altogether."*

"But still, the library, all of the learnings and sacred sites on Sebol!" I argued.

"The others are protecting the island for now, and we are taking what we can with us. The time of the Western Witches is at an end in these lands, Danu Geidt. A new magic must defeat this evil."

I still didn't understand, but I also knew there was nothing I could say that would convince Afar to change her mind. *But I'm not ready!* I thought. *Afar might believe I am – but I don't FEEL like I am.* Would I 'know' when I was a full mage?

Shouldn't I feel more confident about my abilities? But all I had seemed to do was to create disaster and upset around me.

"But Afar, what about my training?"

"There is nothing more I can teach you. There is nothing that anyone can teach that will stop the Darkening now: your only weapons are that which you have always had, Danu – bravery and courage, and your friends around you."

"Afar, no – there is still so much I have to learn! To tell you! We fly to Torvald, to try to get help."

But already my mentor's voice was growing quieter and fainter, and in my mind's eye her image started to fade. She looked much changed, in just the few short minutes that she had been communicating to me. Her wrinkles were deep, and her skin sagged under her chin. She looked almost as old as Chabon. What it had cost her to talk to me, one last time!

"Go to Torvald, Danu. Learn what Saffron has to tell you about magic..." were Afar's final words, which made absolutely no sense. Queen Saffron was a dragon-friend, not a witch, and certainly not a magician!

"Beware the power, Danu – do not drink too deep..." And that was that. She was gone. What did she mean? My brain was too distracted and frightened to sleep, and so I struggled to open my eyes.

We flew over the blue waters that seemed endless, were it not for the fact that I *had* flown over the deep seas before on Crux. Even in my delirious fog of confusion, I could make out that the waves below were different, wilder and higher. To the furthest south behind us there was a line of orange-brown which I took must be the southern hot lands, which meant that we were travelling north. Towards the empire of Torvald.

But we were not alone. Something moved across the waves eastwards. It was still a long way away, but it looked like a dark smear on the surface of the seas. A low, dirty fog bank that was following the waves into the gulf and holding its shape very well.

As I watched, several smaller shapes broke free from under it, they were like tiny seabirds in front of a storm. Small black ships with tattered sails. The Fleet of the Dead.

"Havick!" I breathed, and heard a startled response from Lila, riding ahead of me. She turned to peer at where I pointed, gave out a low moan and urged Crux to fly faster, and higher.

The rest of my journey was little more than fragments and shadows and piecing them together in my mind was like trying to recall the events of a dream. There were green forests and deep valleys rushing underneath me, there was the shriek and call of Halex the dragon in front of me, and somewhere I could hear Crux whistling in his worried way.

At some point, there were rough hands on my face, pulling at my eyes and feeling my brow.

"He needs more magewort. There is a place where it traditionally grows near here. We will harvest some and be back before morning."

And now I awoke to find myself in the almost suffocating warmth of the tent, wrapped in my blankets and feeling like I had the worst cold of my life. My whole body ached, and my thoughts felt odd and out of place. Why was I so ill? Was this what using magic does to you? I had seen how it aged Afar, right before my very eyes – so was that what was happening to me, too?

Snap.

There was a sound outside the tent that drove its way into my mind, signaling its out of placeness. Was it Lila or Rigar and Veen out there, walking around? But for some reason my ears knew that it wasn't. There was no gentle murmur of voices, no sound of cooking-pots simmering, or the heavy sighs of dragons'-breath as they slumbered. Another shuffle of a foot, and then silence, followed by hesitant, wary breath.

"Spirits!" the sudden mind-voice of Crux washed into my mind. Having a dragon intrude into your consciousness unexpectedly was almost as bad as having a witch launch herself into your thoughts. But Crux had a strong mind, under the fog of anxieties that seemed to mask it.

"What do you mean?" I whispered, starting to shift in my blankets.

A snap and the noise of someone saying, "Shhh!" came from outside the tent. Why would any of the others shush their fellows to silence? Would they fear waking me?

"There are spirits surrounding the camp. They are coming for us..." Crux's voice was shot through with fear and worry.

"I'm sure they aren't," I said again, some of his nervousness seeping into my own mind. I had a different view of these things than did Lila, I knew. A dragon's senses were far superior and stranger than our humble human ones. I had never heard of them being able to sense the spirits of the dead before, but they could sniff magic, so why not? The witches had taught me that there was far more to this world anyway, than what our human senses reveal. There were the shades of the departed as well as all the elemental powers, and still stranger things that history had forgotten – creatures that used to call this world their home…

"There… We've found them…" a hushed voice said from just outside the tent. I did not think that this was any undead spirit that Crux was feared of – but that did not mean that whomever was sneaking into our camp didn't also have harmful intentions towards us…

"Crux? Can you tell who they are?" I whispered into the gloom, but the dragon did not respond. I did not even feel the Phoenix dragon in the back of my mind. I shifted the blankets, but my arms felt rubbery and heavy with pain. I wouldn't be able to fight like this.

Sching! The sound of metal scraping on metal, like blades being pulled from a scabbard.

I knew that I had to do something, but what choice did I have apart from magic? Afar had warned me to be careful of magic, but I knew that I could control it, no matter what she said. I was a mage, even if they didn't recognize me as such.

I closed my eyes, and opened my mind to the currents of magical energy that were flowing constantly underneath us all…

CHAPTER 12
LILA AND THE LOCKET

Something woke me in the night, where I lay on the ground next to the fire catching a few moments of sleep in the dark. It was a sound that was out of place. It wasn't the nightmare-moans of Danu, and it wasn't the crash and thud of Halex returning, bearing Rigar and Veen. Moving as quietly as I could, I placed my hand on the scabbard of my sabre that I kept under my bedroll at all times, and moved.

The attacker was big, he wasn't stealthy and small like the last one. He wore the same dark tan and mottled garb as the others did, and with the same hood covering his features, but it looked as though he was more used to fighting in formation than the others, as he bent his legs into a crouch, and raised his longsword in front of him, keeping the fire between us.

We had only stopped at this mountain glen for the night, and it had seemed secluded enough – but somehow my uncle's assassins had found us. What were they doing, scouring the land for us?

Another man jumped from the shadows of the trees nearby, landing on heavy boots next to the first by the fire, and this time raising two smaller blades in my direction as they started to crab around the fire towards me, thinking that I was trapped.

Stupid, I thought, as I kicked the burning coals and logs straight at one, then jumped through the smoke to hit the dirt and grass, rolling to reach my own sabre.

Thud. "Argh!" Pain surged up through my thigh. One of them had struck me! How bad?

"Lila?" I heard a voice mumbling, groaning. Danu, waking up. I rolled on the grass, out of the way of the next booted stomp aimed at my head, but my thoughts were distracted, too busy thinking about saving Danu and not my own life. *I can't let him get hurt. Danu's too weak for this,* I was thinking as I flipped to my feet.

I managed to duck the next sword swipe, but the assassin had followed it up with a foot stamp which connected solidly with my chest, propelling me backward and against the solid trunk of the strange mainland trees that didn't grow green leaves, but green needles instead. My head rebounded off the tough bark and I felt myself sliding to the floor.

No. I can't afford to lose…

"Wave-rider?" It was Crux's fearful voice, small and far away. *"Are you hurt? Injured?"*

My eyes were having trouble focusing, and I had an almighty headache. "No, don't come, Crux," I murmured. "Stay safe…"

FZZAP! The darkness swimming in my eyes was suddenly brightened by a falling star. I heard a muted grunt of pain, and then a thump as something was thrown to the far side of the clearing.

"You shouldn't hurt my friends," Danu said – only it didn't particularly sound like the Danu that I knew. This voice was colder and thick as if mumbled through sleep, and I could feel every syllable burning into my brain.

Danu! I forced my eyes open to see a scene out of a dream – or a nightmare.

My friend the fish-boy had risen from the floor, and he was drifting across the clearing and the ruins of the fire surrounded by a halo of white-purple light. He didn't look like Danu, despite the fact that he was wearing his tattered linen bedclothes and the heavier woolen robes which I had forced him to put on just last night. His skin had a waxy, unhealthy sheen, and his eyes glowed a baleful white. *Like the eyes of the Captains of the Dead,* I found myself thinking. *Like the eyes of my father…*

Was I dreaming this? Had I hit my head that bad? If this was a fantasy, then it was a very convincing one, as I could feel the waves of power pouring off of Danu as he floated towards the two cowering assassins on the other side of the clearing. I could feel the strange winds chilling my skin and smell the humus of the earth.

No, this was very real I thought in horror as Danu started to speak again.

"You will never hurt anyone again," Danu intoned, "because you will not be able to see them." He spoke without malice or any great passion, but instead made quick and strange gestures in the air above them, all the while intoning strange, guttural words.

"*Argh!*" One of the men screamed. "I've gone blind!"

His fellow was still reeling from the smoking burn mark in his back, one which I knew had nothing to do with me and everything to do with Danu here. He must have been the one who had kicked me and had been about to close in for his kill. His eyes were also now a myopic white, but he was writhing on the floor in agony.

"Lila, are you all right?" Danu whispered in his spooky voice.

I wanted to say yes, but my head was ringing like a bell. I tried to struggle to my feet but felt dizzy.

"Lila! Why do you not answer me?" Danu turned his glowing white starlight eyes to me in alarm, and the young man whom I had thought to be my friend pointed a finger at me.

No! His power hit me like a bolt of lightning, but it did not blind or burn me – instead, I felt a cooling, calming radiance unknit itself from the center of my chest and work its soothing magic through the rest of my body. The ringing in my head stopped, the pain vanished, and even whatever sword cut I had taken to my leg no longer hurt. I was healed. I knew it, as sure as I knew that it was all wrong.

"Danu...?" I said, confused. I didn't even know that he had this type of power hidden within him, but he ignored my astonishment as he turned back to the shouting, terrified assassins.

"I do not like hearing your screams. Maybe it would be better if you could also not speak..." Danu started to intone.

"*DANU!*" Someone bellowed, as the trees around us opened. It was a dragon. The thing snapped the pine trees to either side of it as easily as if it were opening a curtain, and on its back was Rigar and Veen, already jumping from their dragon Halex's saddle. Their shout had seemed to disrupt whatever strange trance had been holding Danu in its grasp, as he instantly crumpled to the floor in a heap beside those he would torment.

"Sacred stars – Lila is hurt too!" They must have seen my blood that matted my hair as I jumped to me feet.

"No, no – I am all right, Danu healed me," I called as I rushed to his side (careful to avoid the flailing, blinded assassins as I did so).

"I knew this would happen," said the Dragon Rider called Veen, and I guessed he wasn't talking about my uncle's murder attempt. He stalked past me to the two men and roughly pushed them both to the ground. They screamed at being touched.

"Don't kill us! Don't hurt us. We surrender! Mercy!"

"I am not going to kill you, you miserable fools. Just stop moving and lie still, otherwise you'll end up tripping up and falling onto your own swords!" Veen hissed.

"Did he know what he was doing?" Rigar said hurriedly as he crouched beside me, pulling handfuls of the rare magewort plant from his leather pouches that he and his Veen had gone to collect. He crushed it with his gloved hands over one of the rocks of the disturbed fire, then brushed some of the last bits of coals into it. When it started smoking, he said, "Here," and started wafting the smoke over Danu's face. It seemed to ease his breathing, and a little color returned to his cheeks.

"I don't think he was even awake," I confessed. "He looked…"

"In a trance?" Rigar said sharply, frowning all the more deeply.

I nodded. "Yes."

"Did he say things not in his own voice? Did he say things that were uncharacteristic of him?" Rigar said.

"Kind of," I said. "His voice sounded different, but he healed me, and he used his power to stop these men from killing me."

"Hm." Rigar looked over to his brother, who shrugged a little as he pushed down on the still-writhing bodies of the two would-be assassins.

"What is it?" There was something going on here, something had passed between the two Riders. A warning. "Tell me! I deserve to know!" I spat out.

"When Queen Saffron was younger, she was afflicted with a similar magical ailment," Rigar said slowly, eyes locked with Veen all the time, as if checking how much he could tell me.

"This is an illness? I thought this was because Danu had magic?" I pointed out.

Rigar's eyes widened, and I understood.

"Queen Saffron has magic, too?" I said. It made me feel odd. All my life I had imagined her as a wild island queen, a strong and brave adventurer. Now, it seemed, she might have been more like the mysterious Western Witches. I knew that some of the Western Witches were friendly, even noble-hearted like Danu's mentor Afar was – but still…. You couldn't trust a witch, I remembered my father's words, before instantly feeling guilty. *Danu was a witch though, wasn't he? Could I trust him?* Of course, I wanted to say – but I *couldn't* trust the magic in him. I had seen what it had done to Crux, and that hillside. Magic was dangerous.

"She *did*. It's gone now," Rigar said seriously. "She gave it away."

"You can do that?" I puzzled.

"With a dragon's help," Veen said.

"But, during the days of Dark King Enric, their quest to overthrow him was almost destroyed from the inside by the fact that Enric could use *his* magic to manipulate *hers*, do you understand?" Rigar said.

"Sweet waters," I gasped. "Does that mean you think that Danu…" I couldn't speak my fear, but the question echoed in my head. Could someone else control Danu? But who? Afar? Ohotto Zanna?

"I do not know, and it has only happened rarely in all of recorded lore, so there isn't much to go on – but I rather think that if it was an enemy of yours using Danu's magic, then they wouldn't have stopped to heal you. They would have probably tried to kill you – and done a much better job of it than these men here with blades!" Rigar said.

I nodded. That made more sense to me. "But he still can't control the magic," I said. "It's more like it controls *him*."

"Yes." This came from Veen, restraining the groaning blinded prisoners. "It can go like that, and especially in men for some reason. They can feel the wide expanse of magic at their fingertips, and they open their minds to it too much, and that desire for learning becomes an addiction to power, an illness. Eventually, they become little more than husks as they survive on the magic that consumes them."

Looking at these two ancient faces regarding me, the irony was not lost on me that they knew intimately what they were talking about – but their longevity owed itself to the magic of Halex their dragon-friend here, and not through the use of magic – or at least, I believed, anyway.

"It is more important than ever that we get your friend to

the healers at Torvald – and more importantly, to the dragons," Rigar said, lifting Danu up as if he were a rag doll, and taking him back to the litter. Danu moaned fitfully in his feverish sleep.

What is that magic doing to you? I thought in alarm. It looked as though it was eating him up from the inside.

"What about these two?" I dragged my eyes away from my friend to the two assassins who were no longer moaning but had lapsed into a petrified panic under Veen's fists. It made me wonder just how strong these old Dragon Riders were – did the long generations of dragon-magic also give them unnatural powers, apart from their long life?

"I think they have suffered enough," Veen said heavily. He didn't like me, I knew that. Not as much as Rigar did – and not that Rigar was overly friendly, either. Their long and strange lives seemed to have made them forget how to talk to regular people.

"I wasn't suggesting killing them!" I said, feeling irritable. *How could Veen think that?* But at my words, they still flinched a little. "We will set them free, but what chance have they out in these wilds?"

"Do you care?" Veen looked at me shrewdly.

"Not really whether they live or die, but I care about my conscience," I said truthfully. "They must have had a base or a camp nearby here." The thought suddenly struck me. I still didn't even know *how* they had found us up here.

We had flown for nearly two full days, over the burnt

orange lands of the south and then over the gulf of water that separated the Empire of Torvald from the southlands. It was there that Danu had seen the Black Fleet – but instead of turning east and following the gulf, Rigar and Veen had instead led us north again, towards a series of peaks they called the Dragon's Spine mountains, claiming that they needed to gather more magewort.

Our camp was high in the secluded meadows in the foothills of these peaks, with the snow-frosted heights towering over us.

The Black Fleet had to be leagues away. Days away, even! I thought to myself. *How did Havick get up here so fast?*

"We have a place," one of our assassins breathed from the floor.

"Tell us," Veen growled, leaning closer to him.

"It's only a few hours down the stream from here. Just a camp..." the assassin said apologetically.

"How many of you are there?" I said, feeling that prickle of fear to the back of my neck. *Were there more coming for us?*

"Just us two, I promise," the assassin said.

"Yeah – just us two!" his fellow was desperate to agree.

I believed them, waters help me. I knew that a man in pain and facing the end of his life didn't have much reason to lie anymore. Another thing that my father had taught me. "Tell us everything about your mission. What were you doing? Who gave you the orders? Why now?"

And how did you find us, I scowled.

"It was Havick's witch, Ohotto," the first, more talkative assassin said. "There are teams of us sent to the north and south to look for dragon relics. She sent us out by dead ship more than a moon ago."

More than a moon ago? That meant that Ohotto had dispatched them even before the battle of the lighthouse! I felt stupid and clumsy. I had thought that fierce battle, during which we had lost so many and where I had stolen the Sea Crown, had stemmed their dark tide for a while, given us breathing space at the very least. It turns out that I had been very wrong. Havick and Ohotto had been planning their conquest of the mainland for far longer than I had thought. But I turned my attention to the words that still struck fear into me.

"You came here by Black Ship?" I stepped closer to them; it wasn't hard to sound angry.

"Yes." The first assassin opened and closed his white, unseeing eyes. "When we were just a day out of Roskilde, a freezing fog swept up out of nowhere, engulfing us. It could have frozen the riggings, or drive us into a rock, but no – the dead kept on working. Every night that we travelled in that shroud I had nightmares that threatened to completely unman me. It was...*wrong.*"

Magical fog? Nightmares? That sounded like the evil enchantments summoned up by Ohotto Zanna, all right. "And they brought you here to the northern coast, right?" I pointed out.

A nod. "When the fog had parted, the boat was moored by the northern wilds, and me and the others departed."

"The others? How many?" I asked sharply. "I thought you said that there were just two of you?"

"We were told to go in teams of two or three. We went in a pair. We were assigned a direction to go in, places to scout out."

"For these dragon relics?" I insisted.

"Aye," the man breathed painfully. "There's a scroll here…" His hands moved to his belt, but, as fast as a striking snake, Veen had caught the man's hand, eliciting a worried gasp, and gently pushed it out of the way as the Dragon Rider undid the assassin's utility pouches and threw them to me. I tugged them open carefully to reveal a host of the sort of things that a trained killer might need: tiny blades, hooks, fine cord, pots and unguents of healing salves and creams.

And there, I found a fold 0f waxed cloth at the bottom. I teased it open to see that it was what I had feared. Inside there was a scrap of parchment, almost exactly like that of the campaign maps we had stolen from the Witches' Tower on Roskilde, but this map was of the northern mainland, and more importantly, of the wilder coasts and broken hills. I traced my finger along the visible markers, to see that there were over-large houses for settlements, as well as towers with red marks like a dragon's wings.

Where have I seen those before? I thought, and I wished

that Danu was here to help me. I racked my brains, before I suddenly remembered. "The Torvald Towers!" I burst out.

Veen raised a thin eyebrow at me. "I know of them. They were Dragon Monastery towers before that," Veen said, his eyes flicking to the parchment in my hands. "There were many chapels and holy shrines out here in the wilds, when some of the old Draconis Order monks used to retire to spend their last years contemplating the dragon mysteries, sometimes with their companion dragons."

"And they sound like just the places that would have dragon relics," I nodded, turning back to the assassin. "Tell me. Why does Ohotto want dragon relics?"

"I don't know. I promise you, I don't know," the man begged.

Veen growled. "Probably for her dark magics. It is no secret that any dragon remains are very magically potent."

Yes. I knew that already, and it made sense considering everything that Ohotto had done in the past. From attacking the Haunted Isle for their dragon lore, to attacking Queen Ysix's brood. Now she had set her tasks on the lost Draconis Order, as well.

But all this still left me with one question. "How did you know we were here?" I said to the captives, unable to keep the contempt from my voice.

"This." The man moved his gloved hands to his neck, but once again, Veen stopped him, and pulled aside the man's tunic to reveal a strange pendant.

It was a simple oval of bronze like a locket and under Veen's hands it flipped open to reveal a ghastly secret: a braid of dark hair, sealed under a blob of red wax, with an ugly looking rune stamped on top of it.

"What is that thing?" I said.

"It's your mother's hair," the assassin said.

"What?" I felt sick. The ground lurched underneath me as if I were at sea in a storm. *Had Ohotto found Pela? What has that witch done to her?* "You're lying," I spat at him.

"No, it's true." This came from the second, much more terrified assassin. "Ohotto told us before we left. That we had to wear this every day, and if we felt it starting to tug us in a certain direction, then we had to follow it because it would lead us to you."

"And the Sea Crown," added the first assassin. "That was our second task, apart from the relics. To follow this pendant to you, kill you, and retrieve the duke's Sea Crown."

"It's not his though, is it? It's mine!" I said furiously. "And how did you get Pela's hair!?"

"Who?" the first, more talkative assassin sounded confused. "No, the old queen. The Queen of Roskilde."

"What?" The world seemed to shrink to the circumference of a tiny few strands of dark hair.

"The Roskildean royalty always keep a few relics of their

kings and queens," the assassin told me as if everyone knew. "This is hair from your mother when she was coronated, about the same age as you must be now. They keep it in the royal chapel, along with hair from your grandmother, her mother before her, a couple of old kings' fingerbones…"

I shivered with disgust. "So Ohotto did something to it, to make it lead to me?"

"I don't know what she did to it," the assassin said. "But we felt it starting to pull at our necks just yesterday. We had to follow it."

"Lila?" This was from Veen, similarly looking appalled. "It is not unheard of for this sort of sympathetic magic to work. Your mother would always be yearning to see you again, and so this must allow the witch a way to tap into that instinctive power…"

"Whatever it is, it's gross," I said. "I want it destroyed."

"Wise." Veen snatched the pendant and threw it across the clearing to me, where I caught it, and opened it up to look at the lock of my mother's hair. Dark like mine. Gone dry with age, but I knew that once it would be lustrous and fall like velvet.

I threw it into the remains of the fire, and watched it as the wax melted, and the witches mark bubbled away. The foul smell of burning hair lingered over the clearing, and it made me feel sick.

"How many teams of you are there out here, looking for dragon relics?" I spat at the assassin.

"Five? Six?" he breathed.

"Just. Great," I muttered, turning to go. I'd heard enough. "Veen? Can you take them back to their camp with no trouble, or do you want me to come with you?"

"These two won't offer me any trouble"—Veen hauled them to their feet— "because, if they do, I will just tell my dragon to eat them, won't I?" he said very loudly, as he dragged the men held in his fists toward Halex. The Riders hadn't managed to heal the blinded assassins' sight, but their field medicine had done a lot to seemingly ease the magical pains that Danu had caused. I didn't know if either of them would ever fully recover, and once again I worried about the strength of Danu's magic. All I was doing these days was worrying.

"Thank you." I turned away from them and from the fire, to see that on the other side of the clearing, Rigar was doing what he could for Danu, steeping magewort and making sure that he was warm and comfortable on the litter. I could tell he wanted us to be moving as soon as possible, but I had time before Veen got back to check on Crux. I stepped past the smoldering remains that linked me to a woman that I had never known and walked out under the dark trees.

CHAPTER 13
LILA AND THE FEARFUL DRAGON

"Crux?" I whispered into the darks.

"*Wave-rider...*" his voice was whisper-soft, and it took me a moment to make sense of what I was looking at. He had taken for his bed an outcrop of rocks just below our camp, fenced with tall pine trees. He lay snugged hard under the rocks, and in the night his dark scales made him look more than a little stone-like himself.

"Crux, I am here. Are you hurt? Did the men come here first?"

"*Men? They were men? I thought that they were shades of those that passed before...*" His voice was fragile.

"Oh, Crux..." I sat down on one of the boulders next to him, laying my hand on his side. His scales felt cool to the touch, not their usual warming heat. "What are we going to do with you, huh?" I whispered.

"There is nothing to be done. You should continue on without me. Halex is big and brave dragon, he can carry you along with his own Riders." He lowered his snout to just over my head, and his words broke my heart.

"What are you talking about, Crux? It's you and me! It's always been you and me. Ever since you first turned up for the birth of Ysix's brood. I would never, *never* abandon you."

"Not even if it means your survival?" the once-proud Phoenix dragon said sadly. *"I am but an orphan, Lila. I do not even have other siblings, dragon-sisters and dragon-brothers to call my own."*

It was then that I understood just how deeply the bonds of family ran in dragon society. I said, "*I* am an orphan too, Crux. Don't you see? We were made for each other. You're the only brother that I have ever needed."

"Even if I am a brother who cannot protect you?" Crux said.

"Don't be silly." I tried to sound nonchalant. It felt very strange to be motherly to such a large and ferocious beast. "You will always be able to protect me, because that is who you are inside." I reached out and pressed my hand on his snout and felt him huff back in return. As I felt his breath on my hand and face, I felt a shadow of the feeling we used to have – that fiery, incandescent warmth of belonging between us.

Thank you, Lila Wave-rider. I needed that," Crux said, raising his head from me to regard the stars up above. I did not know dragons were prone to musing, and in him I was scared that it would lead to fretting.

"We will be flying as soon as we are able," I told him – mostly to take his mind off whatever demons he might be entertaining. "We're going to go to Torvald, where the other dragons will be able to help you."

"The other dragons might not accept me," Crux said, his words tinged with nervousness. As much as it broke my heart to hear him this way, it was also frustrating. I could see no reason for this young bull dragon to be frightened!

But then again, I thought. How many times have I felt and thought things that others have thought silly? About whether the Raiders would accept me because of my real parents? Or whether I could live up to my father's boots?

I sighed. "I'm sure that is not true. What do you mean, Crux?"

"Dragons might have a bond, but we can also be very territorial," Crux replied sadly. *"It is one of the reasons why my journey to the Western Isles was so long, and so difficult – as the Orange drakes did not take to me. They were upset at my unusual colors and size."*

I thought about the much smaller dog and pony-sized Orange drakes that had become our unintentional allies when we had been taking refuge on the south coast. They were fierce, and savage little brutes, but they were also cute in their own pointy way. "But look what happened, Crux – you managed to win them over, and now they love you!" I pointed out, and it was true. After they had started to view Crux as an ally and not a threat – as one of their own brood, even, they had seemed enamored of the larger Phoenix dragon, more so than the other Sinuous Blues and Island Greens.

"That was because Danu used his dragon ability to reach out to them, to explain to them that I could bring them fish," Crux said. *"It wasn't me."*

I endeavored to listen to him, even though I disagreed with his assessment. He was still my friend, and even if he was unwell and fearful at the moment, his concerns deserved my respect. "Sometimes, Crux – it takes another person to point something out, or to make a connection from their perspective," I agreed. "Just as Danu helped bridge the gap between you and the Orange drakes, so I, Rigar, and Veen, will help you become friends with the Torvald dragons. After all, Halex *is* a Torvald dragon, right?"

"I suppose so…" Crux lowered his head to look at me with his wide eyes. Was there a hint of that old sparkle that I remember seeing there?

"Come on, wyrm– get some rest before first light. I will sleep here, at your side," I said, crawling in under his wing to find a bit of shelter despite his cool scales. As I drifted off against his belly, it felt for a while just like old times; that we were safe again with each other, and nothing would hurt us.

CHAPTER 14
DANU AND THE GUARDIAN DRAGONS

Awake or asleep, I could sense the strains of magic all around me in the same way that you might hear music. It had started after last night, when I had apparently almost maimed those two assassins for life.

It was not something that I was proud of, and waves of shame over my actions washed up into me every time I thought about it.

"We have all done things we wished we hadn't," said a reptilian voice in my mind, bringing with it the scent of soot and fire. But this mind was not Crux's, I knew that instinctively. It sounded different in my imagination, for one thing, and my eyes were groggily drawn open to peer out past the rising winds to see that it was Halex, the dragon of the ancient Riders Rigar and Veen flying just a little way off from us.

"Skreyar!" Halex let out a large bellow as he soared, and the sound reverberated off the distant peaks, as if he were challenging me.

Dragon language is different from human tongue, that much was obvious. Even though I could hear the dragons' words in my mind thanks to my dragon ability, it consisted of more than words alone. Dragons think in images and feelings and memories and I had often thought that the 'words' that Lila or I might hear was just our own human minds trying to make sense of that.

As Halex's words entered my mind, they came with a sense of forgiveness and ancient wisdom. As Crux's words were always filled with youthful fire—or they had been until worried anxiety had recently replaced that— Halex's words were filled with a hundred changes of seasons, watching the snow settle and melt many times over, and images of countless battles marching beneath him and raging in the skies around him. Halex had been in many wars for the then-Middle Kingdom of Torvald, and I reeled for a moment with the sound of clashing swords, roaring dragons, and the acrid smell of dragon fire.

He knew what he was talking about. I don't know if it was just the act of a dragon's wisdom or kindness, but Halex's few words in my mind brought a sense of peace to my aching and sickly mind. I felt a little clearer, a little more like myself.

"Thank you," I whispered, and the old dragon whipped his tail in response as we flew.

"Danu? Are you all right?" Lila turned in her saddle and called to me. She must have heard my murmuring. "Do you need more magewort? Rigar left a flask with me, if you do…"

"No," I said immediately. That drink, apart from easing my aches and pains, also made me sleepy. It dulled my mind, and I didn't want that for what I had to tell Lila.

"The witches have gone," I said.

"What?" She turned fully around now, unclipping one of the saddle clips in order to do so. I could see from the way that she was looking at me, that she was thinking that I was having one of my frenzied dreams (nightmares, more like) once again, but I saw her skepticism fade as she looked into my eyes.

"I received a message from Afar, like how they contacted us before? The witches are abandoning Sebol, taking what they can and leaving. They will be gone by the new moon," I said, and it was hard to keep the tragedy from my voice. That place had been my home for the longest that *anywhere* had. It would be strange to think of it empty.

"But…how could they? That's terrible!" Lila said, and I had to say that I agreed with her, even if a part of me *did* understand why the Western Witches had decided to do it. The idea of an undead witch, like an undead dragon, was just an anathema.

Witches are supposed to be guardians of life, not of death. Which was what made what Ohotto was doing—playing with the very powers of creation itself, of life and death— so abhorrent.

"I was hoping the witches would be able to hold the west, and that Torvald would be able to attack from the east!" Lila said.

There seemed nothing I *could* say in response. Lila settled for a groan and shook her head, just as a shiver of awareness rushed through me.

"Danger." It was Crux, his delicate senses picking up on something before my puny human eyes ever could. Lila stiffened in her seat a fraction of a moment later, as Crux must have shared his alarm with her, too.

"Where?" Lila said urgently, but I was already turning my head in the direction where it came from. I could *feel* it coming.

We had been flying high over mountain passes and were still surrounded by the taller reaches on either side of us when we saw them. The air was crisp and cold, but our excitement and fear drove the chill from my body. Beneath us were crystalline sparkles of snow, broken only by the grey and black rocks of the mountains that Rigar and Veen were leading us through.

The skies above were a cerulean blue, with gossamer drifts of clouds collecting around the peaks. Everything was peaceful – apart from the three dragons that flew towards us.

They were big, each one easily of the same size as Halex, which meant that they were a little bigger than Crux. These

Stocky Greens were Torvald's fighting dragons, because of their girth and strong limbs. They flashed and gleamed in the bright sunlight, and they held their line with perfect precision.

"What does it mean?" I heard Lila call out to Rigar and Veen, but they said nothing.

"Skreych!" Halex screamed at our neighbors in the sky. She, like Ysix too, was a Sinuous Blue – although her color was dusted pastel, silvered with age. For a brief moment I wondered if this was a trait of the Blue dragons – that they were able to live longer. Maybe because the Stocky Greens have such fierce lives, I thought dismally, feeling Crux's quiverings shoot through my mind.

"Easy, my friend. It will be all right, you'll see…" I promised him, not believing my own words. *What if Torvald decided they didn't like us? We were Raiders, after all?* The tension crackling from Crux and Halex was palpable, shaking me from my groggy thoughts, and filling me with an alert, slightly anxious, energy.

Rigar and Veen weren't Raiders, I reminded myself as Veen, their lead 'navigator' I think he called himself, raised a hand in an apparent ritual gesture. Maybe these new dragon-fliers would respect *them* even if they wouldn't respect *us*.

The three Green dragons and their Dragon Riders ignored him. They grew larger as they swept towards us, flying in perfect unison with their wingtips almost touching – and I saw how they angled their flight so that they would be flying *above* us, not under us. I wracked my brains to remember the Torvald history tomes on Sebol. Did that flying formation mean that they were going to attack?

Rigar and Veen went into action. They seemed spooked by how these three Stocky Greens were flying. They pulled Halex ahead of us with powerful wingbeats and lashes of his tail, as the pair worked in tandem. It was like watching one of the well-crewed Raider ships at full sail, when the entire crew moved as one. Veen leaned his body and Rigar copied his example, pushing out with a foot and pulling on his own secondary reins to give more tension or pull to the straps under Halex's wings or legs. I had thought these 'support' straps an oddity when I had first seen them – why would a dragon need help knowing which way to fly, or which wing to raise or lower? But now, however, I saw this mechanism worked perfectly. It wasn't the same as Raider-riding, that was for sure – but the dragon and academy Riders worked in unison, giving more precision and balance at the precise moments they needed as they swooped up towards the advancing Greens.

Halex flared his wings and scratched at the air, rising higher than the Stocky Greens were – who were now seeking to copy his example.

This was a dominance trial, I thought. I had once seen a pair of the Sea Herons that came to the reed-meadows of Sebol during nesting time do this. They would launch themselves at each other, seeking to fly higher than the other to see who was dominant.

"Go, Halex, go!" I found myself shouting.

All four dragons rose up, high above us – so high that I could not see who was winning – and they were ascending so close to each other as to be almost locking talons.

With shrieks and calls, the three Stocky Greens suddenly broke apart, tearing down out of the sun straight towards us. Did this mean that Halex had lost? Or won?

"Lila…" I said hesitantly, before I was jolted in my saddle.

"Crux, no!" Lila called, just as Crux flicked his wings and shot down towards the snow plains like an attacking hawk. The wind was in my hair and suddenly I was freezing and holding onto the saddle for dear life!

Crux was running away. I couldn't believe what was happening. The bravest, most-savage Phoenix dragon was running away from a fight.

But there was nothing that I could do but to help him. I felt for his worried mind to try to anticipate what might happen next. Maybe there would be a spell that I could use that would help us—

But Crux had walled his thoughts off from me! "Crux?" I said, just as the snow plain swept up towards us in crystal clarity – with the Torvald Stocky Greens just a little way behind – and then the young Bull Phoenix opened out his wings with a snap like thunder, and we were shooting meters above the surface of the snow.

Crux didn't stop there. He plunged and kicked with his back legs down to the snowline, sending up great gouts and clouds of the fine stuff behind us just as the Stocky Greens started to copy our movements.

"SKRAAR!" The angered dragons behind us roared as we rose out of the dragon-made snowstorm, Crux powering his wings again in a tempest of movement as he fought now to get above the dragons.

Another booming call echoed, and Halex swooped down over us, raising his ancient claws in an aerial dive that meant he scraped the air meters above where the three Stocky Greens were. It would have been a devastating attack if it had hit...

"Ha!" Lila shouted, and the tone in her voice made me stop. She sounded happy. Excited. Exultant, even! What was she thinking? We're in a near-death fight against the very people we were meant to ask for help! I turned to see what she was looking at, to see that the Stocky Greens had angled their ascent, flying lower now as they broke their exact formation, one even raising its snout to trill a long set of whistles and clicks at us. What was going on?

"Don't you see? It was a test! Like walking the plank!" Lila laughed as she called out to me.

Remembering the looks of hatred from the Stocky Greens as they had dived towards us did not make me think this was a very friendly test. "Isn't walking the plank when you Raiders kill traitors?" I pointed out.

Lila, to my surprise, looked aghast at the thought. "Is that what you've been thinking all this time? That we kill unarmed people? For shame, Danu!" she said irritably. "We do sometimes force a particularly bothersome captured captain or first mate to walk the plank, but we pick them out of the drink afterwards! We're not monsters, you know."

"Oh." I thought about those battling Sea Herons, and I realized that this was the same thing. None of the herons were usually hurt. It was all just show and feathers and claws to see who top bird was.

"And that was Crux," I thought, feeling suddenly immensely pleased. "Lila – it was Crux who won! Crux outsmarted them!"

"That is because Crux is the best dragon there ever was." Lila grinned widely.

The three Stocky Greens were each backed by two Dragon Riders of the Torvald Academy, in the same rigging as Rigar and Veen wore (although their armor was completely different, and all their equipment looked shiny and new, whereas Rigar and Veen's was old and patched, but well-maintained). I studied their differences between these two sorts of Dragon Riders as we landed on a rocky outcrop, dusted with snow.

"Hail to thee, Riders of Torvald," Rigar said, holding up his right hand in an open gesture. "Hail to thee, Dragons of the Mountain," Veen said, copying his gesture but instead addressing it to the dragons.

The six Torvald riders looked a little uncomfortable at this, but it went down well with the Stocky Green dragons. One made a pleased hiss, and the other two blinked their great golden eyes like a cat. One by one, three of the Riders of Torvald slipped from their beasts. Each of them was the 'second' of their dragon team, leaving their 'navigator' up front. Two of them were women, I saw, and one was a rangy-looking man. They wore red-gold armor that flared at the shoulders and elbows, and helmets that sculpted the wind as it rushed past them.

"You seem to know a lot about the academy, friend?" called one of the women fighters. She walked out ahead of the others, a shield on her back as she leaned on a tall spear-like lance.

"I could say the same about you," Rigar called back, as he walked briskly over the snow towards them, no weapons in hand but hands upraised. I followed his lead and slipped from Crux's back.

"Woah there, we don't know if we can let you into Torvald skies, yet." The woman took a half-step back, and I saw her settling into a warrior's crouch.

Rigar laughed and walked ahead anyway. "What is this? We've had the Challenge of the Dragons, and your three lost, although—" he turned to bow a respectful head to the Stocky Greens, "—I am sure that it was none of your faults, but your Riders!" He boomed with laughter.

"Why—!" The other woman made to lower her spear, but I was surprised as one of the Stocky Green dragons hissed.

"These old ones are right. You would do well, Isolde, to listen to them!" I heard the Green dragon say clearly to his human companion and found myself smirking.

"And what is this?" the Green dragon continued as all three of the Torvald dragons swiveled their head to me. *"A dragon-friend?"*

"Uh…" I felt suddenly nervous under the scrutiny of these beasts.

"Who vouches for this human? What dragon has claimed you?" the first Stocky Green said. Around us, both Rigar and Veen had stepped respectfully out of the way of our conversation, and the other Dragon Riders of Torvald seemed stunned by this sudden interjection.

"I do," I heard Crux say beneath me, his voice sounding like whistles and clicks in my ears, but in all of our heads it was clear and bold reptilian fire. *"I, Crux the Phoenix of the West. Dragon-brother of Lila Wave-rider, have claimed Danu Geidt as my dragon-friend."*

More hisses and thumps of tails. *"We have not seen your family in these skies before, brother,"* I heard the more vocal Stocky Green say. *"Who is your queen? Your Den-mother?"*

A quiver swept through Crux, and I knew that he was scared at their questioning. The Orange drakes had rejected him violently on his way to the West, would these Torvald breeds of dragons do the same, too?

"I have no Den-mother that I can claim." His words were thick with emotion. I wondered what his story was, and why

he had no mother to call his own – was it because she was dead? *"But I am son of Velchmar, son of Daryx and Sol, and for my queen, I call only Queen Ysix of the Western Isles."*

There was an appreciative chorus of hiss and clicks from the Stocky Greens.

"What does this mean?" said the female Rider who had challenged Rigar, and it was Rigar who answered her.

"You new lot, really!" Rigar laughed. "What are they teaching at the academy these days? Some people think that it's us humans who get the dragons to help us with what we want to do with the realms, but it's always been the other way around." He chuckled as he turned back to Halex. "We live in a dragons' world, my young friends – and if the dragons say to trust someone, then the rest of us have to all just get along!"

His laughter was more of a balm to my soul as we all rose into the air behind the academy dragons, than any tincture or potion of magewort.

CHAPTER 15
LILA AND TORVALD

I had never seen anything like it. The citadel of Torvald gleamed in the sunlight like a jewel – its terraces of high walls catching the sun as they marched up the side of the mountain in ever-decreasing arcs.

"It's even bigger than Roskilde," I murmured in awe. I had never seen anything quite so dense as my uncle's stronghold before. Now, though, it made me realize how large the world was outside the Western Archipelago. We had flown across seas, over ruins, over whole mountain ranges and leagues of fields and meadows – and now this.

The citadel of Torvald was built up the side of a broken mountain, with its tall palace gleaming at the top, and spread out into layers down over the foothills. The city itself ended before the bald rocks of the mountain saddle, where I could see another structure, red sandstone, dark against the deep blues of the sky. *Was that...?*

"Skrearch!" I heard the distant hoots and calls of the Torvald Academy dragons, and, to my amazement, what I had taken to be a tower, or a building unfolded its wings from this upmost red fortification, and swooped low over the saddle, its wings snapping as it flew out of view.

Dragons! My heart sang with joy. There were others now, wheeling and descending on the warm, summery airs to the other side of the mountain, away from the city and the academy, where it looked like there was the caldera of an old volcano, like the ones that I had seen from afar in the Western Archipelago.

Something clutched at my heart, and for a moment I trembled with awe. But it was more than just the awe at seeing such a sight – it was also a feeling of *familiarity,* somehow. Something about the shape of it; the mountain, the city, and the home of the dragons nearby made sense to my heart in a way that was hard for me to fathom.

"It is one of the dragon homes," Crux said, his voice still hesitant, but not as fearful as it had been before. I reached my thoughts out to the dragon-shaped space in my mind, and felt again that eternal, confident warmth. Not as bright or as fierce as it had been when we had first met, or before his injury, but stronger than he had been since.

"You feel better," I remarked, unable to keep the joy from my voice.

"Yes. I don't understand it, but something about this place fills me with...." His dragon-tongue struggled to find the words in human tongue, and instead my mind filled with a wash of images. Of gigantic cracked shells, and warm, mewling newts. Of the glorious warmth of a hot summer's day, and dozy sleep as you laze upon a baked rock. Of flying together with many others of your kind, each whistling and calling joyously as you spread out across the world.

"Completeness," I stated. It was how I felt when I was flying on Crux, and it echoed how I felt when I was on my father's flagship the *Ariel,* travelling at full-clip under a favorable wind, with all the crew working in unison.

"Yes. Complete," Crux echoed, and the thrum of happiness ran through him like quicksilver.

"Danu?" Feeling such joy, I turned around to Danu to see what effect this place was having on *him,* too – to see that it was very different indeed.

He was sitting up in his saddle (he had been far more able to sit and talk since we had passed over in Torvald lands) but now he looked like a statue, his eyes fixed on the mountain with a weird intensity. I saw a rictus grin on his features – but it wasn't something that I thought was a good thing, as beads of sweat were appearing on his brow and his jaw was clenched as if he were sailing through a storm.

"Danu? Are you okay?"

He coughed, shook his head, and I saw him blink, focusing

on me as if he had been asleep. "Yes. I think so…it's just – the magic is so strong here…"

It must be the dragon home, if I had understood what Crux had been trying to tell me. This was like some ancestral home to the dragons of the world, and everyone knew that dragons had lived here for thousands of years. Hadn't Danu told me that the dragons were a fundamental part of a witch's magic, or had some vital connection to it? I wondered if what we were doing would be throwing him into harm's way, rather than saving him.

"Here." I passed him the flask of Rigar and Veen's magewort. "Drink it. I won't take no for an answer," I said seriously.

"Yes, yes I think you are right," I saw my friend mumble, and struggled to pull the cork stopper before he glugged heavily at the strange, fragrant-smelling potion. Almost instantly, his muscles relaxed, and a sleepy look fell over his eyes. He jammed the stopper back into its flask and sighed as if he had run a race.

"Keep it with you," I advised, "just in case…" and he nodded.

There was a whistling call at our side, and I saw that one of the Riders of the Stocky Greens had unveiled a long pennant that had been attached to their saddle, green over purple as we few towards the city. It seemed to mean something, as I heard an answering blare from a far-off horn. But what?

The city swept closer, and now I could see how populated it and the surrounds were. Large, cobble-packed roads lead to its large gates, which were laden with carts and wagons and people. Was it always this busy, or was there some kind of fiesta going on? The city itself was a mosaic of peaked and slanted rooftops, with the occasional spire or tower, edged with the green of city trees. Birds lifted from and resettled on the walls, and marketplaces bustled inside.

But the city gates were closed, which made me puzzle. The lines of carriages and people were forming a logjam in a wide area in front of each, as they were carefully let through only a few at a time.

"What's going on?" I called out, but the Academy Dragon Riders were too far forward to hear me. We were flying higher, up the mountain towards the topmost tier, and as we swept over this marvelous land, I saw that the battlements of Torvald were thick with lines of archers with massive long-bows, almost as tall as they were!

This was starting to look like a city at war, I felt with a shock, and my own hand slid naturally to the sturdy wood of my bow. Not that I could do anything with it, of course. *Had the Torvald Riders who had challenged us sent word ahead? Had they recognized us as Raiders?* I gritted my teeth as I tried to do what my mother had suggested. *Be the smartest,* take in all the information I could, assess the situation.

It was hard to stop myself from peering this way and that as I drank in all of the new sights, and smelled baking bread and cook fires and the smokes from smithies and furnaces. There were so many people inside this city, of seemingly all creeds and nations. I had never imagined that Torvald was so well-populated. I guess that, in my mind at least, it would be another place like Ros, the ancestral capital of Roskilde. But it was more advanced than the city that my uncle had usurped. Here there were canals and waterwheels, mill-wheels and tall towers with strange brass instruments. My imagination boggled.

But now all of that ended as the houses grew taller and grander, each surrounded by their own little parklands that reminded me a little (sadly) of the colonial mansion house of my foster-parents on Malata. This tier of the city was the second highest, and we were approaching the high white walls that surrounded the palace of the empire itself.

Gosh. If I had been flabbergasted by the citadel, then I was floored by the Palace of Torvald. It was a little like my uncle's keep, but much bigger. It had several 'wings' of buildings that ended in large round towers and joined with further elegant ivory-colored walls. Different segments of the palace grounds I could see were given over to either green lawns or sandy training fields, and still more bright with formally arranged gardens. *My mother would love this,* I thought – not the high walls and the busyness of it, but that here she would be able to do all the things she liked: gardening – and fighting!

Not sailing, though, I bemoaned Torvald's lack of a coast.

Another blare resounded from one of the higher, slender

towers of the palace, and the lead Stocky Green dragon emitted a whistling call in response. We circled the airs once, then twice, descending in formation towards one of the large areas at the back of the palace grounds, which seemed especially given over to just such a purpose. Small human figures ran back and forth across the court, carrying ropes and what looked like barrels of food to fill large troughs at the further end.

So, this is what a well-run dragon community looks like, I thought, feeling as though my own paltry efforts to help the Sea Dragon Raiders establish a bond were pretty pathetic in comparison.

"Not so, Wave-rider! Although many dragons like to be pampered, not all. The wilder dragons of the islands like to be free to come and go, to hunt as they will, with or without their human allies."

"Are these dragons not free, then?" I said, feeling a sort of revulsion.

"They are free. But they are like prime stallions compared to mountain cobs," he advised me, although I didn't get the reference, as horses in the Western Archipelago were rare.

Despite Crux's assertions, it was hard not to feel slightly jealous of the way Torvald operated, and how the Academy Riders flew together. The three stocky dragons lined up in perfect formation, each one swooping to land and varying their angle of descent by an exact amount as they landed with a skip and a leap behind each other on the long Greens.

The Sinuous Blue Halex, too, made a perfectly controlled descent – although at the last moment he flared his wings and rose a few meters into the air, as if announcing himself to the citadel.

"Our turn now, Crux," I murmured.

"I cannot fly like they do," he said, a shadow of his old anxiety returned.

"You fly as *you* do, my friend." I leaned forward. "Land how a *Phoenix dragon* wants to land, not an Academy dragon."

He chirruped a cough of smoke and did not swoop elegantly as the other Stocky Greens had – or even Halex had, sort of. Instead, he beat his wings to slow his flight, fanning the grass and creating a furious clamor in the air as he hovered for a moment, before settling in exactly the spot he chose. This, I saw, was more of an island dragon way to land, as there aren't very often long stretches of open country in the islands to glide down towards.

I heard coughs and muttered voices from the humans nearby, and I sensed that we had acted out-of-character to this place, but I didn't care. We weren't mainlanders, after all, I reminded myself.

"Lady Rider. Sir!" called out a voice, and a middle-aged man with pepper and blond hair walked towards us, spectacles perched upon his nose. He wore the training leathers of one of these dragon helpers as he waved at me. "The handlers will see that this welcome friend is taken care of, with food, water, and room to fly in." The man smiled warmly at Crux, who had turned his head to one side to regard him suspiciously with one eye. "We have fish," he offered. "The best fisheries in all of the middle lands!"

He must be some kind of captain or quartermaster, I thought with a frown. "Crux?" I whispered. "Will you be all right here, with Halex?"

But the ancient Sinuous Blue, it seemed, had very different plans, as I heard its harsh cry as Rigar and Veen dismounted, carrying their saddles with them. Halex held out his wings, shaking them to settle his shoulder scales a little as he let the two untie and release all of the complicated dragon straps that they used to fly. With a whistle, it raised its snout at Crux, and I heard the Blues hissing voice in my head.

"We fly to introduce ourselves to Jaydra, the Queen – although she will already know of our appearance in her skies."

"The queen?" A tremor shivered through Crux's back.

"Lila?" It was Danu, still groggy, looking at me with worry as he ran a hand over Crux's night-black scales.

"You don't have to do anything that you don't want to, Crux," I promised him.

"Crux, son of Sol. You must meet the Queen of this Den," Halex's call was sharp and insistent.

"No, Lila, I do," Crux hissed in uncertainty, a deep rattling noise that swept down his long gullet. *"But I want to, as well.*

I did not spend a lot of my time amongst other dragons before finding you – but this? This feels right."

Another tremor swept through him, and I knew that he was still apprehensive, but I had to take him at his word. "You come and find me the second you want to. Anywhere I am in that castle. We'll leave."

"I didn't fly all this way to leave so soon!" Crux said with a spark of his old, teasing self. That was enough to make me feel that he was strong enough to go through this challenge that only he could pass, alone. I undid the straps of the saddle and slid down one side of his shoulder, to help Danu undo the pallet that he had been sleeping on during his long illness.

"Ugh, thank you." Danu wobbled slightly on his feet.

"Are you unwell, my friend?" said the blond quartermaster with the spectacles, moving to Danu's side. The man's brow was creased with worry.

"He's fine." I intercepted the man, putting myself in between him and Danu forcefully. As much as I wanted the aid of these people, I did not want them to think that we were weak or could not help our own. I was still worried this was all a ploy and they would throw us all in chains as soon as they found out that I was a Sea Raider!

The man raised his hands in a calming gesture, and stepped back and nodded towards the double doors at the end of the landing yard. "That way will lead you into the palace proper, and there are house stewards who can direct you to whomever you want to speak to."

"Thank you," Danu whispered, leaning on me, and I gave a curt nod.

Rigar and Veen were already ahead of us, striding forward into the hallway beyond that was lined with equipment lockers and cubicles where one could freshen up before they entered the palace. The two older Dragon Riders did not stop but seemed to know where they were going as they ascended the stairs at the far end to another arched doorway from which they beckoned us after them.

"Has this place changed much?" Danu whispered as he lurched at my side. His voice sounded strained, and I wondered if the magic here of this mountain would be too strong for him. *What would happen if he did what he had a few nights ago? Starts levitating and judging who around us deserves to be punished?* These people will kill him, surely. Isn't that what my father or mother would do if he had done just that at Malata?

"It wears new clothes," Veen intoned stoically, which I didn't think was a compliment.

Rigar, however, was more forthcoming as he pointed first down one long flagstone-paved gallery to lead us through an adjacent long hall. Statues stood down the sides, with tall and strange plants clustering under the stained-glass windows. "The palace is very different from when we were first here, under the old Kingdom of Torvald. It grows a new tower every few decades, the tapestries change, old statues are torn down and the ones of the newer heroes are put in their place." He sounded wistful, and sad. "But it remains the same underneath it all." There was a pause as we passed from this hall to another wide passageway, where tables of scribes looked up in shock at our sudden appearance.

"The palace has always been a place of wonder," Rigar whispered as the scribes and clerks frowned, and bent their heads back to their tasks. "When we were young, we would come to great balls here every season, where nobles from across the Three Kingdoms would try to outdo each other with their costumes or seek to marry their prized children off to the best available young lady or little lord." A shadow of a mischievous smile spread across the old man's face, and I tried to picture that time, ladies in whirling dresses or bright pantaloons, gentlemen in their best frock suits. All I had to inspire my imaginings were the occasional children's story books my father had looted from merchant ships for me, so I was left with a confusing image of princesses and knights with swords.

"But the *real* wonder is the academy," Rigar leaned over to whisper in my ear. "Perhaps, if we have time, the king and queen will allow us to visit."

Yes, I thought, thinking of that distant red sandstone building with dragons on its walls that I had seen on the flight in. Even though I was supposedly royalty, I no more felt at home amongst these elegant halls as I did surrounded by miles of land, and not water.

I wonder what will happen at Ros, if I ever manage to

unseat Havick. Another worry blossomed into my mind. I didn't want to be a princess in a gown, locked away in the heart of a castle like a pearl in an oyster.

"Sirs! My lady!" a voice barked before us, and I looked up to see that there was the sudden appearance of four very well-armored knights blocking our path through the open archway that led into a much wider and brighter hall. Their armor was of a burnished bronze, with elaborate dragons stylized on their breast.

"You cannot bring weapons any further," one of them said, his gauntleted hand resting easy on the pommel of his sword.

A Raider doesn't leave their bed without a weapon! I wanted to say but knew that would throw me in their dungeons as fast as if I had killed one of these inland people. I still gritted my teeth, hesitated as I waited to see what Rigar and Veen would do.

"Our apologies, of course." Rigar bowed graciously, carefully removing his sword belt and his dagger, and offering them up in exaggerated caution to these knights. Veen beside him did the same, and I guessed that was my answer.

I will go into that room unarmed? Every word of warning that my father and mother had taught me rang in my ears like a bell. Always be prepared. Always be smarter than the other guy. Smarter, quicker, and braver.

"Ma'am." The knight-captain was looking at me heavily.

"Oh, okay then. Just look after this blade, it's served me well," I grumbled as I undid my sabre and scabbard, then my belt knife, my fishing knife, and I even handed over the set of brass knuckles that I kept wrapped around my ankle. The expression of this knight went from serious to unapproving, but at least Danu was a much easier target to disarm – just his knife and short sword.

"And who shall we say approached the throne?" another of these guards intoned.

"Old friends," Rigar said. "Tell the throne that Rigar and Veen have returned, and I promise they will want to see us."

Oh yeah, I keep forgetting these two had met Saffron and Bower, I thought with a flutter in my stomach. What with the assassins, and then all of the new sights and Danu's magical affliction, I hadn't had time to consider that these two actually knew the woman that I had admired all of my life!

Queen Saffron, I thought. *Saffron Zenema,* so named after the great island Queen Dragon that had raised her as a child. The wild island girl who had overthrown a magical despot and had become a queen herself. It was a fairy story, really. The sort of thing that didn't happen to normal people.

But she was never a normal person, was she? A small thought snuck into my mind, making me feel both ashamed at the thinking of it, and ashamed that I, lowly Lila the Sea Raider could imagine that I would have anything in common with her. Saffron used to have magic, that was what Rigar himself had told me. Great Queen Saffron had been like the Western Witches, born strange and powerful since birth, and *that* was why fate had picked her up to be the Queen of the Empire.

That thought made me feel more than a little cheated, to tell you the truth. My mother Pela had always told me that it was hard work and determination – guts – that got you where you wanted to be in life. I guess I had used my image of Queen Saffron as an example of that: a lowly island girl who had made it all the way to the Palace of Torvald. Nothing had to stand in your way if you didn't want it.

But now I knew Saffron had always had magic? It made me feel even more uncertain about my role and my chances. I had no natural magic like Danu or the witches, and I was trying to stop an Army of the Dead.

"Lila?" It was Rigar, looking back at me from the archway. He inclined his head towards the light. "Are you ready?"

"I guess I have to be, right?" I muttered, keeping my arm around Danu's slightly shaking shoulders as I walked in, doing my best to keep my head held high.

CHAPTER 16
LILA AND SAFFRON

The royal throne room of the Empire of Torvald was not what I was expecting. For one, it was full of plants. But then again, I had only ever seen Havick's throne room, so I wasn't quite sure *what* I should have been expecting.

It was a large hall, long, and with a raised dais at the far end with, as you might think, two adjacent high-backed thrones of gold and plush purple velvets. But the king and queen were not sitting there. It was a room full of light, with impressive arched windows along the walls, next to slightly more shaded alcoves where large paintings were hung.

The main aspect of the room, however, was dominated by central tables upon which sat a polyphony of plants in large clay pots. There was every kind here, thriving in the secluded and steamy warmth of the room – I could see large-leafed lilies next to cacti, even ornamental trees in the center with vines curling around their lower branches. The air smelled fresh and full of life, and rare flowers poked their heads from the varied foliage. I was surprised to see such a large variety of island plants here, in pots of rich granular sandy soils, flecked with quartz; and stranger breeds too – orchids, I think, and climbing flower bulbs which I guess must have come from the warm southlands.

Around these tables walked, tended, and people talked in elegant robes of bright hues, sharing their space with men and women in tan leather aprons who took cuttings and pruned as their lords and courtiers talked the matters of state.

"Refreshment, ma'am?" the blond, be-speckled dragon-quartermaster from before said, holding a silver tray with fluted crystal glasses of something light and sparkling.

"I, uh…" I didn't know what to say. This had none of the feel of the grim and ostentatious throne room of my usurper uncle.

"Thank you," said Rigar, accepting a glass. Veen did not, and I was about to refuse, but Danu croaked at my side, and I took one to press into his slightly shaking hands.

"We have healers, I will call them," said the quartermaster, already turning to disappear into the crowds before I could stop him.

"This way." Rigar nodded through the drifts of people, walking slowly down the line of tables, with leaves brushing his shoulders. I followed him and Veen, with Danu lurching at my side.

To see the queen.

I recognized her in an instant, and it wasn't the simple gold circlet that she wore on her head (nothing like the heavy Sea Crown that was still in my shoulder pack, I noted), it was also her straight-backed bearing, the fineness of her deep crimson and purple robes that flattered her figure, and of course her near-platinum hair. She was nearing her middle-years, I saw, but there was no hesitancy or caution with how she moved.

"Queen Saffron," both Rigar and Veen said as they went down on one knee.

"Old friends." She raised her eyes to greet them, and the aproned plant-tender she had been discussing something with took her leave. Her eyes – so bright! – alighted on me, and I felt instantly embarrassed. *How could I ever think that I was like her!* I thought, as I managed a rough bob of my head, and Danu awkwardly bowed stiffly from his waist.

"Your friend is ill? Let me call Haleth – she can do wonders with her remedies…" Saffron's eyes shadowed with worry.

"Already done it, my love!" said a returning voice, and I saw that it was the dragon-quartermaster from before, who still had on his leather work clothes, but had ditched his silver tray and donned a short purple cape and a golden circlet.

"Lord Bower," Rigar murmured respectfully, as Veen performed a perfect salute.

"He's the king!?" I said, astonished. But kings don't get their hands dirty! They don't go around cleaning up after dragons and handing out wine like stewards – did they?

"Ah, I'm sorry if I surprised you," said Bower, pushing his spectacles a little further up his nose. "Neither I nor my queen really like being bowed and scraped to. We prefer just to get on with the business of the palace…"

"And he likes to see the surprise on our guests faces when he shakes their hand with muddy paws!" Queen Saffron teased him.

"I cleaned up!" he said good-naturedly, holding up his hands which only had a few specks of dirt, I saw. Their manner made me smile, despite the gravity of our mission. My mother would love them, I thought. At his side was a much smaller woman, dressed in simple whites and creams, who *looked* older even that Rigar and Veen. She had mountains of grey hair in thick matted braids, clipped back and set close to her head. Around her throat was a selection of charms and pendants – curious bits of root and rock suspended by fine silver chains.

"And this is our patient?" the woman bustled forward without formality. "I am Gorlas, the healer here – we have the best healing courts anywhere in the world, so you can trust your friend to our care…"

"No," I said protectively, my hands closing around Danu's shoulder. As much as I found myself liking them, I still did not know what they would think of Danu's 'affliction.' Or of Crux's.

"Child, you can trust me. If the queen has asked for him to be tended, I will do everything in my power to help him." Gorlas frowned at me, and I saw something of Danu's mentor Afar about her.

"Danu comes from the Haunted Isle," Rigar said, as if that explained everything. I felt a shiver of mistrust. *How could he spill our secrets so readily?*

There was a slight stiffening from all of those around us. I saw Gorlas's jaw tighten, and King Bower even moved his hand slightly to the dagger at his belt. Even as I was shocked by this, I was more hurt by how Saffron responded – her eyes flicking, eagle-like, between us in a gesture that I knew well, because I had seen it on the face of our trained Raiders every time they measured up a potential enemy.

"He means you no harm!" I said quickly, releasing my hold on Danu's shoulder and taking a half step in front of him. "The Western Witches, despite their reputation, have been great allies to us." I forced myself to admit the truth of my own words. It was a hard thing, as my foster-father had drilled into me the maxim that 'you can never trust a witch' to the point where I *still* didn't know whether Danu shared my goals completely, but I would have to be an idiot to not acknowledge just how much help they had been to our campaign so far. Lifesavers, even.

"I'm sure he doesn't," King Bower said sternly. "But that

does not mean that he won't *bring* us harm." He looked towards his queen. "We have seen what a mage can do."

"But the boy was raised by the Western Witches?" Queen Saffron commented shrewdly. "I did not know much about them during my early life in the isles, as I led such a sheltered existence – but Zenema always talked fondly of them."

"Aye." I nodded, swallowing nervously as I sought to inform the Queen of Torvald. "Chabon, the Matriarch of the Western Witches where my friend here was trained, was dragon-friend to Queen Zenema, mother of the island dragons."

"She was?" Saffron looked startled, her eyes widening as one dirt-tinged hand went to her lips. I knew that she had been raised by Zenema, and that Saffron had taken on her name after the old den-mother had died in battle. The queen turned her head to one side and looked far, as if listening to someone that only she could hear, and beside me Danu mumbled out of his stupor.

"That's true," he chuckled a little, blinking groggily.

"He can hear the dragons," Saffron said, appraising him differently.

"My lady," Danu managed to say, squinting as he focused on her. He tried another awkward bow. "My name is Danu Geidt, and I am lucky enough to be a dragon-friend, and student of Afar of Sebol, under Matriarch Chabon." Even this simple sentence seemed to have cost him, however, as he leaned against me heavily. "It is the magic here, it is so strong…" he whispered.

"Gorlas?" King Bower said urgently.

"I know, sire. Magewort," she said, hurrying from our company.

The situation had changed, but I was still unsure what it meant for my mission, but Saffron seemed to relax – *slightly*. "If the dragons share their thoughts with you, then they will have seen your heart. It is not for me to judge you unworthy of these halls, if the dragons already have placed their trust in you."

"Thank you, ma'am," Danu whispered against me.

A few moments later, Gorlas returned with two other similar white and cream wearing healers, carrying a long sedan chair, which they set under the foliage and helped Danu lie upon. "It would be better in my courts, but, sometimes it's better to get a dressing on the wound than to wait to get to a physician," she said, which was I guessed some rule that she lived by. In her hands, Gorlas held a gourd of something warm and fragrant smelling, which she tipped to Danu's lips. At first, he mumbled and struggled a little, but he drank it all the same.

"Magewort, valerian, and hops," the healer said. "It will ease his mind and block the call of the magic for a while. Until he can learn better to control it."

"Or to give it away," Saffron said in a carefully measured tone. I could see that underneath her concerns, she was like the sea – a deep current of misgivings about magic in general. She sighed, turning to look at me. "I know why I asked these old friends of Torvald to travel far for me – but I do not know who you are yet, or why they brought you here. Will you tell me your story?" With a wave of her hand, more sedan chairs were brought to one of the plant tables near Danu but leaving enough room for the healers to work.

"I…" I looked at Rigar, but he said nothing. "I come from the islands, your majesty. I and my people have dire news, and we are asking for the aid of Torvald."

"This is because of the dead?" Bower said directly as he took a seat beside his wife, and I opposite him. I was surprised once again by their directness, and I felt wrong-footed, which was something that every Sea Raider hated. *What was it my mother had said? How am I being smarter than everyone else now?* I worried. All I could do was agree.

"It does," I said. "I did not know that you knew of them."

"We didn't," Bower agreed. "Not at first. But a little over three moons ago, we were astonished with these two figures out of history; Lords Rigar and Veen on their noble Halex, appeared in our court, and started to tell us that terrible things were underway. That the northern wildlands have seen tides of *shades* rising and travelling westwards."

"Spirits!" I felt Crux's sudden presence in my mind, making me jump. When I raised my eyes, Saffron was looking at me intently, but she said nothing as her husband continued.

"They left the wilds and we thought that we must have

avoided some great evil, until we started losing communication with the Torvald watchtowers," he said seriously.

"I know of them." *I tried to save one for you!* I thought, and was almost going to admit to this, except that would mean admitting that I was a Sea Raider, and we were considered outlaws everywhere in the world.

"Hm." Saffron narrowed her eyes at me.

"We sent boats to Lord Havick," Bower elaborated, and I felt my hands clutch at the arms of the chair in hatred.

"We wanted to ask what he knew of this strangeness, and if he needed our aid – but the boats never returned," Bower stated.

"That is because Havick sank them or stole them." I couldn't contain my disgust for my uncle.

"That is a grave charge, lady….?" Saffron raised her eyebrow at the fact that I still hadn't given her my name.

Now or never. "Queen Saffron, King Bower?" I looked at each in turn. "My name is Lila Roskilde—" *Malata*, I added mentally, "—and I am the rightful heir of Roskilde. Havick is my uncle, he slew my birthparents and stole the throne. Not only has he committed great crimes against my family, but also towards all the people of the Western Archipelago – including the Western Witches and the dragons – and now he brings war to your shores, too."

"So, this is all Lord Havick's work, is it?" Bower's face went intent as he studied the middle-distance. "We have had reports of our coastal towns being attacked, and roads to the major ports being blocked by unknown forces. At first, I thought it was the Sea Raiders."

A chill shiver swept through me.

"But they do not usually raid this far, and they rarely seek to tussle with our Dragon Riders." He tapped on the arms of his chair. "But the dragons have been complaining of an evil magic returning to the world, and there have been reports of the dead walking the land again. You say that this is Havick. Do you have proof?"

"I, uh…" What proof did I have, other than the Sea Crown itself? A Raider's wariness meant that I was still loath to offer the crown up before them – what if they decided that *they* should take it? And would I care if they did? I asked myself. I don't want this damn crown anyway. Nor the prophecy. Wouldn't it be better to hand Roskilde over to these rulers, who know how to rule a realm?

And so, then their Dragon Riders could hunt down us Sea Raiders? I debated with myself. *No,* I wouldn't share the Sea Crown with them.

"We saw the Roskildean galleons attacking their people." I was saved by Rigar stating the facts. "On one side they faced a Roskildean armada, and on the other the Darkening and the dead."

"The Darkening!" King Bower shot to his feet, turned to look at Danu apprehensively, and then back to me. "What do you know of this?"

I bared my teeth at him as I half rose from my seat. I had

no weapons, but I would fight to the last if he meant to imprison us and doom my people.

"Lila!" Rigar shouted in alarm.

"Halt!" Saffron snapped at the two burly knights who had started to rush towards me. "This young lady means us no harm, do you, Lila of Roskilde?" Saffron said, glancing at both me and her husband. "Why don't we all sit down and talk, yes?"

The king held his aggrieved stance for a moment but nodded. "Of course, my queen. You are, as ever, far wiser than me."

"And Lila here knows that she is surrounded. A brave girl like her will know how to count the odds," Saffron said steadily, holding my eyes with her own.

Always be the smartest, I thought as I nodded, and realized that for right now, Saffron was probably that woman in this room. I lowered myself back to my seat and began talking.

"I cannot tell you as much as Danu can about the Darkening," I admitted (earning a look of horror from King Bower, I saw) "but what I understand is this. There is a witch called Ohotto Zanna, trained at Sebol as Danu and the others were, but she went wrong, somehow, and started to explore dark magics. Something to do with dragon blood and dragon relics..."

"Ugh." Saffron looked disgusted, and I nodded in sympathy as it was exactly how I felt, too.

"We know of these dark practices," the king admitted. "But I had hoped that they had been forgotten."

"They haven't," I said heavily. "Ohotto also found her perfect partner in my uncle, Havick Roskilde, and together they have used his navy and her magics to bring the Western Archipelago to its knees. I do not know how long they have planned this for, whether it was Ohotto who put my uncle up to killing my parents, or whether Havick was always an evil man…" I admitted sadly. "But, either way it makes no difference now I suppose. Together, they have found out a way to summon the dead, and now that Black Fleet roams the sea. They are nigh unstoppable, and Havick intends to use them to conquer Torvald as well."

"And the Darkening, Lady Lila," Bower said. "What of the Darkening?"

"I…" I was at a loss for words. "I did not even know what it was, just that it seemed to come with the Dead Fleet. When I first saw it, I did not know it was this ancient evil…" I almost forgot myself, as I was lost in that furious nightmare of the second battle for Malata, the one that we had lost as the fogs of hate and fear had clutched at the Raider's island. *I cannot tell them where I fought it, first! They will know that I am a Raider!* "But Danu managed to find out from the witches that was what it was. He said that Ohotto must have summoned it, and somehow it is tied up with the dead." I remembered the last message Danu had received from his mentor Afar. "Any who die under that evil fog will rise again as one of the dead, bound to Havick and Ohotto's will."

Bower hissed in frustration and anger, and for a moment I thought it was at me, before he explained his outburst. "What you tell me does not surprise me, Lady Lila. When we fought the Dark King Enric, we discovered much about both the good magics of the dragons, and their nemesis – the dark magics. Although we did not face the Darkening itself, it is a force of un-life, a living curse that seeks to pervert and destroy all life. Our histories tell us that it has risen twice before in the past, and was called into being by a powerful mage, using corrupted dragon-magic. It has always been linked to death and to the shades of those departed."

"How do we defeat it?" I whispered.

"How you defeat all bad magic," Saffron said sternly. "You dispel it."

"Mother! You won't believe what I just witnessed!" A voice burst into out meeting, and I looked up to see a rangy young man with chestnut and blond hair walking across the hallway towards us. He was handsome, and tall, and wore leather hauberk over a fine tunic, as well as hard-working trousers and boots.

"Simon, my heart – we're a bit busy," Saffron looked

annoyed but pleased at the same time. *This young man was her son,* I realized.

"And me, too!" said a lighter voice, as, skipping from behind him came a girl with deep, flame-red hair and freckles, slightly stocky, but with her mother's sharp eyes.

"Lady Lila, this oaf with no manners is my son the Prince Simon," Saffron teased. "And the little imp at his side is Princess Robba."

"Oh." I felt a little awkward in front of Simon, as I stood up to give a nod of the head, aware that all eyes were on our meeting. It was strange to be greeted so frankly and openly by such a high royal, as Simon grinned at me and copied my nod.

"You're supposed to curtsey, like this," the younger Robba, who couldn't be a day over ten I imagined, gave a dramatic flourish of her skirts and hands, clearly making fun of the courtly social graces.

"Oh," I said, unmoving. *Raiders do not curtsey.*

"Simon, Robba, this is Lady Lila Roskilde, and that poor man over there is Danu Geidt," Saffron said. "He is a little unwell at the moment, please, give him space." Her words were a little heavy on the last advice, and I wondered if it was for *their* protection that she said that.

"Whatever," Robba said. "I saw a new dragon today!"

"I'm sorry," Saffron said distractedly to me. "They are a force of nature, these two…."

"You don't understand, Momma!" Robba said defiantly.

"A *totally* new dragon. No one had ever seen its type before, and even Jaydra didn't know who its family was!"

Crux. Princess Robba is talking about Crux, I thought, my heart going out to my dragon-brother.

"But he was sad," Robba continued. "He didn't know who his mother was either, when the dragons asked him, he could only say that Queen Ysix had claimed him."

"Your dragon?" Saffron looked at me. "My dear, here, said that you travelled by dragon."

I nodded. "He is a Phoenix dragon," I stated proudly. "They come from the far south and east of here." And then I couldn't help but add, "He is the only one to have travelled this far west, for me."

"There is no bond like a dragon friendship," Saffron said, and I felt again a surge of warmth for this woman. She understood! Maybe I could trust her with all my secrets? That I was a Sea Raider, that I had the Sea Crown of Roskilde?

"I am sorry that your friend has been unwell," the young prince said graciously to me, and I found myself blushing at the courtesy. *What does he want?* In my world, boys who are nice to you want something.

"Yes, it is a…malady," I coughed. "Another curse of the Darkening."

"The Darkening?" Simon looked alarmed.

A small hand tugged on my sleeve, and I looked down into the eyes of the Princess Robba. "But you must be glad he's all better now, at least?" The young princess said the words with a sincerity that almost melted my heart.

"Better?" I said, confused. "We haven't managed to find any cure…"

"You were right to bring him here," Prince Simon nodded enthusiastically. "I was down there working on the paths—"

"And me!" Robba interjected proudly.

"Yes, and Robba – despite me telling her not to! Anyway, we were there when old Halex came to present your Phoenix to Queen Jaydra. Our queen took one look at him, I'm afraid, and instantly called a circle of the other brood mothers. The Giant Whites and the old Crimsons – it was spectacular!" The young prince was full of enthusiasm, and it was hard to not share his excitement about dragons. "They sang and crooned around your Phoenix—"

"And their mouths glowed—" Robba said with wide eyes.

"And the air went all shimmery—" Simon said.

"And sort of like when you're curled up in a nest with all the other eggs and you're sleeping but not asleep, but you feel warm, you know?" Robba insisted that I know this experience, even though I have never been inside a dragon's nest.

"And when the light and the singing faded, Jaydra, Halex, and your Phoenix leaped into the air!" Prince Simon clapped. "They healed him! A real piece of dragon-magic!"

"Crux…?" I murmured under my breath, half turning to the windows.

"I am alive, Wave-rider! I am alive and I am me, and I am

everything that I should be!" His words hit me like a wave of strong sunlight, filling me with joy. "I, uh…" I turned back to the royal family in alarm. I had to go to him. I had to see my friend Crux as he should be, cavorting across the skies with his new friends, unafraid of anything.

"We understand," Saffron said quickly, even moving to my side to lay a cool hand on my arm. I was shocked by this moment of tenderness. "Let us all go out to the gardens, as I know I would dearly love to see this new family of dragon that Jaydra approves of!" she said with a laugh, and it was like the shadows of our earlier conversation were entirely dismissed.

"Not *all* of us, my queen," her husband said behind her, looking between Danu and the healers, and me.

I felt torn for a moment, but knew that I had no choice but to go to Crux. "Look after him." I prayed fiercely to the king, who nodded gravely.

"We will. I promise you, Lila."

CHAPTER 17
DANU AND THE KING

Torvald was like a whirlpool. The magical currents of this place pushed and pulled at me like I was just a tiny boat in the middle of a sea, rocking fiercely in the waves.

Only, it's not the citadel, is it? I thought. I could tell that this power washed up and through this ancient palace, and the stones and terraced streets beneath it. Almost like it was leaching upward from the ground itself…

Behind my eyes I could see washes of colors as well as voices, sensations – even temperatures like sudden breezes of fierce cold, being drowned out by raging warmth. I didn't know if I was asleep or awake, or whether this was all a vision. Distantly, I was aware of what was happening around me, the movement of white-garbed men and women as they put cool hands to my brow or raised my wrist to check my pulse.

A woman named Mori, a mother of two boisterous boys. She'd only been working as a healer under Gorlas this past winter gone, after a king's messenger sought her out in Monger's Lane. Mori had a reputation for being good with herbs and helping her neighbors with their ailments. "We want you to work for the Court of the King and Queen," the messenger had said, and although the honor was great, she worried about her boys in the palace nursery…

"Argh!" I pulled my hand away from where Mori was taking my pulse. I didn't want to know any more about this woman's life, her secrets. How did I know that? It was as if I had shared her mind, just briefly – as I did with Crux.

"Danu, hush. Quiet yourself." This was the voice of the Healer-in-Chief, Gorlas. She hadn't touched me with her bare skin yet, so I did not have access to her thoughts.

"I can't. It's too much…" I said. The little boat of my mind was tipping over and letting in too much of that magic stuff. I was going to drown, and a part of me wanted to. To let go, and to fall into that sea – the magic here was so strong, it was a power. A power that, if I allowed myself to, I could drink of it.

"*DANU GEIDT.*" This was a familiar voice, but it reverberated with a power that I had only ever heard in a Den Queen Dragon's voice. It was the King, Lord Bower of

Torvald, and he approached me through my magical sight – but he looked different. His body was consumed by a red and golden light, from within, and as he reached my side I tried to pull away from him.

"Don't touch me!" I tried to warn as he reached out a hand to lay it on my head. I was panicking. I didn't want the King of the Torvald Empire to share his secrets with me. That would be too much responsibility on my shoulders. I was just a fisherman's son, I was just a boy from the islands—

Too late, I thought as his cool and calloused hand lit upon my brow. Immediately, I felt his story, his life, wash into mine.

The king, unsurprisingly, was born a noble. But he was a noble in the time when many of the old noble houses had fallen, corrupted and abandoned.

In a rush of emotion, I saw Bower's entire, terrible childhood under the shadow of the Dark King Enric and his Iron Guard. The forever looking over your shoulder, the never being good enough for the sneers of the other noble children, the constant fear.

I saw images of him travelling, alone, far into the wilds where a beautiful, wild girl with white-blonde hair found him, and her island sea-green and turquoise dragon, Jaydra. My heart thumped with the wave of fierce love for the girl who had become his wife, and a love for the dragon as well.

But that memory was shrouded by flying over frozen wastelands as ice formed on Jaydra's wings. By long nights watching the feverish younger Saffron anxiously as she struggled against her own magic. The horizons that were filled with the black smoke of pitch-fires and dragon-flame. Screams. Cursing and bloodshed.

In the heart of it all, I saw a young, handsome man with fine features and a luxurious head full of hair. He looked straight at me, as if seeing me inside Bower's memories, and started to grin…as he did so, his skin peeled back, his cheeks sank, his hair disappeared, leaving a grinning corpse still obscenely alive, clacking wicked yellow teeth at me as he rose one skeletal finger to point at me—

"No!" I recoiled.

"DANU GEIDT," Lord Bower's voice once again, full of power and authority. "I am the chosen guardian of this place. This holy mountain. If my authority means anything, if the power vested in me by the dragons means anything, then hear me now. Remember who you are, Danu Geidt. Find your center."

His words buffeted me as strongly as the winds of magic had, but they had the effect of shielding me from the worst of the storms. *What type of magic is this?*

"It is no magic. I have no magic," Lord Bower said once again. "But I am like you, a dragon-friend. And the dragons gave me everything that I am."

I tried to do as he bid. Who was I? I was Danu Geidt, student of Afar and Chabon, and dragon-friend to Crux. That meant something. It meant that they believed in me, as Lila believed in me, and that trust gave me courage. I remembered the calming meditation that Afar had taught me, almost one of the first lessons I had ever received at Sebol. That little boat on a calm, tranquil sea, soothing and restful. I was safe in the boat of my senses, and I had the skills to sail it anywhere I chose…

Ah. The magical clouds and waves receded somewhat – although I could still hear their torment out there, as if behind a port window on a boat.

"He's coming round," Healer Gorlas muttered as I shook my head and tried to open my eyes again. "Which is good, because I don't want to give him any more magewort. He's already had enough to send an ox to sleep!"

I had? I felt a little slow, my limbs were heavy and I was a little groggy around the edges perhaps, but I wasn't in danger of falling asleep. If anything, underneath that soothing grogginess I felt the buzz of excitement.

"He's powerful, then," the king mused. He was no longer clothed in radiant gold and crimson light, and his voice did not ring with authority like it had done.

"What was that?" I asked, sliding my feet from the sedan as I looked up at him.

"Woah, steady there. You shouldn't be walking around yet!" Healer Gorlas said.

"But I feel fine," I said.

"What *that* was, my young friend," the king said with a serious smile, "is a gift, and a burden. This place here that we are standing on? Not the palace floor, but the mountain itself is one of the ancestral homes of the dragon-kind."

"Really?" That made sense, thinking about the power that I had felt even approaching the mountain of the citadel. "That would explain why the Dragon Monastery and Academy were built here."

"Yes." The King seemed pleased at my understanding. I had heard the witches say (a little disparagingly, actually) that he was a 'scholar-king' but I had not expected him to be so enthused about sharing knowledge. "From what I have discovered since coming to the throne, there are three such dragon mountains we know of here in the northern part of the world, but the dragons have told me that there are more. These 'home mountains' accumulate and concentrate some of the power of the generations of dragons that have lived here. Humans, too, at first mystics and the mad, were drawn here to the dragons' power. I do not understand the mechanism yet, maybe it is the same as when a dragon bonds with its home, that place, too, becomes a source of power?"

"It could be." I nodded, intrigued by the idea. "The Western Witches have long known that there are certain places that can be discovered in the world that hold great reserves of power – both good and bad. They warn of dream-seas, or patches of seas where nightmares and visions abound, or else of sacred trees, where it is said you can heal and rest your mind."

"The Western Witches, I see." The King's face was grave. "I have been wanting to send an envoy to them for so long now, but there have always been pressing matters; bandits and border skirmishes and crop rotations." His voice went low. "Perhaps, I too had hoped that the evils of the past had finally been laid to rest, and I did not want to involve Torvald with the witches, and magic…" His eyes slid to the far doors, where outside the queen and Lila appeared to be laughing. "Maybe one of the things that we can do while you are here is to arrange an expedition."

Ah. My face fell. "That would be, uh, difficult, your majesty," I said in a softer voice.

Bower looked at me with consternation.

"The Western Witches have gone. Left."

"Gone?" The king frowned. It was not as daunting as having a dragon frown at you, but still, the sight of the most powerful ruler in the known world frowning at me did make me gulp nervously.

I didn't know where to start. There was so much to tell, the war against Havick, the treachery of Ohotto Zanna, the division amongst the witches, the Darkening… What was worse, was that Healer Gorlas was standing just to one side of me looking at me under heavy brows as if she would be personally insulted if I dare to keel over and fall ill again, and there were other healers and courtiers moving between the plants, talking quietly.

"Have no fear of what you can and cannot speak here, Danu," Bower said sternly. "I grew up in a time when to even mention certain words could get you imprisoned. Now, my queen and I operate a policy of complete honesty, wherever we can."

I was shocked by his approach. After the witches insistence of silence and secrecy usually being the best option, and I opened my mouth to tell him so. "Sometimes, some pieces of news are too dire to spread so freely," I quoted one of Afar's sayings.

In response, the king just looked away, pained. When his voice returned, it was low. "I have done wrong by you people of the Western Archipelago, and it is my fault. My lady queen has always counselled closer relations with the islands of her birth, but I have always looked to the borders of Torvald and the encouragement of the dragons back to their enclosure here." He signaled for water to be brought forward.

"I have heard some of the news, from Rigar and Veen as well as from my forward scouts. I know that the archipelago has been facing a terrible foe. It does not surprise me that your mentors, the Western Witches, advise a policy of silence." He cleared his throat. "But that *is not* how we do things here in Torvald. Your tutors are very wise, but fear that their mission to keep alive all the lore and knowledge that the Dark King attempted to stamp out has made them fearful. Whereas, I and my queen know that you cannot give in to fear before a tyrant. You have to face them."

Well said, I thought, and told him what my mentor Afar had told me just recently, about the witches taking the Western Track, about their fears if a witch ever became one of the undead, and what we knew of the Darkening.

"Then it is worse than I had ever feared." Bower looked away and out of the windows, to where dragons were playing in the skies out there. Who would have thought that such a world could also have such a very great evil within it?

"Danu, your tale is revealing me more than you know, pointing to truths about *our* history here in Torvald," the king continued, sitting down heavily on the nearest chair as wine was pressed into our hands. "It has been hard work for me to piece together the history of Torvald, when Enric the Dark King spent so long suppressing it. But this is what I know. When he took over Torvald, the heirs to the throne, and all the Dragon Riders that couldn't fight, fled to the corners of the world with what knowledge they could. They didn't want it to fall into the Dark King's hands, you see."

"I know," I nodded, "a lot of that knowledge was entrusted to my Matriarch Chabon, of the Western Witches."

"Precisely." The king nodded. "What most people *don't know,* however, is that some ten years after that initial supply of books, grimoires, and histories were taken into protection, *another* shipment was sent to the Western Witches."

He was right, I had never heard of this story before. "But I thought you said that this Dark King had taken over? Who sent it? What was sent?" I asked.

I watched the king shake his head, as if the answers were mostly beyond him. "I have been able to offer rewards and encourage learning once again for all of this lost knowledge, but so much of it is scraps or clues. You must remember that, at the time, Enric was thought of as a hero by the enchanted people of this very citadel. All of the accounts and personal messages of the conspirators were deeply guarded. However – there has been evidence that ten years *after* Enric came to power, a group of Dragon Riders came back to put a stop to his evil. They failed, but at least one of them did manage to escape Enric's clutches with something called the Dark Book of Enlil."

That name rang a bell. Why? Where had I heard it before? *Something that Afar had said. Something about the Dark Book and Ohotto…?*

"En, clearly, refers to Enric, and *'lil* in the language of the old region of Maddox, where the Dark King came from, means *lore* or *knowledge*."

"The Knowledge of Enric," I breathed.

"Yes. A grimoire collected by the most evil man in all the lands himself. It was rumored to have contained not only his personal spells, but also everything that he had learned about how to pervert the magic of the dragons."

"And summon the Darkening?"

"Yes, presumably. Although, thankfully, he never got to

put that plan in motion. The connection of the Darkening and dragon-magic goes back millennia of course, far longer than even Enric Maddox walked the earth, but if *he* had managed to crack the formula?" I saw Bower shudder. "As it was, by the time that we faced him, Enric could already communicate mind-to-mind with humans as the dragons do. I dread to think what he would have been capable of had he been allowed to keep developing his studies."

Mind-to-mind? I thought in alarm. Isn't that what I had just done, before the king had used his power to calm my thoughts? I had skimmed that healer's life. I had read the king's memories as easily as if they were my own. *Bower said these were the Dark King's abilities. And the Dark King was evil.* This was why the Western Witches were always wary of training me, a new mage. I didn't – couldn't – blame them. *I was scared of what I was becoming now, too.* I coughed and forced my thoughts to return to the conversation.

"But now Ohotto Zanna has the Dark King's personal spell book," I said. "All of the magic of the Dark King and the worst bits of dragon-lore put together."

"And she has managed to raise the dead with it, aye," The king said gravely. "That *has* to be our priority, although I feel for your friend, but Torvald's history is tied to what is going on in the Western Archipelago, and it appears that we may even have a hand in their cause."

The next sentence that Bower said chilled me to the core. "If we allow this black witch Ohotto Zanna to continue her work, the evils that she has summoned are sure to undo the entire world of both humans *and* dragons."

"So you will help us?" I said. "You will help Lila?"

"Torvald will not rest until that book is destroyed, and peace returns to the Western Archipelago," the king said, his face marked with grim lines.

CHAPTER 18
LILA, WHAT A QUEEN NAMES YOU

"**L**ook at him!" young Robba said a few steps in front of me on the sward of green that stretched outside the palace hall.

"He's handsome, isn't he?" I laughed in pleasure. It was a delight to see one so young as the princess taking such an honest delight in the creatures that flew overhead.

Crux flew with a grace and force I couldn't remember *ever* seeing in him. His scales gleamed in the sun, and his calls were sharp and clear. I could have wept with relief at the change that had overtaken him. He swooped low over the palace (making some of the wall guards duck in alarm, I saw with a grin) but was not reprimanded by the other dragons or, more importantly, the queen nor her eldest child behind me. In the air around him were other dragons – I saw a Crimson Red

(I had only ever seen one of those before) as well as at least two Stocky Greens, a Sinuous Blue, and one of the smaller turquoise sea dragons, that seemed to be delighting in Crux's efforts as she followed his antics.

"He has a fast turn of speed, huh?" said Prince Simon, his grin as wide as mine as I appreciated Crux's powerful wing beats and aerobatic display.

"He does. Fastest dragon in the land."

"You think?" Simon raised a cheeky eyebrow at me. "I bet that my Flagg could give him a run for your money."

"Ha. No chance." I shook my head, feeling a little giddy. "No mainland dragon could even come *close* to what Crux is able to do."

"Now, that is where I *know* that you are wrong…" Simon dared me. "What do you say to a little wager?"

"Simon…" Queen Saffron's voice struck a note of warning, but the thrill of seeing Crux in the air once again filled me with bravado. There is nothing like seeing a dragon in full capacity. It lifts the soul and gives a feeling of wild joy.

"Why would I do that? You'd lose. And anyway – you have a kingdom of riches, and I…" A shadow crossed over my mind. *What do I have, apart from my people many, many leagues away to the south, possibly embattled right now?* The thought sobered me up in a trice. "No," I said firmly.

"What? I thought you Raiders liked a challenge!" Simon laughed.

Raiders. He knows. My face froze, a chill clutching at me.

How does he know? Did Danu say something? Crux? Instantly, in the Raider way that I had, my eyes swept to the nearest guards, the gates, could I rush in, seize Danu, and call Crux to carry us away.

"Simon!" Saffron said sharply, her eyes needling her son.

Oh no, I had been right all along, I thought. The queen came from the islands, before the rise of Havick when the Sea Raiders were unanimously feared and hated by the Free Islanders. She would hold those same prejudices – *and perhaps for good reason, too,* as the Sea Raiders back then had far fewer qualms about raiding anyone they could. It was only the rising dominance of Roskilde that had caused us to turn our attacks against the fat Roskildean merchant vessels, and away from the smaller, Free Islander vessels.

"What, Mother? You were the one who told me!" Simon laughed it off.

She knew? My eyes caught the queen's, regarding me shrewdly. Would she order her guards to throw Danu and I in prison? Would she refuse our plea for aid now that she knew who— what – I had come from?

"Lila, easy," the queen said instead, but she made no gentling or calming motions with her hands or eyes. She wasn't going to budge an inch from her views, I thought. But what *was* she going to do, then?

"I *did* know that you were from a Sea Raider family. I saw it the second that you walked into our courtroom. The way you held your back straight, the defiance in your eyes, the way your eyes turned to check every exit, every guard, despite the fact that you were half carrying your poor friend."

Danu. How do I get him out of their clutches without causing bloodshed? I fiercely wished I had my blades with me.

"You knew?" I said out loud. "But then, how did your son…"

"Ah." Saffron appeared momentarily embarrassed. "I must apologize, a little detective work. You know that turquoise dragon that is currently trying to bite Crux's tail? That is Jaydra, Den mother and queen to the dragons of Mount Hammal."

The turquoise dragon that bonded with her at birth, in the islands.

"We have spent a long time in each other's company." Saffron smiled. "Now, our sharing of thoughts and memories is so natural that there is hardly a moment when we are not thinking together." As if in agreement I heard a sharp, screeching call from above. "It was an easy thing to talk to Jaydra, and for her to share her senses with me of you and your friend Crux."

"And so Jaydra smelled Raider on me?" I said, and my voice sounded defiant even in my ears. It was strange, being the *target* of a dragon's powers.

"You are bonded with Crux, you know that a dragon's senses are not like our own. They can detect where we have been and who we have surrounded ourselves by just by the merest elements of sand, surf, or fragrance."

"Malata," I said.

The queen's voice grew heavy. "Yes. The Isle of the Raiders. I only knew of it through the stories of the island dragons, of course. They regarded the Sea Raiders as interesting, bold—for humans— but also dangerous." A note of rebuke crept into her voice. "The dragons respected how they flew along the sea on their boats, faster than any other sailor—"

Wave-rider, I remembered Crux's term for me.

"—but they also couldn't understand why they caused so much mayhem and bloodshed amongst their own kind." Saffron now fully frowned at me.

This is it, I thought. I was sure that I could get past Simon and Saffron on my own, even without weapons – but the court guards? *I would call Crux,* I decided, and reached upward with my mind.

"But you need not fear, Lila-Roskilde-of-Malata." Saffron's voice stopped me. The reminder of who I was and where I had come from, the burning wreckage of the Raider Island shook me. "Jaydra also sensed the destruction of Malata. The terrible loss to your people. The panic and torment that the Darkening and the dead have caused to you."

To my surprise, the queen sounded truly sorry for us. *Why would the monarch of Torvald care?* It was a fact that, before

Havick grew so powerful, there were a fair numbers of Torvald merchant ships that had also lined our booty chests!

"No one should lose their home as you have, Lila," the queen said softly. "I have been lucky that my home still exists, under the care of Queen Ysix, and that I have found such a welcoming home here too, with my husband," she explained. "But that does not mean that I do not remember feeling lost and alone, strange and rootless for many years of my younger life."

My throat closed as my head struggled to catch up with what my heart knew. *All these years I have looked to her as my role model. Is this really happening? That the fierce Island-Queen Saffron Zenema is saying that she is like me, in some small way?*

"And from your answers in my court just now, and what Jaydra sees in your Crux, and how you have acted towards my own family..." the queen's eyes flickered to little princess Robba, her mouth open in delight as she completely ignored us and watched the tumbling, playful dragons above. "I know you are not any ordinary Sea Raider. Reading between the lines and through the gaps in your tale, perhaps I can see that there *are no* ordinary Sea Raiders now."

Saffron raised her chin, and a look of fierce pride crossed her features. "It took a lot of courage to come here, to this court, when you must have known the people of Torvald might reject you. That is true island-courage, Lila, and I like being reminded of it."

Tears formed in my eyes.

"What you and your people face, Lila, the machinations of a cruel tyrant are what I, too, faced here with the old king. The evil magic that has torn apart lives and homes are something that I, too, have fought – although my adversary was Enric's stolen magics, and not the Darkening itself. I truly believe that you are attempting to take the Western Archipelago – *my original home* – down a different path than the horror that is presented to it now. For that I thank you, Lila Roskilde, and I will give you a new name to add to your others, Lila Roskilde, dragon-friend of Malata—I will always think of you as the Protector of the Western Isles."

"Thank you, Lady Saffron." I bowed my head to hide my tears, but in return the woman I had always admired almost as much as my own foster-mother crossed the few grassy steps between us and enfolded me in a strong island hug.

And with that gesture and those words from this strange, brave, beautiful queen, I felt my past and my present, my struggles and all my joys jam together in one knot. But where before I had always felt as though my identity was a puzzle that I couldn't unpick – was I a Raider or a Roskildean? A guardian or a rebel?—suddenly all those elements fit.

I was Lila of the Western Isles, no more, and no less. And I would fight to protect my home from all the perils that threatened it.

PART III
REVENGE

CHAPTER 19
LILA, LEADER, CAPTAIN, COMMANDER

"I look stupid," I muttered to Danu. He stood at my side, clad in long robes over a new tunic and breeches, just as I was. Before us was the marble-slabbed promenade that led from the main doors of the palace all the way to the front gates, and we weren't alone.

On each of the broad steps stood two of the palace guards in shining, bronzed armor with red cloaks, one on each side of us. At the foot of the stairs stood the royal entourage–Lord Bower wearing his purple and red cloak, and Saffron wearing her green and purple one. Their crowns shone and sparkled in the sun, and at their side stood tall Simon wearing his own finery and matching circlet, and little Robba wearing a white and cream dress. Another double line of the palace guards on either side, bearing tall lances in their hands and beyond them sat the dragons.

The Torvald dragons lined the route like sentinels. Some were large and stocky, while others were much smaller and had tails that extended far into the grounds.

The air above us was filled with the sound of hisses and chitterings, and I saw that the mainland had smaller breeds of dragons the size of dogs; 'Messenger dragons' they called them – had settled on the crenulations and towers all around. I wondered distantly if they were related to the Orange drakes. Anything to take my mind off what I had to do.

"Lila, you'll be fine. This is just a formality," Danu mumbled at my side, wavering on his feet and his eyes slightly glassy with the massive amounts of magewort that Healer Gorlas had been dosing him with. But at least he looked better, I thought. A whole lot better. We'd only been here for one night, but somehow in that time Bower had managed to do something to my friend that meant that he was much more in control of his powers.

"You're looking well," I complimented him.

"The power of the king," he murmured, smiling a little goofily, and looking at the distant mountain peak as he did so. Up there we could clearly see the Dragon Academy, and once again I felt a pull in my heart to get in there and investigate. What did they teach the potential Dragon Riders of Torvald? Could it help my Dragon Raiders?

But alas, there was little time for such things. Just this

morning over breakfast in the throne-garden room (with servants bringing in trays of sliced fruit and mixed bowls of a corn and wheat delicacy, topped with honey and raisins, and the whole thing slathered in fresh cream) the king and queen had heard reports that their coast was being threatened by more ships of the dead. They had lost contact with another port-village, and there were reports of a strange, terrifying fog lingering on the shores of the great estuary-inlet that bordered the mountains of Torvald.

It was time to act, and the rest of that morning had seen courtiers and Messenger dragons winging and running through the sedate halls, creating the show that we were about to put on for the people of Torvald.

"Why can't we just fly down there with the dragons though?" I hissed through my teeth, looking at the proud creatures that dwarfed the crowds beyond them. They were different from the island dragons – even the ones that were of the same breed, like the Sinuous Blues of Island-Turquoise Jaydra herself. They were quieter than the dragons of the archipelago for one thing, and they did not have that watchful predatory stare that many of Ysix and Sym's brood had, I saw. Instead, they appeared *proud,* if that made sense. Calmly and self-assuredly ignoring the humans that moved around them, as if sure of their position in this strange dragon-society.

They don't mind the harnesses, either, I thought, seeing that every one of the dragons below me had their wide leather and iron fixings prominently displayed. If anything, these dragons wore them as a badge of honor.

"That's not how things are done here," Danu said. He had apparently become an expert in the city ways of Torvald overnight, since chatting with the king, and I wondered if he was going to remain to be this insufferable for the rest of the day. "A city as big as Torvald takes time to act. Lord Bower needs to appease the dragons as well as his counsellors and nobles, otherwise they won't let him take out the armies."

"Hm." I shrugged as if it was all a waste of time, when we could be fighting, but I could reluctantly see the sense in it. Kinda. It was a bit like one massive Raider's Council, with all these nobles like captains of their respective ships, arguing their case with the chief. The difference was, however, that with us Raiders, each of our captains and quartermasters had proven their worth through sweat, blood, and toil, and so my father and mother had a natural respect for them.

Kasian. Once again, the shadow fell over my heart. Should I tell Queen Saffron or the healer about the horrible sight of my father, lurching towards me with the glowing eyes of the dead? I haven't even told mother yet, I thought, my heart sinking a little. No. It was a fantasy. A dream, I was sure. A nightmare.

"It just takes so looong," I whispered, before my wait was ended by the blast of the horns from the tower walls, startling the Messenger dragons who took off in a whirling chorus.

The palace horns blew once, twice, and then a final time

before silence fell over the assembled throngs. In between and on the far side of the dragons I could see crowds of people—nobles, counsellors, and notable civilians—who had been invited to attend and witness this event: Torvald's declaration of war.

BWAAARM! A different call rang out across the mountain, this one from the distant Dragon Academy. It was deep and sonorous, and reverberated in my heart as well as my chest. In unison, each of the assembled dragons rose their great snouts in its direction.

"That's the fabled Dragon Horn of the Academy, a bronze tube that they have used to call and summon their dragons for hundreds of years," Danu said. "Bower was telling me that even their tyrant-King Enric couldn't melt it down!"

"Good for them," I thought, frowning slightly. It was a damn good idea to use horns to signal to the dragons, I thought, for those Riders who didn't have the close bond with their dragons that we did, but still… *What's the point of training to be a Dragon Rider if you don't develop the bond?* I thought wildly. Now *I* sounded like an expert in dragon-training, I realized!

With the echoes of that blast cascading from the hill, there rose into the air from the distant academy small shapes, growing smaller as they spiraled into the air in perfect timing, like watching a whirlpool.

"I wish I could get our dragons to fly like that," I said jealously. "One thing that you *can* say for these city sorts: they've had a lot of time to practice and train!"

"*Am I not a good enough flyer for you?*" Crux's soot-soaked voice welled up into my mind and I was pleased for the sound of his good-natured annoyance. With his dragon-thoughts came the knowledge that he was still flying low over the far side of Mount Hammal, exploring this new and strange place as I wanted to.

"*I found a lake of silver river fish. Creamy flesh without any salt!*" He teased me with his good fortune. "*What do you say then? Do you want me to come when you whistle? To pirouette? To dance?*"

"No, wyrm." His harsh humor was a balm to my Raider's soul, and I knew he bore no ill-will to the Torvald dragons, but I also knew that he would not brook me telling him how he should fly!

"Huh?" Danu looked over at me with blinking eyes. Once again, I remembered that the magewort worked to blanket not just his magical abilities, but also his natural gift as a dragon-friend, too.

"It's nothing," I wanted to laugh at Crux's words, but Danu's fogged mind only made me worried. *Would he ever recover properly?* No time even to worry though, as below us the king himself started talking.

"Friends! Dragons! Nobles and kin!" His voice carried clear to my ears and further, but he stepped forward so more of his subjects could see him.

"I have summoned you all here with grave tidings. You will have heard of the strange attacks that have beset our shores, and now, we have news of their cause!" He and the other royals turned to regard us both.

"We have been visited by none other than the Princess Roskilde, a Queen-in-waiting for her people, whose home in the Western Archipelago has been savaged by the same dark magics that threaten our very own shores!" he called out, raising a hand towards me. That was our cue (as the palace head steward had informed us) and we descended the stone steps, one at a time. This is ridiculous, I thought. All show and performance.

But Danu was right, the city moved slowly, and these things had to happen if I were to win their support. I could put up with a bit of frippery for the sake of my people.

"She comes to us as a friend of dragons herself, and she asks for our aid. Will the people of Torvald refuse her? Will we, who have known terror and tyrants and foul magics ourselves, turn our backs on our historic allies?" Bower called.

Who's he calling historic? I frowned. He must mean the Roskildeans and Free Islanders – again, I felt that touch of old Raider ire. Would King Bower be able to get the nobles on his side if he had told them that they were about to support the savage Sea Raiders of the Western Archipelago?

There was a murmur from the crowd, rising louder in our ears as we drew towards the royal family. By the time we reached the final steps, the chant was deafening.

"*NO! No! No!*" My heart thudded in sympathy and gratitude, and especially now that we were close enough to see and hear little Robba at the side of her mother, shouting louder than all the rest.

"Then, my friends and countrymen-and-women, I ask for your support in sending a phalanx of Dragon Riders, trained at our academy, to help our embattled allies. Will you show the people of the Western Archipelago – the very same birthplace of our beloved lady, Queen Saffron – that they can look to Torvald in their hour of need?"

"*YEAH!*" the crowds of nobles (and Princess Robba) roared back, followed by cheers and chanting "TORVALD! TORVALD!" I felt another moment of familiarity with this ritual. It was a just like during the Raider's gatherings when the various captains of the boats would try to boost the morale of their crews before they embarked on a new raiding mission. *'Get them believing in you, get them believing in themselves,'* my father would say. My poor father.

After the speech, the king and queen welcomed us to join them on the wide plaza-type area, before we paraded (slowly) forward to the lines of watchful dragons. I felt a little nervous at the humans' eyes watching me. Seeing the looks of both curiosity and pride in the nobles' faces, as I wondered how many of these nobles had I and my family stolen trade goods from? However, my shyness was overcome by a larger fascination with the Torvald dragons. They gazed at us unblinking, like a cat might do, and one – a large

Crimson Red, gently reached down to sniff the air over our heads.

"Don't worry about Flagg. He's just checking you out," Prince Simon said jovially, making me feel a little angry.

"Of course, I'm not worried," I laughed back. If anything, I felt more concerned with how quiet these dragons were. I was used to the island dragons, who expressed their emotions more freely. I wondered what had made the Torvald dragons like this; they didn't look mistreated, in fact; they looked positively radiant with health with broad muscles and a good shine on their scales. But they were just…reserved. *It must be all that training they do,* I thought.

Further down the line, Torvald Riders were already mounting. They wore shining metal armor over their banded leather jerkins and greaves, with helmets that had swung-back horns fixed. They moved with a regimented simplicity, performing the checks of their harnesses and equipment with great care. I had to admit that the soldiers looked a little fiercer in the flesh than even I had imagined them. I couldn't help but compare their side-mounted spears, bows, and lances, and their long scabbards at each hip to the ragtag and haphazard Raider-Riders I had been training.

"They weren't always like this." Queen Saffron had followed my gaze. "You see that one?" She pointed to a pair of large, burly Dragon Riders clad just the same as the others, though each had bushy red beards and wore slightly different ribbons of color on their belts. "They were from the northern mountain tribes. Very similar to the folk that this Army of the Dead came from," she whispered to me as we walked.

You shouldn't mention the army, I thought, though of course I would never say such a reprimand aloud to the queen. It made me feel superstitious to even think about that great evil out here, under the bright and open sky.

"When I and my husband retook Torvald, we did so without any of these Dragon Academy Riders. The Dark King had done his best to destroy the academy, you see—and we had to enlist the help of the mountain tribes and the Island Dragons instead."

She was trying to make me feel better about my mission, I thought, feeling a little silly and foolish beside her. It was true that our stories *were* similar; two island girls who raised a flight of dragons to defeat their enemies, but next to the great Queen Saffron, I felt like a fraud. She was a character out of myth, and at times she didn't even seem flesh and blood.

But she also had magic on her side. The thought crept, unbidden, into the back of my mind. That was what Rigar and Veen had said, wasn't it? Despite my chat with Queen Saffron just the day before, despite our bonding over our shared love for the dragons, the fact of her magic made me feel *more* different from her somehow.

How could I even hope to do what she did—overthrow a tyrant— when I didn't even have any magic?

"You have me." Crux's fiery voice broke over my mind, as

brash and rude as he always had been, and I felt instantly grateful for his rough confidence.

"Ah, Lady Lila...?" the king mumbled, as I saw a flash of deep midnight blue and black scales, a hint of orange and green of his side-scales as Crux swept low over the walls and appeared to dip towards the crowds. To the assembled good and great of this city it must have looked like one of the dragons had gone rogue and was flying directly at them, and they began responding as any unused to seeing wild and free dragons might—with a degree of alarm.

Crux pulled up before he could raise any serious panic, but he had created a commotion and a shoal-like surge in the crowd all the same. I tried to hide my grin as Crux landed, not behind the line of regal dragons nor in line with them facing the promenade but used the actual marble flagstones as his landing route, as if this whole ceremony had been for him and him alone.

"Bulls," I heard a different disdainful voice in my head and was shocked. It was undeniably a dragon's voice, but very few other dragons had shared their thoughts with me, apart from the Queen Ysix.

"Easy there, Jaydra," Queen Saffron cooed, as she walked towards one of the smaller turquoise-green dragons who was eyeing my Crux with clear annoyance, her tail lashing back and forth on the grass behind her.

"I'm sorry, Lila, but Jaydra..." Saffron started to say.

"No need to apologize!" I laughed out loud, startling the

human queen. "My Crux is a bull dragon. And I wouldn't change a thing about him."

As Crux loped up the path towards me, I watched as Jaydra, herself a Queen of the Torvald dragons, reached forward and nipped at his ear as if in rebuke.

"Skrech!" Crux hopped back lightly and made an odd little coughing sound in response, but he lowered his snout in deference to her all the same.

"I think she actually quite likes him," Queen Saffron whispered behind her hand to me, her previous alarm transformed into one of amused curiosity at this play between our dragons.

"What's not to like?" I agreed, as I walked up to the young Phoenix bull and he lowered his snout to me, also, allowing me to hug him in our familiar embrace.

"Right, well – if we're all set?" Bower said, nodding to the dragon handlers who stood at the sides, all dressed in padded leather armor.

Aren't we going to get changed first? I thought in alarm, as both the king and the queen climbed up the legs of Jaydra with ease, and Prince Simon ascended his own Flagg. Little Princess Robba was pouting and stamping her foot, but the Healer Gorlas had already sternly taken her by the hand and held her close as the rest of the Torvald Dragon Riders followed their king and queen and mounted their dragons.

"We're going now?" I muttered, following Danu who had already ascended Crux's leg. I hurried up, feeling that familiar electric shock of joy and recognition as I always had on reuniting with Crux.

"It's good to have you back," I whispered as I took my seat.

"It's good to be myself again," the dragon agreed, already tensing his rear leg muscles to pounce into the air. But I noticed that he held off, waiting for Saffron's dragon Jaydra to be the first before following behind. We watched as the small but spirited turquoise green queen surveyed her dragon subjects coolly, as if assessing for herself just what had to be done, before she made a low chirrup to her riders, and Saffron leaned forward to pat her neck.

Those two are close, I thought, pleased at the sight. Behind the queen, her husband had secured himself with a familiarity that he did not look as though he would possess, before setting one hand to his wife's hip in an affectionate gesture that came from years of companionship. As if that was the signal, Jaydra arched her neck and roared her challenge to the skies, tensing her back legs and springing into the air, as fast as a speeding hawk.

"Skreyargh!" Crux roared as he leapt, eager to join the smaller turquoise queen, and then other dragons joined us. Instantly, I felt that rush of enthusiasm and joy, looking down at the palace grounds as they receded below into a toy-like display in seconds.

Behind us, the ancient Sinuous Blue of Rigar and Veen's dragon, Halex, and behind them came what Lord Bower had called a 'phalanx of dragons' with Prince Simon at their head on Flagg. There had to be over twenty assorted academy dragons taking to the air, one after the other in perfectly-timed procession. I saw another Crimson Red, as well as a large number of Sinuous Blues and Stocky Greens, each leaping from a standing start as the one before it rose into the air, while the one after it tensed. It was like watching a flower unfolding, only if its petals were made of scales and teeth.

It's beautiful, I had to admit, but I had no time to teach the Sea Raiders such complicated aerobatics. We just had to learn how to fight well, and together, and that was all that we needed.

Jaydra wheeled ahead, heading up the mountain to perform a fly-over of the Dragon Academy, and both Danu and I craned our necks to look down jealously at the large fortification with its specially-constructed dragon-landing towers. Red and purple flags were raised, and cheers came from the guards on the walls. Inside I could see a system of courtyards and training grounds, as well as what appeared to be a large kitchen garden.

There was no time to examine its secrets, however, as Jaydra led us onward, over a barren rocky saddle in the mountain and over a sudden gulf that opened out behind us.

"Home." I felt the kick of Crux's emotions in my stomach and his feeling of belonging and confidence found its echo in me.

"I know it isn't, but it also is at the same time," Crux

whispered in my mind, and although I couldn't make sense of that sentiment, my heart could, somehow. Some places felt so right that they were a kind of home to us, even if our lives belonged elsewhere.

"I have shared with you just a little of how I grew up," Crux said as we soared over what the humans called the dragon enclosure – a wide, blasted-open crater of an extinct volcano, with high rocky cliffs as walls. Inside I could see lush, hot-house vegetation and great slabs of rock thrown up from the innards of the mountain. There were ledges and the sudden openings of caves, and as Jaydra passed by, I saw snouts rising from the dragons as they watched their glorious queen in flight.

"I never knew a home, not in the way that this place is a dragon-home." Crux was being uncharacteristically unguarded with me, and I wondered if this was partly the effect that this sacred mountain was having on him, or perhaps the effect of his illness. *"I was born in a nest, but half of my brood-mates were stolen, and the other half were eaten,"* he told me, and I recoiled in shock. *"Not all dragon colonies exist the way that you do here, in the west of the world,"* he confided in me. *"So, it is strange, and new, to be invited into a dragon-home such as this one,"* he told me.

Invited to join? I thought in alarm. *He wasn't going to leave me, was he?*

"Ha! Foolish human. Crux would never leave his Wave-rider." The Phoenix swept me up in his thoughts and joy, and

in that rush of strong, bright wind and hot sun – and mostly the glory of flying with dragons once more, my thoughts took on a surreal, day-dreamy quality. *Maybe the point of it all is to connect up all the places where you feel at home,* I thought, thinking about what those places would be for me.

The sea. Being on a Raider's ship under full sail. Listening to my mother tell me stories of raids as we sparred. Riding on Crux's back as we flew through the air. And yes, even a little bit of me had felt comfortable in the Palace of Torvald, I thought as I looked back on the last, couple of strange days. Not that I was comfortable with the pomp and circumstance or the tall walls or having servants at every doorway and corner, but rather with the throne room that was filled with plants, and the easygoing nature of Queen Saffron's court, where anyone could talk to their monarchs at any time that they chose. That felt right, and home-y.

And my people had been raiding them for years. The thought hit me as we flashed across the last cliffs of the enclosure and made our way to the wilder lands on the far side of the mountain. These Torvaldites weren't so controlling as I had thought them to be. And neither were they all like the rich merchants I had helped plunder. I saw deep woods and lakes, and the occasional ribbon of smoke from what I thought must be woodsman's huts. Beyond the confines of the mountain, I saw that the land became more rural once again, with the patchwork greens of fields and meadows, and the distant hazes of villages and towns.

It's not that I have any love for this landlubber existence, I told myself. It was odd to see so much green and nowhere near enough water. But I had felt Crux's hammer of homesickness as we had passed the Dragon Enclosure, and that made me view Torvald in a new light.

These were real people, living their lives. I realized that I *could* feel this now, much more so than I ever could before, because I had met the Torvalders and ate with them, talked and even laughed with them a little. The ones in the palace were wealthy, yes, but Torvald wasn't just a palace – up here I could see a whole landscape of villages and people's lives, as they struggled to make ends meet.

Some things are universal, I realized. Everywhere you go, whether on land or at sea, most of the everyday people – like us Raiders or the Free Islanders – were just trying to make ends meet. That is all. While kings and queens and wars fight overhead, they just want to live their lives.

I was thinking about my mother and what was left of the refugees in the southern kingdom, of course. I was thinking of how much they needed a bit of peace.

And us Sea Raiders have been plundering Torvald's merchant galleys for generations, I reminded myself. Merchant galleys that had brought valuable food and goods and profit to the people of both Roskilde, the Free Islands, and Torvald here.

"*It is in the way of the world to hunt for your food,*" Crux warned me. "*You should not be so angry with yourself.*"

Maybe he was right, but it was also the same effect as seeing my dead father Kasian. Once you had seen the fact of your actions, there was no unseeing it.

The Raiders would have to stop raiding Torvald boats if I was to win.

CHAPTER 20
DANU, WOULD IT BE ENOUGH?

The flight from Torvald was a blur, but it was also a pleasing one. It felt like a long time since I had felt no pain and no threat of losing myself in the currents of magic. I don't know how or what Lord Bower had done to me, but I was thankful for it.

It's easier with the king near, I realized. Even with something as silly as when Crux surged ahead, trying to outrace Jaydra and so that meant that we pulled alongside the smaller turquoise and green dragon, during those moments I would feel a deeper wash of calm.

"King-dragon's voice," Crux informed me sagely as we flew high over fields and woodlands, rivers and villages.

"What?"

"As a Brood Queen is everything to her nest, and den, as

Jaydra is everything to the dragons that live nearby because of where she lives," Crux said, *"in that same way, a king or a bull who is the chosen mate of the queen has the same ability to calm and connect the other dragons of the den and brood."*

"And Bower is the king of the sacred mountain, and mate to Queen Saffron, so he gets to command them?" I said, wondering how that meant he could calm my magic just with his presence.

"Not command. Connect with. Because you have shared your soul with me, and with Lila, you are open to his gifts," Crux informed me.

I still didn't understand it, but that didn't mean that I also couldn't be grateful. I was. Very. Even though my feelings were still surrounded in cotton-wool from Healer Gorlas' magewort, I also now had room to think, as well.

Room to think about where we were going, for example, which was down towards a river plan beside a wood, where there were already lines of pavilion-style tents.

"*And fish!*" Jaydra called out, raising an excited chirrup from Crux and even the more reserved Torvald dragons behind. We swirled in a great arc, the other academy dragons following us in in the same way that flocks of seabirds gathered around a nesting island. Jaydra went first, choosing the river for her landing. She raised her wings and beat them strongly, legs outstretched, as she skidded across the river, sending up plumes of water on either side. She screeched and whistled joyously, and through my dragon affinity I could feel her satisfaction at the cool, refreshing liquid.

Ourselves and Crux were next, and although he tried to copy Jaydra, the island dragon's graceful landing, (she now looked like a swan, wing half-folded around the king and queen) he was not designed in the same way, and Lila and I ended up with soaked boots and calves and laughs on our faces.

One-by-one the other academy dragons came in, most to the river, though some landed on the grass, flicking their tails in excitement. They let us humans dismount onto the banks of the meadows, and it wasn't long before I saw that there was a full dragon-bathing event happening, with Crux being the loudest and most-boisterous as he splashed the other dragons and joke-bit them on the ears.

"Fool of a wyrm," Lila said as she looked on, and I could see she was doing her best to remain serious despite the smirk she couldn't keep from her face at the Phoenix's antics.

"Jaydra wanted them to have their fun, before the long flight ahead of them," Saffron said behind us, still wearing her fine robes (as we all were) as she stripped off her crown and earrings, and placed them into a leather drawstring bag, embroidered with the seal of Torvald. Lord Bower beside her did the same.

"Oh, thank the sweet waters," Lila mumbled, clearly pleased at the thought of changing out of our Torvald fineries.

"This is one of our landing sites." Bower nodded to the

wooden huts and pavilion-style tents that edged the field. Already, I could see the resident workers racing to open it up, draw water, and start fires. "We have many across the kingdom, at key crossroads," he explained. "We have changes of clothes for everyone, food and rations, as well as spare weapons should you need them.

"Thank you." I nodded, watching as the other Academy Dragon Riders were already moving to the tents with their backpacks.

"We'll stay here to break our fast, and to allow the dragons to eat and drink their fill," Saffron took up the conversation. "And then—we're splitting the force."

"What?" I heard Lila say, looking between me and the royals. "I'm sorry, your highnesses, but we really need all of you—"

"The book," Lord Bower said, looking at me seriously.

I had told Lila about the Dark Book of Enlil, of course, but so far, I hadn't heard of any plans to retrieve it. It seemed that we were going to learn of them now.

"The welfare of your people is precisely why we are splitting our forces, Lady Lila," the king said gravely. "The phalanx will ride to the southern kingdom, there to give aid where they can to your foster-mother and those you have saved."

"…and to entreat with the southern princes," the Queen of Torvald mentioned, shrugging. "Torvald has a sometimes-difficult relationship with the southern hot lands. We wish to make it known to them that your people, Lila, are under our protection."

I saw Lila stiffen a little at that and wondered why. Did she resent Torvald's aid? Did she dislike the thought of being somehow less autonomous? It was clear that the king and queen here were very good at taking over, maybe Lila felt a bit sidelined by all these grand gestures?

"But I and my husband, and we thought you and Danu as well, will not have to go to the south to reunite with your people if you agree," the Lady Saffron said, keeping her voice low as she said this.

"What?" Lila repeated, before a moment later I saw comprehension dawn. "You mean to try and recover the Book of Enlil, don't you?" I saw her say.

"It is the only way to stop the Army of the Dead," Lady Saffron said.

"And the Darkening," Lord Bower added.

"And that means," Lila took up the thread enthusiastically, "if we can dispel the Army of the Dead, then we will just have the Roskildean Navy to contend with." She grinned fiercely. "And us Sea Raiders have always been very good at fighting the Roskildean Navy."

"*Your* navy now, Lady Lila," the queen said pointedly.

"Yes." Lila nodded, her eyes going far away. Still, even after everything that we had gone through, I found myself wondering: *is Lila still too much Raider to ever look on the Roskildeans with anything but mistrust?*

But of course, my friend had changed. She had grown up before my eyes over the last few seasons. She was taller for one thing, and she *looked* like a princess as she raised her chin to stare calmly and coolly at us all.

"A lot of things are going to change if I win," she said, "*when* I win."

I wondered what she meant.

"Well, time enough to plan for the future when we've won the war," Lord Bower said with a wry grin, as if he knew *exactly* what sort of thing that Lila was talking about. I guessed that with his experience, he did. "After we dispatch the dead of course, you will also have a phalanx of trained Torvald Academy dragons to liberate the islands, so... This has to be good news for the campaign, does it not?"

"It does." Lila smiled, and nodded, before adding in a quieter voice. "And thank you, for thinking of my people first."

"You forget, Lady Lila," Queen Saffron said, "they were once my people, too."

As we walked up to the tents however, to smell the already cooking food and to join the Academy Dragon Riders as they stretched and prepared, a part of me was wondering if this was all going to be just so easy as Lord Bower had seemed to think that it was.

When we went to retrieve the Book of Enlil, we would have to face Ohotto Zanna and her cabal, I knew. Perhaps these Torvaldites didn't realize what that meant, as there were few people in their lands with natural magic. A witch in the fullness of her own natural abilities can raise storms and sink ships, I had been told. Witches were powerful, and the Western Witches of the Haunted Isle were perhaps the most powerful.

And Ohotto Zanna was one of the most powerful even of them, I thought grimly. *Could we pull off what my mentor Afar and old Chabon had failed to do? Even with a king and a queen and a queen dragon?*

CHAPTER 21
LILA, A DRAGON RAIDER'S MERCY

We bid farewell to the Dragon Riders of Torvald in the late afternoon, as the sun started to burn the sky to the west.

"Go well, and fight with honor," Rigar told me seriously, before sharing a look with Danu. "And you, young man – I would advise not using your magic at all, if you can help it." He sighed before adding, somewhat mysteriously, "There have been very few mages in this part of the world, and even fewer people who know how to train them. But with the Lord Bower here, I have confidence that you will be able to control your powers."

"Thank you," Danu said, as Rigar swung himself up onto ancient Halex's back, and set off after the phalanx of Torvald Academy dragons headed to the southlands. Even though the academy dragons were under the head of Prince Simon and his Crimson Red Flagg, it was Rigar and Veen who I knew would be invaluable to their mission. The two old Riders would act as the go-betweens and messengers between Pela and Prince Simon, and their slightly removed nature would work to win the trust of the Raiders and the Free Islanders, I hoped.

Give her my love, I had told Rigar, who had nodded just as seriously as if I were Queen Saffron giving him a sacred task itself. It was strange, this living and working with royals and legends. They were nothing like I had imagined them, at the same time more natural in their manners and different than anything I had ever expected.

We rode into the burning west of sunset, finally free to give our dragons the speed they longed for. There was me and Danu on Crux, and Lord Bower and Lady Saffron on Jaydra. That was it. Not for the first time, I wondered at the audacity of these two monarchs flying together to defend a kingdom that wasn't even theirs, but I respected them for it as well.

It was something Kasian and Pela would do, I thought with a smile as I looked ahead at them on the back of the smaller sea-turquoise dragon. They had discarded their fine robes and jewels and didn't even wear the sculpted armor of their own academy Riders, instead opting for stiffened and banded leather jerkins, hauberks and greaves. I watched as the Queen Saffron (riding at the front of their dragon, as I did with Crux) leaned back and stretched, before releasing her clouds of almost platinum-white hair into the brisk wind, her mouth wide with laughter as she did so.

I wonder if the life of a queen meant that she didn't get to ride her own dragon-friend as much as she would like, I thought with not a little bit of alarm.

"Dragon-sister!" a reptile voice swam into my mind, correcting me. It was Jaydra, the Queen of Mount Hammal, sharing her thoughts with me. I was a little surprised as I was learning that it was rare for dragons to freely talk to other humans that were not their own dragon-friends, but Jaydra's mind felt warm and mirthful, as her human sister Saffron looked.

"I'm sorry," I corrected, wondering if I should start calling Crux my dragon-brother.

"You can call me what you like, wave-rider, I call you mine," Crux croaked into my mind at the same time, and I felt a sensation like psychic vertigo at sharing my thoughts with two dragons at the same time. He breathed soot and fire through my thoughts, clearly staking his claim over me to the Queen Dragon.

"Bulls. Always so jealous," Jaydra said and I saw her flick her tail ahead of me, before withdrawing from my mind.

"Skrech!" Crux cawed back at her, and Jaydra put on a burst of speed that was an obvious excuse for a race.

Queen Saffron was right, I thought, as I flattened myself forward over the makeshift saddle. Our dragons liked each other. Maybe it was because Jaydra recognized in Crux another outsider, in some way. He wasn't from the mainland and neither was she.

Jaydra was one of the smaller sea-green and blue-turquoise dragons that I had spent my youth seeing every now and again (usually in high summer). She had a shorter, sharper form, like a hunting hawk compared to the Phoenix underneath me. It meant that she could dive much faster than the bigger Phoenix could, and was also far more maneuverable, pulling off much quicker turns and stalls than we did, but Crux also had the larger wingspan. The midnight-blue and black Phoenix seemed to be of a size with the Crimson Reds I had seen, and were what I considered to be a 'classic' dragon shape.

"I think you are trying to be nice…" Crux huffed at me, giving me a mental shove that made me laugh.

"I am," I said, explaining to him that whenever I *thought* of a dragon, whenever *anyone* thought of a dragon, then it was his shape that they thought of. He didn't have the long necks and winding bodies of the Blues, nor the short legs and barrel shape of the Greens. He wasn't monstrously gigantic like the Whites or the Yellows, nor small and stubborn like the Orange drakes, nor wingless like the Browns.

"Hm." He huffed as he tried to follow Jaydra's darting flight (and failed) but I could feel through his thoughts that he was secretly enjoying himself all the same.

In fact, I only just realized how big he had gotten since I first met him. He had been so much smaller than the Crimson

Red I had seen on the island, and now he was as big if not bigger than Flagg, at least.

"Dragons grow fast when they are young, then grow slow when they are old," Jaydra informed me casually, and I realized then that she could wander into my mind and out with an ease that made Crux annoyed. He whistled and dove down after her, playfully snatching at her tail, but Jaydra shrugged her wings and zipped away as fast as a darting swallow.

It felt good, to be giving ourselves over to dragon games for a little while, until we came to the shadows of the mountains.

"Up ahead!" Danu called out and I followed his pointing hand to the shadowed southern gap in the mountains that we were heading towards. At first I thought it was blocking out the last dying rays of the sun. Only it wasn't just the natural shadows of the rock and land, was it?

It was drifts of dark smoke, caught in the hollows and foothills.

Saffron waved in a sweeping motion towards it, and I got her message immediately that she wanted to take a low, circling flight around to see what it was. Immediately, the Queen Dragon dropped her earlier enthusiasm and concentrated, one-pointed, on the movement. Crux's muscles tightened underneath me as he, too, dropped his bullish joy and stretched out his wings. With our wider reach, we easily outpaced the smaller dragon, taking the lead—which Jaydra didn't seem to mind at all.

It felt good to be flying together, working as one, I had time to think. *Maybe this was what made Torvald so strong. Could I do the same thing with my Dragon Raiders?* I allowed my daydreams of an island academy of dragons to play out as they drowned out my anxieties of what we were going to find.

A part of me already knew what we were going to find, anyway. I had been seeing the palls of smoke hanging over the archipelago islands for the past couple summers.

"Smoke and blood and terror," Crux agreed with me as we swept down.

Lord Bower was signaling at me, but I couldn't make out what it was.

"He says that we should be in sight of the coast down here," Danu said behind me.

"How do you know he says that?" I frowned, before the mage told me that it was 'king magic' like it was some sort of explanation. *Whatever.* I would rather trust in my eyes and my sword, as now the smell of the smoke reached up to me.

The mountains stretched further west of us, and this land underneath us was broken into foothills and wilder humps of ravines and woods, speared by long roads. I reasoned that this must still be Torvald land, but it looked to be a part that was sparsely inhabited.

Black smoke, constrained by the cooling night airs, hung

in pockets between hills and over dales, always nearing one of the roads. I urged Crux lower and closer, and we saw, rising out of one of the sites, the ruins of a stone-built tower, blackened halfway up. The fires had died down, but the smoke was still thick.

"The king says these are old watchtowers and what he calls dragon shrines," Danu informed me.

That made sense, I thought, knowing Havick's previous plan to cut the islands and Torvald off from each other by attacking the sentinel watchtowers.

"And he sent assassins out for the dragon relics, as well," I reasoned. There were so many patches of destruction, and so regular, that it seemed to me that it had to be this continuing work of my uncle.

And the dead.

"Skreyarch!" Crux roared both into the air and in my mind, as his ears suddenly twitched forward. *"I can sense them,"* the Phoenix whispered at me. *"The spirits. I can sense them underneath us."* I was worried that he was about to fall back into that frightened, nervous dragon that had advised us always to flee the dead, but no. This time it was different. Crux was not sensing the natural dead, but, through our shared mind I knew that it was the magical stench associated with the Army of the Dead.

They were down there, somewhere, in the murk.

A sea-change rippled through us, and it took me a moment before I realized that it originated with Jaydra. Suddenly I was white-hot angry, and my stomach felt fluttery and upset with the depth of emotion that the Queen Dragon was exuding.

"Abominations!" Crux hissed into my mind. He was no longer afraid of the spirits of the dead it seemed, or else the nearness of the Queen Dragon was giving him courage. He swept downward, circling the blackened tower and through the dark smokes.

I coughed and hacked, my eyes stinging before we broke the layer of blackened smoke and saw the destruction that lay underneath us. The tower itself had stood on a promontory of rock over what must have been a small collection of huts and wayside buildings – but now all of them were broken open and blackened, and the ground was the churned mud as if an army had marched through here.

And there were people still there, standing in place, unmoving.

"Who are they?" I had a moment to wonder, before my connection with Crux informed me precisely. The dead – only these dead did not look like the others that I had fought. They did not wear fur cloaks or wear great broadswords at their hips – no, these wore the simple tabards and tunics of normal village folk. Well, normal village folk who had hideous wounds and had skin turned a ghastly pale.

Crux roared, his neck swelling to pour his dragon fire upon them.

"WAIT!" A voice shook through us, and then I saw that it was Jaydra, Saffron and Bower descending through the smokes. The voice had been Bower's, and it had been filled with kingly majesty.

The dead were already moving towards us in jerky movements as they awoke from their stationary vigil. Crux obeyed the king for a wonder – but I think that he was more obeying Jaydra.

The Queen Dragon flared past us and landed, a good hundred meters further up the track, holding her wings high in tense aggression, as Lord Bower and Lady Saffron slipped from her side.

"No, they'll attack!" I shouted, snarling in frustration as Crux set down beside his queen, allowing me and Danu to race after them.

"Lady Saffron – no! There's nothing left of the people they were now!" I called as my boots hit the mud. Behind me, Crux hissed a warning threat at the dead as they started to shamble and stutter towards us. They did not move as the Army of the Dead moved, with grace or ease. I wondered if that was because they were second-generation dead, or whether even the undying had to take time to learn their new mode of life.

"These are my people!" Lord Bower called, "I have to try!" He stumbled forward towards the nearest one, holding out his hands to the woman in a black and purple tunic, with blonde-grey whisping hair held back in an unkempt bun. I could not un-see the horrible stain of dried blood across her side.

"HALT!" I heard, and *felt* Lord Bower call, through my connection with Crux. I did not think that whatever strange ability the sacred mountain for the dragons had conferred on him had any effect on humans – only dragons and dragon-friends, but it seemed that the King of Torvald was desperate to try every tool he had at his disposal all the same.

The deceased woman did not halt. Instead, she bared her teeth and lurched forward, hands raised into cruel claws to scratch and maim the King of Torvald.

"Careful!" the queen moved fast for a woman of middling years. I was still moving forward through the mud and she had already tripped up the dead woman and pushed her to the ground, standing in front of her husband with her teeth bared.

The dead woman floundered in the mud, reaching to scrabble at Saffron's boot.

"How do we reverse this?" Lord Bower looked appalled at the woman, and I realized then, with crushing clarity, what one of the many pitfalls of being a leader of your people actually was. Lord Bower had spoken a fine speech and had done the right thing as far as we were concerned, but he was still a monarch on a distant throne. Most of his decisions came from reading and studying reports, and hearing the advice of his wife, the dragons, and his counsellors. He had not seen the dead up close. He was just as appalled and repulsed by them as I had been. *And he did not know how to deal with them.*

I unslung my sabre, and swept it high into the air—

Thock!

When I raised my eyes to look at the monarchs of Torvald, I saw that Lord Bower was staring at *me* in horror, while Queen Saffron's eyes were guarded as she sprang back. "It takes a lot to kill the dead, your highnesses," I said unapologetically. "You have to break their bodies and burn them. Crux?" I called out, as we gave ground under the shambling, lurching forms of the dead Torvaldites.

"Wait, but—" Lord Bower gasped as his wife pulled him out of the way and Crux did what I knew he had been waiting to do. With a roar, he released his dragon flame to scour the recent battlefield, engulfing the last of the huts and houses and the lurching bodies, as well. There was a roar beside him, as Jaydra added her flame to his, the waves of scorching heat rolling over us.

When it was done, we couldn't see the bodies, but there was a lot of steam and smoking mud. I didn't know if that would be enough to destroy them, but it had stopped them from getting close to us.

"We should just be thankful that the Darkening wasn't here as well," I said, collapsing back against Crux's foreleg. "Because it *was*, otherwise these poor folks wouldn't have stood back up again." When I looked back up, I saw that Lord Bower and Lady Saffron were looking at me in alarm.

"What?" I asked.

CHAPTER 22
DANU, A QUEEN'S OFFER

We left that accursed place gladly, but not before Lord Bower had insisted that we see the ruined dragon shrine. His manner had changed, both his and the Lady Saffron's, after seeing Lila attack that woman so casually.

I knew how they felt. Lila had performed a blow worthy of a knight, or a barbarian, and she had done it with the calmness and efficiency of someone who was used to violence. It's not that I thought that these two were faint-hearted, or would shirk from a fight, but I could see them re-appraising this fierce island girl they had taken into their hearts.

"We need fierce, now," Crux had advised me, and I was sad that I agreed, or at least a part of me did.

The dragon shrine had been little more than a one-room

tower, with alcoves on the inside with broken statues of dragons holding up the inner walls. Without them there, half of the building had fallen down, and it was impossible for Lord Bower to ascertain if the dragon relics inside had been stolen or not. But it was highly likely that they had. This had set a quiet fury into the king's heart, I could feel, as we left that place and flew further up into the mountains, to find a place far enough from the destruction where we could spend the night. The king seemed so appalled by this sacrilege that he became taciturn and clipped in his speech, even refusing to speak to anyone at all as we laid the fire, ate our rations, and settled down for the night.

"Danu," a voice murmured late in the night as I sat by the fire, watching the night stars slowly wheel above. It was Saffron, rising from her tent and wrapped in a thick, embroidered robe. Both the king and Lila were in their tents, sleeping.

"Your Highness," I struggled to get up (as it seemed the proper thing to do for a queen, after all) but she shushed me back into my place.

"It is my turn to take watch. Go, rest now," she said wearily.

"No, Lady Saffron – I'm good until Lila—" I started to say.

"Danu. *Go to bed*," she said with a little more force. "I think it's important that *you*, of all people, get enough rest."

She was talking about my magic. And my inability to control it, wasn't she?

"And as for Lila… I think it's best if we let her sleep, as well," Saffron said with a frown. My puzzled look was all it took for the queen to explain.

"Ah Danu… How to say this?" I saw the queen in the firelight suddenly not as who she was now, but perhaps who she had been some years ago. A girl who was used to sitting on the dirt floor and prodding a campfire with a stick. "My husband is upset," she confided in me, and I felt suddenly nervous. *Should the queen of a distant land be confiding these things to me?* I was painfully aware of the awkwardness.

"Lord Bower has lived a hard life, he travelled to the archipelago with me, and he came back here, through those mountains behind us, through the snowdrifts, the avalanches, we faced wild shadow-dragons, the northern tribes…" She shook her head. "But for all this, he grew up in his secret libraries, surrounded by books, in a noble family." She smiled fondly at her own memories of her husband. "That upbringing was hard enough for him – he was being raised to think like a king; like an honorable man in a city that cared only for strength, pomp, and circumstance. It is one of the reasons he makes such a good ruler to his people now," she confided in me, before continuing.

"Lord Bower did not grow up in the archipelago, as we have. He did not face the harsh realities of storms and starvation, sea monsters or what have you. I fear that when Lila finished that poor dead woman so suddenly, and so finally, and when she called on her dragon to destroy them, that Lord Bower was not seeing them as they are now – puppets of an evil witch, of the Darkening – but as the people he was sworn to protect."

I opened and closed my mouth, unsure of what to say. *The king has to realize that these aren't his people any more,* I wanted to shout – but how do you shout at a queen about her king?

"I know, Danu, I know…" Saffron had appeared to read my thoughts. "This is just one of the worries that has been keeping me awake this night." She gazed into the fire. "We need to find a way to bring the Western Archipelago and Torvald together, in a way that both parties will agree to, will feel honored by. For too long, my home islands have looked on Torvald as the enemy, as a fat goat to be stolen, and the people of the mainland have viewed the Western Archipelago as little more as a home to heathens and savages." She sighed. "And look what happens when our two peoples ignore each other? A tyrant rises in the west and threatens the east. Our world is too fragile to be separate anymore."

I couldn't agree more, but I dared not admit that I shared her husband's worries. *Would Lila be a true Queen to Roskilde? Or would she turn it into a Raider-state?*

"And *you* have been worrying me, Danu." She surprised me by changing the subject quickly.

"Me?" I said nervously.

"Yes," the woman said simply, and directly. I could see some of that dragon upbringing of her girlhood showing through her. She had a plain honesty about her speech that didn't care if I agreed, or what I thought about what she said. *What must it have been like, to grow up amongst dragons!* I thought in wonder.

"You have a mage's gift. We all know that. Rigar and Veen recognized it, your own tutors recognized it, and the dragons see it in you," she said softly.

"And mages are dangerous," I concluded for her, feeling my stomach turn over. "I know." *Do you know what it feels like, for everyone who has ever talked to me about this, for all my teachers whom I love and respect to have the same look in their eyes?* I thought at the queen. *That I will turn bad. That I have a bad soul?*

"They are," Saffron said directly, as was her wont. "I still don't know all the history of them, or why this is the case, but it is true. Mages come about once in a generation – a person with extraordinary magical power – and they can easily be consumed by that power."

I thought of the collapsed hillside that I had brought down on the Army of the Dead. The way that Lila had looked at me afterwards, when I had unwittingly stolen Crux's own lifeforce to do it.

"Enric, the Dark King, was a mage," I stated.

"He was," Saffron said flatly. "Which is why I worry about

you, Danu. I worry that, when the time comes, you will not be able to say no."

"To do what you did?" I whispered. Rigar had told me the story. "To give your power up?"

"To *return* my power." Queen Saffron said with a smile, reaching out her hands to stretch out her fingers, as if she could still feel the rill and run of power through them. Maybe she could. "I returned it to the world, and I could teach you how to do the same, right now, if you wish."

Yes. No. "I…?" I didn't know what I wanted. My whole life I had been in training, gearing towards the day when I would no longer be an acolyte, but a mage proper, one schooled by the Western Witches.

"I don't know," I admitted. "We will need my magic to defeat Ohotto and Havick."

"Will we?" Saffron was looking at me sharply. "Because, if there is anything that my struggle with the Dark King taught me it is this – you don't need magic to overcome evil. What I always needed, every day, was the belief and support of my friends at my side, and that was all." She smiled into the fire. "It took me a long while to realize that, of course, but it's true."

And that's why you're Queen Saffron Zenema, I thought. *The island girl raised by dragons who became queen of an empire.* I was no such thing. I thought of the loss of my mentor Afar, and all the other things I had not been able to save. I hadn't stopped Lila's father from dying; I hadn't saved

Malata; in fact – I wasn't sure how much there had been that I *had* managed to do.

"Thank you, my lady," I said in a dour voice. "I will think about your offer, but I can't go and face Ohotto Zanna without magic to counter hers with. I just cannot," I said as forcefully as I dared.

"I know," the island girl said sadly. "But I needed to say that – and you needed to hear it."

CHAPTER 23
LILA, THE UN-FREE ISLANDS

It took us two days more to reach the Western Archipelago, during which time I was aware of a growing sense of unease, both from Crux and Jaydra and their human riders.

What's up with Danu, for instance? I thought as once again he seemed lost in deep thought, biting his lips as we flew.

"Is it the magic?" I asked him as we flew – one of the rare times when we were gliding high enough over the weather fronts to allow us to scrabble back and forth across Crux's back with little fear of falling.

"No! Of course it isn't my magic!" he said with an aggressive edge, as if this were a long-standing argument between us.

"All right! Don't break my ear off!" I snapped back at him,

figuring that it was probably the long flight that was making him and the others grumpy. I knew Crux was tired, after all, as I could feel it in his muscles. But he had flown through much worse conditions, like when we fled Roskilde the first time, with the Darkening hot on his tail.

It's probably not his magic, anyway, I reasoned, noting that Danu had seemed far more alert and less in psychic or real pain than he had been near Mount Hammal. *Ugh.* Boys, I thought, thinking of Danu and the king. Lord Bower had been positively sour with us ever since leaving the mainland behind —and while I could understand homesickness—I wondered if there wasn't more to it.

I knew that the king was in contact with the other dragons in the phalanx, as just yesterday he had told me that they had rendezvoused with Pela and the others and were escorting them to a nearby southern city. But no matter how I tried to ply information from the king about my people, he had remained somewhat aloof.

Of anyone, I had thought the queen would be happy to get back to the Western Archipelago. She did indeed seem to be a little easier in her mannerisms, leaning back and letting the wind roll through her hair and fingers, but when I tried to talk to her about her childhood out here, she was curiously guarded.

Maybe this was a bad idea, I started to think, before what we saw on the second day made all of my own personal concerns seem petty to say the least.

"What is that?" the king shouted, flying at our side.

I stammered, not even knowing what to call the storm gathering over the northern Roskildean edge of the Western Archipelago, and not just any storm – but a superstorm.

I had never seen the like of such a weather front in all my years on the oceans, but especially here, in the Barrens, where the winds were strange and the currents subdued.

The entire northern half of the archipelago (as far as we could see, anyway) was enveloped in a thick, black, storm. We were still a way off from entering it, but the thick black and purpling thunderheads boiled as they eddied and moved around.

The center of that thing will be a vortex, I thought, trying to calculate where its epicenter was by what islands I could see. I should have guessed: *Roskilde.*

CHAPTER 24
LILA AND THE STORM

As we dove through the thunderheads, we were battered and pressed by sudden gusts of freezing rain-laden wind. Crux half-folded his wings, allowing him to twist and turn like Jaydra with far more accuracy as lightening flashed over his right shoulder. Everything was a whirl and a blur of noise and rain – the water hitting so hard that it felt like pinpricks of ice being thrown at my face. Even Crux seemed to be having trouble keeping his direction as we were buffeted by the strong gusts of storm gales. The black clouds below were like a blanket, wisps spiraling upwards at times as it roiled from internal forces.

"Wait. This is something that my magic *is* good at!" I head Danu call.

The hairs on the back of my neck rose, and then a wave of

warmth rolled over us. Though, it was much nicer, and I could feel that even Crux agreed – he still had to contend with the wind.

We shook and bounced as we tried to stay above the clouds, but the winds were getting fiercer if anything. Ahead Jaydra struggled as well, as her claws dipped into the tops of the storm clouds as she fought to stay upright.

Crux growled deep in his throat – but I couldn't hear it, only feel the reverberations rattling through his neck and shoulders.

No, I don't like this any more than you do, I thought – before suddenly we had broken free of the last cloud layer and were out into the drenching rain.

Below us were islands, surrounded by Roskildean war-galleys.

"Havick must be trying to hide his operations with this hellish storm, now that he has attacked the mainland," Saffron shouted across the gulf of air towards us. "He knows that Torvald will retaliate with dragons, he wants to make our progress harder."

"They're fortifying," I thought, watching the movements of the smaller ships back and forth along the islands, as the other, larger galleons patrolled the harbors.

"I can see men and women bearing stone, and I heard shouts and screams," Crux informed me, confirming my fears. My uncle had effectively taken control of the entire

archipelago and was now shoring up his defenses as he attacked Torvald lands.

"*Crap!*" There were more ships than there had been before. Many, many more since when we raided Ohotto's tower in the citadel. These islands below were the more traditional territory of the Roskildean island-state, and so they had naturally become a staging post for what looked to be an armada. *But no ships of the dead,* I thought. At least they were still far away.

Rain was playing on my back and on Crux's wings like we were the skins of a drum. I wondered just how long we had before—

BLARR! The burst of a war horn carried up to us on the teeth of the gale, before being snatched away just as quickly. I couldn't tell which ship it had come from, or what direction – but I didn't need to pinpoint it, as warning flags were run up the main masts all around.

"They've seen us!" I shouted, and my words were stolen from my lips as soon as I screamed them into the rain.

PHOOM! The blare of the cannon was accompanied by the white muzzle flash as one of the galleons spat fire at us.

"*Two can play with fire...*" the Phoenix dragon snarled in my head, but I forbid him.

"No! There are too many!" I said, as still more cannons blared below us as they attempted to track our movements through the air. In this storm it was fairly easily to outfly them, as Crux did just that, turning to climb through the air towards the island's ridge of higher hills, away from the sea.

"*WATCH OUT!*" Lord Bower's voice shook through both Crux and me as we soared over the ridge to see that it was crowned with Roskildean watchtowers. We didn't hear the snap and hiss of the ugly little crossbows that they had, but suddenly the air was filled with arrows.

"Skrech!" Crux swerved, throwing his right wing up and arching his neck and head low as he protected me and Danu from the brunt of the shot. The Phoenix dragon grunted in pain as several found their way into his flesh. *Don't be poisoned, don't be poisoned,* I begged, as still more clattered and broke on his strong scales.

"Crux! Get out of here!" I shouted, as Jaydra peeled away around the far side of the watchtower, heading for the other side of the island – *but there were other galleons over there as well,* I thought in alarm. We had blown it. Havick and Ohotto would know that we were coming for them. Maybe a messenger bird has already flown to Ros itself, by now...

"*Ia Cyrrhus...!*" Another shiver of unease went through me as Danu's magic swept forward, and the black storm clouds overhead dipped down towards the attacking watchtower. He meant to use the natural elements to attack this one, as he had done previously.

But I couldn't let him. I threw myself as far backward as I dared, unclipping one of the belt hooks that secured me to the saddle as I slapped at Danu's outstretched hand. He had been sitting bolt upright, his eyes filled with that eerie glow that they had when he was using his magic, with one hand outstretched as he pointed to the watchtower. That was the hand that I slapped out of the sky, making him startle, and the light fall from his eyes.

"Lila! Why did you do that?" He looked at me angrily.

"You said yourself – there's a coven of witches under Ohotto! Do you really want to let them unleash their magic on us now, when we haven't even got to Ros yet?"

Danu grumbled, but he must've seen my point because he didn't try again and instead hunkered down to let Crux fly as best as he was able.

"THIS WAY!" Again, it was Bower's 'king voice' that I heard through Crux's connection, and the Phoenix was already swerving down over the island's trees and hills to follow.

Jaydra and her riders had found a small opening in the defenses of this armada – a jetty where the ships were mostly fishing and merchant galleys. They flashed over this tiny cove and were heading low over the rainy seas to the north.

PHOOOM! More booms of cannons as the nearest of the Roskildean ships attempted to give chase, Crux wheeled to one side and the jetty exploded with cannon shot, and then we were out, racing over the water and outpacing those who chased us.

"We won't have long!" I called to Danu as we pulled nearer to Jaydra and the others. "That was Watch Island. It's only a little way from Ros itself!"

"Then you need to come up with a plan, and quickly," Danu said, his tone sharp, revealing how hurt he was that I had forbid his magic.

Maybe now was the time to use it, I thought – especially when the dark shapes of ships loomed out of the storm towards us.

Galleons. Probably dispatched to apprehend us.

These galleons were undoubtedly Roskildean in origin – but of a new design I had not seen before. They stood taller and prouder in the water than the other Roskildean vessels. "One, two, three…" I counted the different levels and ended at five. That was huge. If the Army of the Dead wasn't bad enough, each one of these mega-galleons could probably level a port all by itself.

Torvald-killers, I thought. My uncle built these specially to attack Torvald.

"Lila! What do you want me to do?" Danu shouted, and panic ripped through me. How could I have not prepared for this? What was it that my mother had always said? Be smarter. Be brave. Have a plan. Our plan amounted to launching a two-dragon attack on one of the most well-defended islands in the world.

The mega-galleons had a forest of sails that stretched up high into the sky, dominating our eyeline, and almost making me forget the storm above and beyond them. I watched in horror as Jaydra angled her flight *around* one. She appeared no bigger than a cart horse next to a medium-sized ship.

Each one had a strange prow though. Gone were the bowsprits, and instead the prows had been reinforced with hundreds of plates of metal, almost in mimicry of the scales of the dragons that were their enemy. They ended high in a backwards curl of cast-iron; looking like the perfect battering-ram. But it wasn't that which was strangest part of these megagalleons, it was the way that two of the largest 'scales' swung downwards on either side of the prow ridge, revealing the muzzles of enormous cannons, far bigger than the ones on any other cannon.

"Heck! That's big enough to take out a wall!" I swallowed nervously. *Or a dragon.*

It was at that very moment that Jaydra ahead of us appeared to ripple in the air, and fade from view.

"What? Hey!" *Was it the witches? Had they done something to the rulers of Torvald?*

"It's magic. I did the same spell, remember, when we attacked Ros the first time – and I don't intend to be sitting ducks out here now!" Danu hissed as I reeled on my saddle.

"But I thought that Saffron had said that she didn't have magic anymore?" I whispered, as Danu started to hiss and croak his strange words, drawing his hands through the air around us as if cloaking us in the very vapors of the storm itself.

The sea below and the mega galleon took on a washed-out, slightly blurry appearance (which didn't appear very different from its current rain-lashed self, to be honest), but what *was* different was the tides of magic that I could feel emanating from Danu. And if *I* could feel it, then I was sure that Ohotto and her coven, fully trained in the delicate magical arts, would be able to as well.

We flashed between the first and the second mega-galleon, just as the vessel fired its wall-destroying forward cannons. The flash was bright, intense, and the sound was so loud that it instantly went into 'non-sound' – which I had only experienced before when I had been too near my father's small cannon as it had fired. My ears started a high-pitched whine, and Crux hissed in pain through my mind. A plume of smoke the size of a house erupted from the front of the mega-galleon, and I knew that if we had been anywhere near that, then just the force of the shot probably would have blown us out of the sky.

I dragged my attention away from the devastating galleons to check on Danu. His shoulders were hunched, curving inwards over his chest, his head bowed, and eyes squeezed shut as he mumbled the invisibility spell.

He looked like he was in control of it, though I was no expert on magic. How would I know when he was about to get a god-complex?

Instead, I turned to concentrate on the waters ahead, trying to see where the next threat would come from.

CHAPTER 25
DANU'S SIGHT

I could sense where Lord Bower, Lady Saffron, and Jaydra were. Even though I had my eyes closed, I could still see a picture of them in my mind, as well as a dim, dream-like picture of the seascape around us.

The storm was a deep purple froth and wash of colors, and I knew in that moment that *yes,* it was indeed a magical storm and though it was not malicious, it had no intelligence or direction, it had been summoned by Ohotto and her coven to hide their activities.

Jaydra and her two human riders shone in the murk like a green jewel, sparkling ahead of us like our own personal star, guiding us onward. I had never seen a dragon look so alive as the smaller turquoise island dragon did at that moment. Not that I thought Queen Jaydra was happy, but that she was full of life in a way that other dragons rarely were.

One of the benefits of being a queen, maybe... And then on her back were her humans. Bower seemed to have a glow about him as if he had taken on some of the qualities of the Queen Dragon herself. But it was the image of Saffron who surprised me, by the fact that she did *not* glow or radiate power as the other two did, but instead was crystal clear in being herself, without magic.

Then how did she make their dragon disappear? I thought in confusion.

There was no time to be confused, though, as my magical sight also brought the image of rising, heavy shapes of the docks and seawalls of the port city of Ros. Even though it was bright with the many street lanterns and torches and candles in windows, the city still appeared somehow *heavy* compared to the dragons.

"There is little life here," Crux whispered into my mind, answering my unasked question.

Many of the inhabitants had fled? Or been press-ganged into Havick's ships? I wondered.

"I see the shades of the dead, everywhere." Crux continued, and a tremor ran through his wings. *"They congregate thick in the streets, drawn to this misery and war."*

But what was worse, was that beyond the immediate city I could also sense *them*. The witches.

There was a sickly red glow piercing through the storm,

turning darker and darker into a deep purple as it spread out into the storm, and, from the layout of the city, I could tell that glow was coming from the tall Witches' Tower where we had found, not the Sea Crown we'd been looking for, but Ohotto's battle maps. The power I felt was too great for just one witch, and I knew Ohotto must have her coven with her as well.

Just the merest act of thinking about them seemed to bring my awareness closer to them, just as it had in the magical dragon-sight that Crux had shared with me. *All of these powers I have mimic dragon powers,* I thought as I flew into that red light, getting closer and closer until I could see the tall spike of the tower itself, lit up from within.

But it was too dangerous to be this close to the other witches, even if I wasn't doing this physically. I knew full well there were other forms of dangers associated with the mind and the soul, as the red glow started to intensify, grower sharper and sharper – drawing me in as it did so...

"Danu," a voice said.

It was her, I knew it. Ohotto Zanna. Not that I recognized the voice – it sounded strange and croaky in my mind— but it *felt* like Ohotto's mind in a way that I knew, without even having to question, what Crux's mind felt like.

I recoiled instantly, pulling back my thoughts from the red-shining tower and throwing up my protections and walls like veils of gleaming, brilliant blue light.

"Danu? What is wrong?" Crux said. He must have sensed my magical fumblings, and instantly I felt his warm, soot-filled presence surround me.

"I'm fine. I was just shocked, that's all. I think our enemy sensed me. No. Not think, I *know* that she did," I whispered into the night. My magical sight faded from my eyes, leaving me feeling shaky and defenseless, somehow. *I can't see them, the witches now. I don't know what they are doing.*

"You did the right thing," Crux informed me, and then went on, ever the wise wyrm. *"All minds are noises. Human thoughts chatter all the time. By using your magic, you are broadcasting where and who you are."*

"We have to warn the king and queen," Lila whispered back to me, having overheard at least half of my conversation with her dragon. Our spell of invisibility had faded now that I had pulled my mind back into the confines of my body – but so far, the sleeping port-city of Ros hadn't spotted us.

The storm was still high, and Crux skimmed the clouds as high as he dared without ascending into the thunder-fronts entirely. Below us, the home of Lord Havick was laid out in concentric circles of dotted lights from the street lanterns and glowing windows. What time was it? I wondered, guessing that it had to be near midnight. A perfect time for a witch's work. That was what Ohotto and the others were up to, high in that tower.

"Ssss!" There was a hiss close by – it had to be close, as the wind was strong in our ears, and for a moment I saw a greenish blurry flicker of a shape—Jaydra with her human riders cresting the gales just underneath. But the Queen Dragon appeared to be annoyed with us, as her thoughts broke into all our minds.

"What are you doing? You must hide yourselves, immediately!" Jaydra scolded us.

"We can't," Lila whispered into the night air, knowing her thoughts would reach the dragon, or Jaydra's sensitive ears would pick them up anyway.

"It's the witches," I whispered into the night air. "They're close, if I use my magic…"

"Not your magic, human!"

Having a Queen Dragon scold you is like passing your hand through a fire. It was hot, painful, but not enough to scorch – yet.

"Crux's. Why would he need you to use your magic, when he has his own?"

"I'm sorry?" Lila said, clearly as confused as I was. Below us the streets passed by, occasionally turning into the darker, open areas of plazas or parks.

"A dragon has their own magic. It's in our blood!" Jaydra snapped. *"Now stay out of this, humans. I need to talk to Crux alone."*

And at that, our minds were shoved forcefully back into our own heads, making me shake my head at the sudden almost-vertigo. "It's true that there has always been tales of dragons having powers," I whispered to Lila, remembering my studies on Sebol. "Legends of dragons that could summon storms, cause nightmares – and of course we know that they can read thoughts whenever they want to…"

"Pfagh!" Crux suddenly washed into our minds, making me reel and Lila blink painfully. *"There is so much I do not know! That my own accursed brood never told me!"* he snapped. *"Hold on. Jaydra told me how to tap into my magic…"*

A wave of power rolled out from his heart, and for a brief moment it was like falling asleep only to jolt awake with a powerful burst of energy. The world around us blurred, as it did when I cast my invisibility spell – but this time it was coming from Crux! But then we had snapped back into focus again, as visible as before. Ahead of us, was the citadel of Ros Castle, the ancestral home of the Roskildeans and Lila's birth right. It stood over the port city on a bluff of cliffs that cut into the land, its tall walls topped with leaping, curved wave-like battlements. The walls wore a coronet of burning torches, guttering and flaring in the wind, and rising from the top even of that were the towers, with the very highest being the one that I had seen in my vision.

"Easy, dragon-brother," Lila whispered to the Phoenix below us. "You can do this. I know you can do this."

"I can. I am Crux!" He hissed, and once again a wave of energy expanded outwards from the dragon's heart. This time,

as the power rolled upward over me I felt woozy and sleepy, but when I blinked and rubbed my eyes, I realized that I was now looking at the world through a thin, blurry gauss of light – just like it looked when *I* had cast my invisibility charm.

"You did it!" I congratulated him, knowing how much it cost me to perform such an enchantment. "Be careful it doesn't tire you, my friend," I advised him.

"Tire me? Why would such a little thing like this tire me?" Crux snickered in my thoughts, reveling in his new-found abilities.

It seemed like there were many advantages to being a dragon, I thought. Maybe *he* should have been the one to train to be a mage at Sebol!

"Heckh!" A derisive lizard-laugh in the back of my thoughts. *"Why would a dragon spend so much time learning dead words from dusty, dry scrolls? I have the magic in every heartbeat!"* He built up to a roar, but a calming, soothing sound from Lila subdued him (thankfully).

This dragon-magic also appeared to be 'cleaner' or more natural in a way. There was none of the harsh, buzzing head or the surges of manic energy that I so often experienced when casting an enchantment coming from the edges of Crux's mind (well, no more than the exuberant confidence that the young bull always felt, that is). I hoped that meant that this was also a magic that the witches couldn't detect – but we had no way of knowing.

"Crux? Can you pass on a message to Jaydra and the

others for me?" I whispered to him. I didn't want to shout as we slid through the storm-lashed night.

"Easily, Danu."

I told him to relay the information to the king and queen that I had gleaned from my vision; that Ohotto's cabal of witches was probably waiting for us. The information buzzed as it passed through the air as the dragons relayed messages to each other, before Jaydra herself spoke to all of us.

"We have a plan, although I do not understand why we cannot just knock the tower down—"

(Just like a dragon, I thought)

"But my sister-Saffron advises me that we are only here for a book, so we will draw the witches out, and you will steal into the tower to get it."

"But my Queen!" I said. "You will be flying against a coven of the most powerful witches left in the world!"

This time I really *did* hear a distant, muffled snort from the hidden dragon. *"You mean that they will be dealing with the most powerful queen in the world, surely!"* Jaydra reprimanded me.

Okay. Best not argue with a Queen Dragon, either.

"I will fly at her side, Danu dragon-friend. Have no fear. I could not sit and wait in the shadows anyway," Crux informed us both, and, with a shared look with Lila, mouthing the words 'what can we do' though we had no choice but to agree. It was strange working with others again, other riders who knew as much if not more about fighting with dragons.

Crux glided high over the castle walls just as we had done last time, but as we avoided the wall guards and their waiting torches, spears, and crossbows, headed for the patch of castle roof where we had landed before, we saw our earlier attack had inspired Havick to change things here. This time there were now large iron spikes that had been mounted on the roof.

"*Ssss!*" The Phoenix dragon flapped hurriedly to hover, eliciting a few querying calls from the guards on the walls opposite.

"Did you hear something?"

"I thought I felt a breeze…"

"It's just this storm – you idiots!" another guard said, as we flared and circled the collection of buildings, halls and towers, searching for a suitable place to land.

"There!" Lila whispered, spying a small stone courtyard at the back of one of the halls. It was tiny, absolutely no room for Crux to land, and I doubted if there was room for more than four people to stand there either – but I knew what Lila was already thinking as I saw her unclip herself from the saddle and start to slide down the shoulders and legs of the dragon. "Crux can drop us in there. Crux can do anything."

I felt an agreeing purr from the dragon as I unclipped myself from the saddle, wiped the rain from my eyes, and started to climb, hand over hand, on the other side of Lila.

The wind was strong – fierce, even –driving the rain constantly into my eyes, but the Phoenix dragon also curled his claws around us both as he flared and flapped, angling his great wings over the tiny courtyard. It was some kind of washer's court, I thought, or a servant's area, as he lowered a little more, a little more…

"Skreyarch!" There was a sudden screech of dragon call above, and I looked up to see that Jaydra had thrown off her invisibility and was swooping around the Witches' Tower, snarling and shouting. She was met by the high-pitched, shrill shriek of a voice and a sudden cloud of purple and red light rolled out from the tower, as fast as smoke from a cannon. Jaydra tucked her wings, rolling away, but I smelled acrid chemicals scorching the air, dissipating quickly in the rain. *It was now or never.*

"Go!" Lila called, as Crux released her, and we jumped from the dragon's foot.

The stone floors were slick, and I slipped, tumbling until I hit the brick wall at the far side with a thump, and rubbed my head. *Ow.* All we had to do now was to get up to the tower, and through a palace of loyal guards, witches, and—possibly—the walking dead.

CHAPTER 26
LILA, MY PEOPLE

We were in the servant quarters, or one of them, anyway. From my previous time here in the palace – although it had been short and tinged with panic –I had gotten a sense of how this place was put together. These servant halls, quarters, and rooms would sit behind and slightly below some of the larger royal halls, and there would be guards' chambers at every level. It gave me enough to work with so that, as we tiptoed through a long hall filled with barrels of soaking sheets, that I knew that we would need to be heading to the left and up.

"Wait," I hushed Danu as I leaned against the open archway at the end of this washers' hall. There was a voice coming towards us, gruff, weary.

"I tell you, I don't like it… If I had my way, I would be leaving this place at first light – it's just not natural!"

An agreeing noise came from the second person. They were getting close. They would see us when they walked past. I tensed and pointed at the barrels. Without saying a word, we crouched down behind them.

"Did Griff tell you he saw his son not two nights ago? Walking through the street in the dead of night, next to a band of others, and heading for the docks." There was a pause in their speech before the man continued. "The poor boy's been dead a year!"

"Heavens and waters!" the first man coughed. "I know what we're being told – that the dead protect us from the dragon-fiends, but still… It doesn't *feel* right to me…"

My heart shook, and not with fear but with rage. I had the sudden, unstoppable sense that *these* people were normal people just like us Raiders or Free Islanders. What horrors was my own uncle putting them through? *They understand that my uncle is evil. They can see the horrors he has brought into the world.*

"It's not right," I said, rising from the shadows and startling them as the two older men walked past. They were servants, I had guessed right, wearing the simple brown habits and over-tunics of their station. *Servants. Raiders don't have servants,* I thought with righteous anger.

"Gah! Who're you?" One of them, a slightly shorter, thinner man staggered back. Both were in their later-middling years, and I wondered if this was why they were relegated to being down here, and not manning the mega-galleons along with the other able-bodied men and women.

"Havick and his witch have raised the dead. You've seen it, and I'm here to stop him," I whispered. Their eyes flickered from my face, to Danu's spooky countenance at my side, and to the bare sabre in my hand. Fear in their faces, the hesitation.

"We mean you no harm. I won't harm a hair on your head, I promise," I said, feeling my words grow thick. "I am only here for Havick."

"You–you're from Torvald?" the second, larger man said, backing away, looking back and forth down the corridor.

"No," I shook my head. "I'm from *here*."

※

The two servants, Russ and Gam, led us quickly through the servant's halls, down the back ways and narrow stairwells that avoided the guard patrols. The sound was muted down here, in the heart of my enemies' lair, but I thought I could hear the distant sound of shouting.

"Is that your army?" Russ, the smaller man said as he led us up toward the throne room. He looked as pale as a sheet, but he was determined to do the right thing in leading us to our goal. I was touched by this act of faith and defiance from the older man.

"Not *my* army," I muttered, as there was the sudden blaring sound of a gong being rang further inside the castle.

"That's the warning bell!" Gam whispered. "The soldiers will be coming out..." The larger man looked at me. "Lady – I don't know who you are, but tell me this truthfully now, I beg you – should I get the servants out of here? I don't want to see any more of my friends turn into the dead."

Anyone who dies under the curse of the Darkening will turn into the dead, I remembered. "No," I said. "But get them to their rooms and barricade the doors. There is only me and —" I didn't want to tell this man about the two dragons flying above us somewhere in the night airs, bearing the leaders of Torvald against the Witches' Tower, "—and my allies. No armies, I promise you."

Gam looked hesitant, as if he might suddenly call for the soldiers to come *here* but Russ made a decision. "Here. Discard your cloaks, wear these." He took off his habit and tunic, revealing a dirty, shabby vest underneath as he handed them to me. "It won't hide you for long, but you'll pass at distance for a servant. The soldiers don't pay any attention to us anyway."

"Thank you," I said, as the other made the same offer, and soon we were dressed as the serving classes of this place, a fact that made me feel slightly proud. *I'll walk up to you, Uncle, looking like the very people you have trodden on all your life.*

"Go now, up those steps and straight on. You'll see. If you

can end this madness, then I wish you well!" Russ whispered, turning and taking his larger friend Gam with him as they ran back into the servants' halls to hide.

Here we go. I tucked my sword into my belt, kept my head down as I reached the top of the stairs to find a narrow door that creaked as I pushed it open and stepped into a throne room full of massing Roskildean soldiers.

I froze, and even my breath seemed to stop in my chest. Had Russ and Gam betrayed us? But then I remembered our robes.

The throne room was just as I remembered seeing it before, a long marble hall lined with pillars, alcoves and tapestries depicting the great deeds of Lord Havick, Defender of Roskilde, and at the far end was the semi-circular nave with its many oil paintings of the Roskildean noble line – including my own birth mother and father, around the gilt throne. I couldn't be more aware of how different this throne room was from Queen Saffron's, which looked more like a greenhouse than a throne room.

Right now, however, this place was an unofficial staging post for the castle's soldiers. Men and women buckled on breastplates, wound the taut cord of their crossbows, and secured their helmets.

"Lila! Move! They don't even notice servants!" Danu hissed, reminding me of Gam's words, keeping his head down as he crowded at my shoulder.

Yes. Be a servant. Right. Biting my lip and keeping my hand on my sword under my tunic, I walked forward.

"Blue Team! Form up!" a captain barked, as still others were attempting to sort themselves out into military formation. *They mean to fire on Crux and Jaydra,* I thought, as my anger tightened my hand on the pommel of my sword. *I can't let that happen.*

"Lila! Come on!" Danu was already a few steps ahead of me, skirting the edge of the hall, heading for the knave of the throne room where we knew there to be a door that led to the higher levels of the castle, and from there to the Witches' Tower itself.

"Wait," I had a sudden idea. How many doors were in this place? It was a throne room, which meant that it was pretty essential to the running of the castle- but also that it had to be defendable. I saw the main double doors at the far end of the room, and then a further set of double doors on both the east and west side of the room, leaving only the single knave door left.

"Lila, time!" Danu hissed at me as the soldiers filed into ranks.

"Can you lock those doors?" I whispered as we walked quickly. "With your magic?"

"I could – but when I use my magic, the witches will know that I'm here!" Danu whispered back.

"They already know, Danu – you told me so," I pointed

out. *And besides, surely, they were busy trying to bring down two very large and very angry dragons...*

Danu didn't argue, but nodded, his steps slowing as we neared the knave, before he finally leaned against the wall and shook his head. "I need to concentrate," he said, closing his eyes.

He was muttering something, his chin on his chest as I felt waves of eerier power trickle from him. It made the hairs on my neck stand up and my teeth itch.

One of the nearby soldiers looked around, clearly sensing Danu's magic too.

"You there, servant!" he shouted at me. I tried to ignore him.

"Oi! I'm talking to you – get over here, wench!" the man snapped. He was tall with short grey-black hair and stubble. He had his front breastplate on but was having trouble cinching the back.

"*...go drink bilge-water...*" I muttered as I walked up to him, keeping my head down. Was there any chance that he would recognize me? Right behind me was a painting of my birth mother and father...

"Sort these straps out for me," he said. I gingerly reached up, looking nervously over at Danu who was still concentrating. On the other side of us, one of the doors closed as if the wind had pushed it and wobbled slightly as if something had fallen across it on the far side.

"Well, I'm waiting!" the man barked, and I reached up to grab the straps and pull them, *hard*.

"Ow! Wait...!" the soldier gasped, as the tightening breast and backplate forced all the air out of his chest. "Too tight...!" he gasped.

"Oh, I'm sorry, sir—" I tightened it a bit more, just to feel him wince.

"You little... I'm going to..." the soldier gasped for air as I hurried back to Danu. Maybe I shouldn't have done that, but it had felt so good and the offensive soldier had no time for rebuke, anyway, as he was called into the line of crossbowmen and women.

There was an audible thump as the main double doors shuddered, and Danu and I were on the move again, up the nave, behind the thrones, and to the narrow door that was almost hidden behind the tapestry. How many of the soldiers even knew it was here? I turned back to look, seeing that each of the doors were still closed. Whatever Danu had used to barricade them must have been on the other side. It wouldn't hold the soldiers for long, but even pausing thirty or more crossbows was a worthwhile goal in my view. We slipped through the narrow door to a not very wide, but very elaborate stone passageway. Before we went, though, Danu concentrated and held his hand over its hasp.

Clunk. It locked in place, and he tuned to give me a weary smile.

Then a purple fire erupted around us.

CHAPTER 27
DANU, BATTLE-MAGIC

"**D**anu – down!" Lila body-checked me to the floor as the duke's passageway to the Witches' Tower filled with an acrid, burning purple light. I didn't even have a name for whatever sort of curse this was, but the purple fire evaporated in moments.

"Danu Geidt – Afar's brat!" sneered a voice that I recognized.

"Calla," I said, crouching with Lila at my side. "You've finally chosen sides then?"

The last time I had seen Calla—the auburn haired, young protégée of Ohotto, only a few years my senior—she had been trying to convince the rest of the Western Witches at Sebol to throw their luck in with Ohotto because, she said, Chabon the

Matriarch was gravely ill (thanks to their secret curses!). It had all been a ploy, of course.

"Some of us never *questioned* where our loyalties lie," Calla shot back. "Not like you, Danu. First Afar, and then the Sea Raiders, and now I see that you've shacked up with those arrogant Torvaldites. I guess we should have seen it coming, as a mage is drawn to Torvald as a fly is to—"

"Shut up," I said, throwing my hand towards her and releasing my own magic at her. *"Aqueris!"* A jet of ice, frost, and snow coalesced into a lancing shape and struck Calla in the chest. It bowled her over, back into the wider hallway below the gated entrance to the Witches' Tower, the lance itself shattering upon impact. As much as I hated her, I didn't have the heart to do her serious damage. But it gave me and Lila time to get out of this passageway, where we were sitting ducks—

"Mord!" Calla was tougher than I had expected, throwing her hands towards me from the floor, sending green tendrils of light from her hands to wrap around my arms and chest.

"Agh!" Even though this was just light, it was like being held by poison, as a burning sensation stabbed into my skin and I fell to my knees.

"Get off him!" Lila jumped forward, sabre singing from her belt as if she meant to cleave Calla in two.

"On your knees, whelp!" Calla snapped as she batted Lila out of the sky with a wave of invisible force before she could strike her blow.

"Lila!" I watched as my friend skidded across the flagstones, and somewhere above us Crux's frustrated wail resounded. I struggled, but the pain was too great. It was like suddenly being ill and injured all at once, like I was reeling from the desert sun and being strangled by knives at the same time. *I can't let her win. I can't let her win.*

"You're pathetic, you know that?" Ohotto's student staggered to her feet. "To think that the coven was worried, scared even, of Danu Geidt!" She cackled, twisting her hand so that the green poison-light tightened around my body. I was sweating, and my heart was hammering, and I didn't know how much more of this I could take...

"'Oh, Danu Geidt, the mage-in-training,'" Calla sarcastically scoffed. "It doesn't look like you're a mage, Danu. You haven't even mastered battle magic yet. But then again, you have been running around half the world with dragons and that feral little girlfriend of yours. Have you ever wondered that maybe you *aren't* the mage of this generation, Danu? Who says it has to be a boy, anyway?" Calla held up her hands, as purple-red flames burst from them. "Maybe *I'm* the mage, little Danu." Calla smiled as pleased as a cat and extended her hands towards me.

"Enough of this." Crux's angered voice roared into my head, and with it came a surge of his dragon-power, freely given. I knew what this meant now. Every time he did this, opened his heart and poured his soul into mine (or I dipped my hands in and took it from him) he lost years, perhaps even

decades of his life. I didn't want to take it, but I had no choice as the dragon power filled me up, flooded through my body, and the green poison-tentacles burst apart. I staggered to my feet.

Calla stepped back, her hands wavering in the air in confusion. "You're not that powerful!" she whispered in horror at me.

"No. But my friends are." I threw my own outstretched hand at her, and a whirlwind of air slammed her against the wall so hard that she slumped to the floor with a pained moan.

I could kill her right now, I thought, filled with the dragon energy. I probably should.

"Danu?" Lila looked up at me from where she now stood and it was then that I realized that I was floating a foot or two off the floor. Likely my eyes were glowing with borrowed power as well.

No. My feet settled on the floor, and the terrible light faded from my eyes and mind. I would not use this gift of my friend to kill. I was better than that. I could be better than that.

"Oh, thank the sweet waters…" Lila whispered as I returned to normal, at least outwardly, for Crux's power still raged inside my every heartbeat. It was enough to wave a hand at the finely sculpted, iron gate across the stairwell that led up the Witches' Tower – to break it from its mountings, crumple the metal and send it sliding across the floor.

"Come on." Lila was already heading for the stairs.

"Wait," I said, and slipped past her to be sure I went first up the stairs.

CHAPTER 28
LILA AND THE WITCH

Whatever had happened to Danu, it had seemed to cleanse all of his previous hurts and weariness, as he raced up the circular stairs to where we knew Ohotto's chamber was. Up there was a secondary, ritual throne room with a gold throne surrounded by sconces of torches and incense – it was from here I had retrieved the Roskildean battleplans the last time– and beyond that the room had been filled with Ohotto's jars and bowls, crystals and scrolls and magical equipment, as well as detailed maps of Havick's invasion plan. It seemed that was the place where my uncle and his witch had spent a lot of their time trying to manage, manipulate, and control the future of the Western Archipelago – and now the rest of the world.

It was also glowing with a baleful, ugly reddish glow, that

shone down from the open door to illuminate our faces as we ascended.

But it was met by a healthy, bluish light shimmering in front of Danu. I had never seen him perform such an act of magic, and I could feel the power of it crackling through the air.

"Setak!" A vile word muttered from above, one that I didn't understand but hurt my ears as I heard it. I gasped as a plume of purple-red flame shot out from the open door to strike against Danu's protective shield.

"Danu!"

He grunted in concentration, but despite being pushed back, the shield held.

Can he withstand them? How many witches were up there?

"Skreyarch!" A roar shook through the stones of the tower —Crux, bellowing his fury at the witches inside, matched by Jaydra's high angered keen. They weren't attacking the tower, but their fury was enough to make the witches above us *think* that they were.

"To the windows! There!" a woman's voice shouted, and there was a sudden *whoosh* as some cruel little spell was cast out of the windows.

"Crux! Are you all right?" I sent a desperate thought out to him.

"I am Crux! A little fire will not slow me down!" came back his ferocious response.

"It's him! The mage-boy – stop him!" Another shriek, and

this time the purple fires filled the doorway, flaring around Danu.

"Lila, down!" he hissed, hunching his shoulders as if he were holding the blue shield with his hands, and not his mind. Once again, the flames did not manage to penetrate his defenses.

"*ENOUGH!*" The bellowing voice shook through my mind, bringing with it the combined fury of King Bower, Queen Jaydra and Crux as well. That was when I realized the dragons and the king were teaming up to send their magical might to Danu! A fierce, feral joy rose in me, setting my teeth together as my limbs jittered with the strength of the gift.

"Not too much, Crux, please!" I did not want my dragon to squander his vital life-force away for us.

"Not squandering, wave-rider, sharing," Crux snapped at me, and redoubled his efforts, a wave of purifying dragon energy filling both me and Danu.

"Enough." I heard Danu echo the king's command, and his voice sounded deeper, fuller, like Lord Bowers' himself. I looked up to see that Danu had risen from the floor, his form defiant as he pushed through the doorway into the witches' chamber, sending the dome of blue light before him in a devastating shockwave.

"*Aiii!*" There were thumps, bangs and screams as Danu sent another wave of blue force into the room, before the light flickered out and I entered the tower room behind him, to find it empty of attackers, its contents destroyed.

The dragons roared victoriously around the outside of the tower, even as the warning bells of Ros continued to chime. It wouldn't be long before the soldiers had their crossbows and cannons trained on us, I thought in panic, looking at the scene of devastation that was the witches' ritual room.

There were only two moaning and groaning coven witches up here, both younger women dressed in heavy black robes. They must have been catapulted against the walls. Neither was mortally injured, but Danu was hovering over them, one hand held up with a blue corona of light shining around it all the same.

"Don't move, if you value your life," he intoned, his voice gradually losing its timbre and returning to normal as his toes, and then his feet settled once again on the floor. He had returned to us, *almost* to normality, although his eyes still had a strange, glowing intensity to them.

And that left Ohotto Zanna, who was crushed by the golden throne. I levelled my blade at her, to find that she was not what I had expected.

Ohotto Zanna looked old. No, she looked *ancient*. Her skin was bone-white and wrinkled, and her hair was a frizzy grey and white. Her claw-like hands shook as they scrabbled at the throne pinning her down, but I doubted she had the strength to do more than breathe.

"Where is it?" I snarled at her. "The book." This was her?

This feeble old woman was the person who had twisted my uncle's mind and caused such destruction to my home? This is she who killed my father? My anger jumped in me, aided by the recent influx of dragon-power. And this was she who was responsible for raising my father from the dead again. Was Kasian still aware, somewhere in that un-life? Was there still a part of him that realized what he was now, and was tormented for eternity?

My hand itched to drive the blade into this old woman. It would be a mercy, after all. Like the Torvald dead on the mainland. She had to pay for her crimes.

"Reverse it," I snapped at Ohotto, but she clamped her mouth shut. "Reverse the spell!" I said, pressing my blade to her throat.

"I can't," the old woman breathed.

"Ohotto?" Danu asked, his eyes wide as he saw Afar's old rival for the first time in years. "What have you done to yourself?" He seemed shocked by her appearance. *So, she hadn't always looked like this?* I thought. I had never seen her in the flesh, I wouldn't know.

"The magic.... Lars. He took the life from me," the decrepit crone whispered.

Lars. I knew that name. It had been forever seared into my memory, the night I had seen my father die. *Lars Oldhorn. Captain of the Dead.*

But before I could think what Ohotto might mean, Danu did something I was not expecting him to do. He cast a brief look at the other two sobbing coven witches, their wills broken, at least for the moment. He turned quickly and, with a gesture of his hand lifted the throne off of the most wicked witch in the archipelago. Her ragged breathing eased just slightly.

"Why did you do that?" I cried. "She's evil."

"She was once a student of Chabon," Danu said softly. "Maybe there is some good still left in her."

Some good? My world shook around me, and outside Crux echoed my frustration and fury. Where was the good when she had summoned the Darkening? Where was the good when she had attacked Malata? When she burned out the Free Islanders? When she attacked our limping fleet? How many good sailors and souls had died because of her? Hundreds? Thousands? Tens of thousands?

I watched, astonished, as Danu knelt at her side and put his hand over her shaking claw of a hand.

"Ohotto? You recognize me, I am Danu Geidt, student of Afar, student of Chabon."

A look of vile hatred scrunched the old witch's face, and I almost finished her then and there.

"You will tell us where the Book of Enlil is. You will help us find the spell you used to summon the dead," Danu said seriously.

And then we can kill her? I scowled. Outside, the wind was dying down now that the witches magic was dissipating, but it was being replaced by the distant sounds of shouting guards, and the *phwip-phwip* of crossbow bolts. I asked Crux how bad it looked out there.

"*Nothing I can't handle. A few beestings, that is all. But Jaydra sees ships approaching. A fleet.*"

"We don't have much time." I gestured menacing with my sabre at the witch.

"There. In the throne," Ohotto whispered. "But I cannot reverse it. Nor do you have the strength to do what I cannot, for Lars Oldhorn is no longer bound to me."

"He is the beast you summoned? From the grave?" I spat, my mind filled with the images of my father falling before the dead captains' life-sucking grasp.

"He and his clan. They are the Dead Fleet, but…" Ohotto coughed weakly. "He turned on us. On me. He has bound his life with Havick, and now he does not need me nor the spell to stay in our world. Only Havick can reverse the spell by speaking those last words, with his will, or by his death."

"Then I will kill him, too," I said, drawing back my sword—

"Lila, wait!" Danu cried out in alarm. His magic had almost entirely faded now, and he looked almost like the scared, normal young fisherman that I had first met.

"You are Lila. Of course." The witch squinted up at me, hatred and bile evident in every thin bone of her body. "You should have given up and died a long time ago, child. What have you brought to the islands but bloodshed and death!"

"Me?" Rage filled me. "How dare you!"

"Yes, you!" Ohotto cried out, daring to point a finger at me. Beside us, Danu had reached the throne and ripped aside the wooden seat, to see a hidden compartment where a heavy black grimoire was sat. "The Prophecy of Roskilde should never have come to pass. You must have read what it says – that you will rise from the ocean with blood and fire and death in your wake. Well, look around you, Lila Roskilde, and what do you see? All of my work has been to *stop* the islands falling into destruction and death. To *stop* you!"

It was like a lightning jolt to my system. How could this horrible, evil woman believe that? "What could you possibly mean?"

"You've read the prophecy, girl!" the witch snapped. "The girl will seize the crown, to be followed by blood and fire and death – and look around you! I couldn't let you get the Sea Crown. And then when I divined that you were a dragon-friend, I knew you would use those beasts to enslave the rest of us! Roskilde was the only hope against the tyranny of Raiders and dragons – *and* Torvald's self-righteousness! I made it so that Roskilde would be a force to be reckoned with. A power in the world to rival any!"

I had never wanted to have a prophecy written about me. I had never wanted to be Lila of Roskilde, but Lila of Malata. Was all of this really my fault? Did that mean that my foster-father's death was my fault, too? Did the fact that I had dared to stand against my uncle mean *I* had set this chain of events into motion?

"Yes, you see the truth of it now, whelp!" Ohotto cackled. "The worst thing to happen to your parents – both your birth parents and your Raider ones— was *you!*"

"No!" I shouted, and in that instant, one of Ohotto's coven raised a hand, brimming with purple light. She threw her arm forward, towards Danu. The mage reacted just as fast, bringing up his hand with blue light crackling around him, but Ohotto was moving now, too, purple light flickering at her shaking fingertips—

I lunged forward, driving my sabre into her. "This is for my father. This is for the parents I never got to know. This is for Malata!"

"Lila – no!" There was a loud *bang* as Danu threw his blue shield at the attacking coven, flinging them to the wall where they slid to the floor, unconscious. He turned back to look at me in horror. "What have you done?"

"She was going to attack me. Or you," I said, cleaning off my blade on her robes.

"She was a wreck!" Danu said in astonishment. "The magic had sucked every ounce of flesh from her body! I doubt that she could have done more than light a candle in the state that she was in!"

"She was still responsible for far more evil than me," I snapped. The look on Danu's face made me feel ugly, and annoyed. *How dare he?* "Ohotto was once one of the most powerful witches in the entire archipelago, maybe the world."

And she turned Kasian into a walking nightmare. "It would have been foolish to allow her to live."

"But Lila..." Danu shook his head. "Now that you *are* Lila of Roskilde, the Protector of the Western Archipelago – you can't just kill people anymore. Even if they are your enemies! You are a leader, a commander, a hope for a new way of life," he said, exasperated and upset as he pleaded with me. "The Western Archipelago needs to be based on justice. On laws and justice – not just killing people who do bad things!"

We had no time to argue, as there was the approaching sound of running feet coming up the stairs. The guards had apparently managed to break their way out of the downstairs throne room and trace our steps. Outside, distant cannons rumbled.

"We have to go," I snapped, rushing to the window. It was the way we had left before, and I hoped that we could do so again. Danu said nothing as he heaved the book to his chest, cast a look at the remaining coven witches, and shook his head at their stupidity.

"Go," he told them. "If I were you, I would run, and never come back. The dragons know what you did to their hatchlings, and they will be hunting you from one end of the islands to the other. I could punish you, or kill you, but I do not think you will live long anyway."

The windows had been thrown open, and I looked out to see the approaching shape of Crux, having sensed our actions inside.

"It is not over," he said as he flared his claws and grabbed onto the roof and the tower rocks with his hardened, black talons. In my thoughts he sounded guarded, reserved, and I wondered if my actions inside the tower had even managed to annoy a bull Phoenix dragon, as well.

But if he did feel reproach towards me, it did not change his actions as he flared his wings against the clatter of crossbow bolts, and I jumped down, to catch onto his neck and tines, shifting out of the way as Danu slid down Crux's neck behind me. With a grunt and a roar, he kicked off from the tower, accompanied by the boom of small cannon, and the whistle of the wind.

CHAPTER 29
DANU, WAR COUNCIL

We flew inland from the port city of Ros, flying this way, towards the mountains on the island-state of Roskilde, because the way south was blocked. The mega-galleons had drawn themselves up around the coasts, and there were hosts of smaller warships converging on their capital. And yet, all the time that we flew, my mind was filled with disbelief.

How could Lila kill Ohotto? The witch I had known as the young, beautiful blonde had been turned into a shadow of her former self by the evil magics that she was using. Perhaps she was near death anyway, I tried to rationalize. Perhaps Lila spoke the truth when she said that Ohotto had tried to cast a curse in that last moment of her life. But I did not want to believe that—I found I could not trust what Lila told me. Still,

I had to agree when Lila had said that Ohotto had been one of the most powerful witches in the archipelago.

"Any person who is that evil does not give up their hate so easily," Crux informed me sagely as we flew.

"I know," I muttered under my breath. But was killing Ohotto really the only way? It made me worried about the future. Maybe Lila Roskilde was really still Lila Malata, a Raider who believed in revenge and retribution only, not justice and democracy, as Torvald did. Maybe Lila was the cause of all the death and destruction, just as Ohotto had said.

It was then that the words of Queen Saffron rang in my ears, when she had told me Lord Bower did not trust Lila. I had been angry at that revelation – but now I wondered if I was guilty of the same disingenuousness.

However, for all of their misgivings, it seemed that the king and queen still flew with us, even though Jaydra must have informed them of what she could sense had happened inside that chamber. I wondered if the king was rethinking his alliance with the archipelago and wondering what actions the empire of Torvald would have to take for its interests out here.

Everything is spiraling out of control, I thought in desperation as we flew through the night, passing barren fields and huddled townships as we sought an escape. Everything that I had been working for, the path that Afar had put me on, was to make the Prophecy of Roskilde come to pass. To put a rightful heir on the throne of this isle, and to restore peace and order to the archipelago.

But what if Ohotto Zanna had been right? What if I had been wrong to aid Lila in coming to power? What if Lila was the worst thing that had ever happened to these islands?

※

"Things are bad on the mainland, and we have little time to act," Lord Bower informed us as we sat on a rocky ledge rimed with frost in the sharp cliffs and rocks of north-eastern Roskilde. Even though dawn was rising in the east, this far north and this high up, the world was forever locked in cold, and the grey and black seas below thrashed the cliffs and were flecked with drifts of sleet and snow.

On the ledge Crux had managed to light a fire of old driftwood and scrubby cliff bushes, around which we sat, while Saffron distributed our rations.

"Eat, all of you," the queen said. "This war won't be won if we are starving."

The Lord Bower had been in communication, through Jaydra and his own abilities, with both his phalanx of Dragon Riders in the south, as well as the dragons of Mount Hammal. Through them, he had received news that was both distressing and serious.

"The Darkening has made landfall on the wild coasts, and has spread into Torvald lands, with the Army of the Dead marching in its shadow," Lord Bower said. "Any who dies under its spell rises again, and that means that Torvald forces are loathe to attack them." The king's words and glances were heavy. He must have hoped that our mission here, last night, would have put a stop to this evil, but it seemed all it had done was to reveal instead who—or what—the true enemy was: Lars Oldhorn, the captain of the Army of the Dead.

"And he is tied to your uncle now, in some act of evil magic that I do not know about," Saffron shook her head sadly. "I had hoped that we could avoid an all-out confrontation, that we could dispel the Darkening by removing its source." The queen's eyes fell on the grimoire that sat on the ground beside me. The Dark Book of Enlil, the personal spellbook of the Dark King.

"I feel that we are somehow responsible for this," Saffron said to her husband quietly. "We should have acted more to try and eradicate all traces of the evil that the Dark King left in the world."

Lord Bower frowned, but I could see that he felt shame as much as the queen did.

"We all do what we can, when we can." Crux's sanguine voice breathed his sooty wisdom into my thoughts. *"We act according to our natures, and that is all."*

"We all have to do what we can," I echoed, using the dragon's words, as I thought about Lila's actions in that tower. Had she been right to kill Ohotto? Or should she have shown mercy? I was suddenly tired and weary of this endless cycle of blame and shame. *All I knew was that now we had a great evil to stop.*

I had been searching the dark book all night, on the flight (as much as I was able) and here as we grabbed a scant little time to rest – but I could find no word of any spell or enchantment to dispel the Darkening, or to break the hold that Lars Oldhorn had on Havick. It seemed the Dark King had been far more interested in gathering evil knowledge, not in learning how to undo it. All I had seen was the spell to summon the dead, and the final passage that Havick would have to speak to end their contract.

I kept on coming back to that one, ultimate solution: that the answer lay with Havick. "Ohotto said that he was the lynchpin now. The seat for the dead and the Darkening's power." I did not add in what we all knew had to happen next, for it appeared obvious. We had to find a way to put a stop to him, somehow.

"I have summoned the Dragon Flights, all of them save a skeleton crew left to defend the citadel," Lord Bower said with finality. "But I still fear whether it will truly be enough. If our only weapon against the dead is dragon fire, then we will need all the fire we can muster."

We could not hope to burn every single member of the Dead Army though. Of this I was certain. But what were our options, save capturing Havick?

"You mean to defend Torvald." Lila nodded, looking back over the dawn-lightening island. I wondered if she thought Lord Bower and Queen Saffron were abandoning her, to deal with the Roskildean mega-galleons on her own.

Which she can't do, when all that's left of the Raider warriors are many thousands of leagues to the south. And even then, there weren't enough of them to rout out the Roskildean navy.

"No," Lord Bower said. "If we can defeat Havick, in one way or another—"Lord Bower squinted his eyes, bringing his hands together in one gesture—"then perhaps we can cut the head from the snake. Perhaps we can stop this evil with him."

"Havick is *my* uncle," Lila said defiantly, rising to her feet. She looked tall, and proud, and I wondered what she was going to say next. Was she going to bid them good riddance? Or was she going to join with them? "I must undo the evil that he has caused. I will fly with you, Lord Bower and Lady Saffron, and I have my own flight of Dragon Raiders, who will be able to help."

Saffron's eyes gleamed with pride as she looked at this fellow daughter of the islands, but what I saw in Lila was something different when she turned to me.

"I know, Danu," she said, her face etched with determination, "that you have doubts about my actions – but they are mine to make, and I believe them to be right. The Western Archipelago isn't the same as the mainland, the north, south, and maybe even the closed councils of the Western Witches. We are a wilder people. We judge people on what they *do,* not on what they say." I was surprised to hear Lila talk for the whole archipelago. Strangely, she sounded more like a leader now than she had ever before. She turned back to King Bower and Queen Saffron. "And the people of the Western Archipelago will gladly give aid to Torvald, as I have seen what they have done to help those in need." And, as much as I might not like her tactics, I had to admit that she spoke like the kind of leader that the Western Archipelago would follow.

"This is not your decision alone, humans. Why do you just not ask us!" Crux informed us all, raising his head to blink slowly at Lila and the rest of us.

"You humans think that this is just your fight. That this is a war between humans, but you forget that Ohotto's Coven was attempting to steal dragon newts and dragon relics for her magics," Crux said. *"Her coven was casting magic against Queen Ysix and Sym's island to stop us archipelago dragons from talking to each other. Now that the coven is gone, we can talk to them again. We can seek their help."*

He was right! I thought about the cruelties Ohotto's Coven had inflicted upon the dragons of the islands. Ohotto was evil, through and through. She had taken the ancient dragon affinity that had built the Western Witches and corrupted it, abused it, and made it a mockery of everything Chabon had ever held dear.

I knew in that moment that Ohotto would never have stopped at releasing Lars Oldhorn – even if the undead chief really did betray her in the end. She would have continued to use the dragon relics and dragon blood. Hadn't we found her assassins on the mainland operating with those very orders?

I looked at Lila and her dragon once again, staring at each

other in the ruddy glow of the firelight, and for a moment they almost seemed alike. Two savage wild creatures, proud of what they had achieved and – yes – where they had come from. Neither of them was the genteel or civil heroes that King Bower and Queen Saffron now were, but then again neither were the islands.

"Crux, you genius!" Lila said with a sudden laugh, shared by Queen Saffron, who stood up. "I had not thought that with Ohotto gone, we could apply to the dragons for their help yet again."

"Yes. The island dragons could help us all," I cleared my voice to say, and for a moment I could see it almost as Chabon had—to see the possible futures that she prophesied. The Western Isles would never be safe, and they would be harsh, a place where actions and oaths mattered. But it would be free – and perhaps even happy, of a kind.

And with that thought, something like peace flowed through me. There. We had found a hope for the future, that the islands and the mainland could indeed work together for the good of all. Finally, the last of my loyalties to the Western Witches crumbled. Finally, I could fully trust in Lila and her leadership, and work together with her wholeheartedly, knowing that she was thinking of all her people, and not just the Sea Raiders who had raised her.

CHAPTER 30
LILA, THE ATTACK

"*It is done,*" Crux informed us, as he lowered his shoulders and legs for Lila and me to climb back up. The morning sun was now rapidly rising in the sky, and both he and Jaydra had spent the little time we had keening into the skies their long, ululating calls. I could not hear a response from Queen Ysix or Sym or any of the other island dragons, but it must have gone well, as Jaydra and Crux were whistling and chirruping at each other, eager to get moving.

The plan was simple: to fly as fast as we dared, back to the mainland and join up with both the island dragons and my Dragon Raiders, under Senga and Adair. At their side would also be the dragon phalanx under Prince Simon that the Lord Bower had sent to protect my people.

And then? We would use the twin dragon flights in a pincer movement to attack the Darkening and the.

We would have to leave the navies of Roskilde, for now. That thought stuck in my mind like a thorn, and it was strange to think that my destiny lay out there somewhere, not here in the islands.

I had to ask myself if I was doing the right thing, but my heart was certain and steady. *Yes.* If this was what we had to do to defeat Havick, then this was what we would do. For the islands, and for all of us. For the world.

It was time. "Go!" I whispered to Crux, and we jumped into the air.

It took us a further few days to fly within striking distance of the mainland, during which time we once again passed the burning ruins of Free Island villages, and the seas swamped with Roskildean ships. But now, they weren't the essential enemy. They were men and women, soldiers and sailors like the servants we had seen in the palace.

The real enemy was Lars, and the way to defeat him was through my uncle, Havick.

But, when we left on the third morning with the mainland an easy flight away, I saw that it had already changed.

A heavy sea of fog had amassed over the broken coasts,

completely obscuring the cliffs and islets that we had flown over just a few days ago.

"The Darkening," Danu said with a shiver. It would still be a few hours before we drew close to it, but even the sight of it was enough to fill us all with dread. I wondered how many dead feet were marching under its heavy clouds, and how many people were being raised back up, even now.

"Friends!" Crux lifted his snout in the air to the south, and we saw a speck of dark colors turn into a cloud. As we circled and waited over the open waters, the cloud soon started taking on the iridescent shines and colors of the dragons. It was Senga and Adair, Rigar and Veen and the others, and their joyful chirrups and whistles reached us over the high airs.

"Where are the island dragons?" I asked Crux, who immediately sent me a mental image of them flying, already having crossed the Barrens and soaring high and fast – a great river of dragons with the long-necked Ysix at their head. In that ethereal way that dragon-sight did, I could share just a little of their thoughts and feelings, and felt outrage, pride, anger, as well as the distant image of Roskildean mega-galleons struggling to keep up with them as they flashed across the sky above them.

It wouldn't take them long to get here. Should we wait? I knew Lord Bower and the queen would already be impatient to get going to save their people.

"We fly!" I called to the other dragons, to the flight of

Senga and Adair, throwing my arm forward and up, in a gesture I hoped they would understand.

They did. Effortlessly and without direction, the approaching dragons split into two forces, Danu and I joining the Dragon Raiders, and the king and queen joining the Academy Dragons and their son Prince Simon. As a pair, we flew in two interweaving streams, separating into rivers as we flew high over the grey mass of the Darkening, seeking its forward edge.

When we found it, it was skirted with flames and death, just as the prophecy had foretold.

The dragon flights from Torvald had already found the Darkening and the dead, it seemed. I could see small knots of Crimson Reds, Sinuous Blues and Stocky Greens descending out of the skies to run strafing runs against the forward edge of the creeping Darkening fogs. The skies around them were filled with the rise of steam and black smoke, as well as the boom of cannon.

Cannons? I wondered if Torvald field-forces were engaging the enemy as well, but that was madness since every Torvald soldier who died would also rise to fight for the enemy.

But then the fog of the Darkening was disrupted as a small projectile shape rose out of the mist to strike at a Torvald dragon. The great Green beast suddenly flapped its leathery wings awkwardly and stagger-flew out of the sky and away.

It was the dead. They had brought their cannons with them, and their crossbows. There were swarms of the terrible little black quarrels rising out of the fog all along the front, and I wondered how many of the dragons thus wounded would end up like Crux had been, poisoned by the evils of the Darkening.

Casting a look over to where the Lord Bower and Lady Saffron were leading their dragons, I choreographed my movements. Our flight was partly made of the larger Greens and Blues, but mostly made of the smaller and faster Turquoise island dragons, which meant that we could fly in fast and low, and not have to make the larger swoops that the academy dragons did.

Crux signaled my intentions, and they matched their flight to follow us as Crux angled sharply, spilling his dragon fire in a blistering line across the front of the Darkening fog.

Phwip! Phwip-phwip!

Storms of bolts raced up on either side, clattering against the Phoenix's hide, but Danu shouted something, and a blue shield just as before rippled into existence under his belly, turning most of the projectiles away. I prayed that the dragons behind us were lucky, and fast, as Danu did not have the strength to shield us all.

It was almost impossible to know where the targets were beneath the fog of the Darkening, but I copied the academy dragons' example by directing the Raider dragons' lines of fire to be laid across it. The flames hissed and disappeared into the fog, causing disruptions and frothing quakes in the magical cloud as if I were watching stormy waters, not a cloud.

You're an idiot.

You're a failure.

How could you let this happen?

All of my fears and worries amplified and battered by the Darkening, but I tried to remember what Danu had taught me, and how we had escaped the fears the last time. *Crux,* I thought, opening my heart to his warmth. It filled me with confidence, and hope, and helped to push back at the fears that the Darkening grew in us.

And up! We rose out of our attack once again, Crux catching the updraft to soar high and wide out of the range of the dead's cannons and join the Torvald dragons from the mainland. I looked back, counting back our Dragon Raiders as they performed their attacking runs to safety.

Senga and Adair... Rigar and Veen... I scanned the returning Raiders, seeing most of the faces that I knew and remembered, and a few that I did not. It appeared that Senga and Adair had managed to get some new Free Islanders to join our Dragon Raiders.

They flew and attacked awkwardly for the most part, but they *flew*, which was the important thing. They were not the choreographed, perfect flights of the academy dragons but they were sharp and expressive, the river of Raider dragons breaking apart into a storm and choosing their own fast, low paths of attack.

At least it meant they didn't form one solid target, I thought, grinning as the last of them completed their attack run—

And then disaster hit. The Darkening convulsed, and a patch of the grey, cloying clouds suddenly exploded upwards like a water plume, engulfing the last island dragon and wrapping it in thick tendrils.

"No!" I shouted, turning Crux to return to it as the dragon struggled, shook and convulsed.

"Lila – it's over!" Danu shouted, and I knew that he was right. The island dragon was already sucked down into the murk and swallowed whole.

No. No. No. I thought in anger, feeling helpless as we had no room to attack now that Lord Bower and Queen Saffron were also beginning their diving fire-run. This time, it seemed that the Darkening fog and the concealed Army of the Dead inside were more prepared for them, as the fog performed that tendril-plume attack three more times and managed to capture at least two more dragons.

Does that mean that when those dragons die, they will rise to be reborn once again? I thought in horror. We couldn't let that happen. An undying, unkillable dragon too great a threat to the world.

This had to end now. I had to find my Uncle Havick.

CHAPTER 31
DANU, THE LOCKET

"You're in charge now!" Lila shouted to Senga as she leaned back, and Crux wheeled up and away from the Raider flight.

"Me?" Senga's face was at once fierce, worried, and excited. She would know what to do. She was a fighter, through-and-through.

"Lila? What's the plan?" I asked, knowing that she, just like Senga, would have one. She was quick-witted like that.

She waited until we had risen into the cleaner airs, back from the battle as different flights of both academy and Raider dragons swooped and rose, and tried not to get hit by arrows or cannon shot or the grabbing tendrils of the Darkening itself. When we were a safe enough distance away that we couldn't hear the screams and shouts of the other Riders, Lila turned to me, her belt knife in hand.

"Do you remember my mother's locket?" she said, her face pinched with worry.

I nodded. It was the magical item that the assassins had been using to track her.

"I want to know if you can make one," she said, grabbing one of her braids and yanking it tight, to slice through the end with one clean movement.

"But – why?" I asked in confusion as she handed me her braid.

"Ohotto enchanted my mother's own hair and the locket because it was connected to *me,* the body that the hair came from would remember me, and would lead the wearer to *my* body, right?"

"Okay...." I looked at the hair. *Was she asking me to find her dead mother?*

"Well, I figure that if it works that way, maybe it connects with anyone who shares the same blood. Havick is my uncle. His parents are my grandparents. There has to be a connection there, right?"

Lila really was a genius, I thought, holding the lock of her hair and fumbling in my saddlebag for the Dark Book of Enlil. I had seen the spell that Ohotto had used to make those lockets just this morning as I had been trying once more in vain to find some spell that would reverse the Darkening, and I was sure that I would be able to fiddle with the magic to make it fit Lila's request.

"Careful.... Bad magic," Crux whispered as soon as the grimoire touched his back.

"Don't worry, I will..." I said, flicking through to the pages that I needed to go to, and started mumbling the words.

"You who were once whole, remember your parts,

You who are parted, remember your whole..."

The words flowed through me, as I recanted the words and syllables in the correct order, setting my thoughts on Havick, and Lila's parents as well as I could.

The spell ended unexpectedly, with a feeling like a wrenching in my chest, and I coughed, rubbing my ribcage gingerly.

"You've just lost three years, foolish human," Crux sniped at me. *"That is the cost of dark magic, and why dark magicians steal others' lives."*

"I did?" I looked at the braid of hair with disgust, before I was aware that it was also pulling me in a certain direction. "It's working," I whispered to Lila, handing her braid back to her.

"Good. Then we can follow it to my uncle." Lila held onto one of Crux's tines with one hand, and her enchanted braid with the other, as she directed Crux to fly out against the Darkening once more.

CHAPTER 32
LILA, FAMILY

My eyes found my uncle even before I realized which way the braid was pointing. It was like I was drawn to him, blood to blood, as if our meeting once more was fated. He was standing on a small promontory in the battlefield, with the Darkening's fog ebbing around the hill, and the shadows of ghostly dead figures marching on either side.

Of course, I thought. The Darkening plays tricks on the mind, and Lord Havick won't want that if he can help it, will he? That was why he was here, in one of the places where the fogs were thinnest.

"Uncle!" I roared, screaming out of the sky as I shoved the braid back into my tunic and drew my sword.

"Lila – the dark book," Danu said hurriedly, producing the

grimoire and handing it to me. "You remember what Ohotto said. Only Havick can reverse the spell now by finishing those words."

"Or by his death," I said, although I still shoved the book into my belt, just to please Danu. I had no intention of trying to get my uncle to speak some silly words, when I could just run him through instead.

Havick opened his mouth to answer me back, but before he could he was violently shoved backward by a bony-white hand. It was Lars Oldhorn, the Captain of the Dead and the barbarian leader of this clan. He had white skin that was drawn back and desiccated on his bald skull and wore large furs of a cream-white bear, and in his hands was a mighty double-headed ax.

The Captain of the Army of the Dead was grinning as he raised that ax towards us—

"Skreyargh!" Crux opened wide his maw to roar his dragon fire at them both, but with a sudden convulsion he was thrown off-aim, and the fire shot uselessly into the skies.

"Crux?" I looked down to see that his legs had been caught by the Darkening's fog, and it was wrapping itself tighter and tighter around him, drawing my dragon down.

"Lila – go!" Crux snarled into my mind as he thrashed his tail back and forth. *"You must defeat Lars. Danu will free me, now go!"* He bucked his neck and I jumped as I saw his intention, sailing through the air to hit the ground with a roll at the base of the promontory which Lars and my uncle occupied.

"Child. What a pleasure to finally meet you," the captain croaked, looking down at where I crouched. He held his battleax ready but casually in his hands, seemingly unconcerned by the young woman come to challenge him.

I wondered if the large man might be right, as my mind was reeling from contact with the Darkening – but I knew that I had an inner reservoir of strength, of hope and of life and courage in the belief that my friends Crux and Danu had in me. Still, it was nearly all I could do to stand up, raising my sabre with a shaking hand.

"Finally, I can have almost the whole family! You Islanders will make good warriors for my army," Lars said, and, underneath the torment of my thoughts, I wondered what he meant. The unliving barbarian stepped closer towards me, nodding to a shadow that emerged on one side of the hill, and then separated out into two forms – one thin, and the other lurching.

It was Havick. My uncle. And beside him stood Kasian.

Father! My heart reached out to him. *He hadn't been a dream. He hadn't been a nightmare vision of the Darkening.* It was undeniably him – the same man who had taught me how to sail and how to tie a reef knot and a sheet-bend. He was still broad, but he was no longer stocky, and his face was sunken around his cheekbones, and taking on a ghoulishly pale hue.

"*Luh-luh...Lil—?*" my father croaked, stumbling forward around the mound of dirt towards me.

His eyes. They had changed, taking on the clear, sharp cerulean blue of storm waters. His face twisted into a snarl as he raised his scimitar threateningly towards me.

"Father – no! It's me, Lila!" I staggered back, my eyes flicking to the only other living man there, Havick. His once-fine features were now emaciated, and his eyes haunted. He still had rich dark hair and a sharp nose, but he had taken no care in his appearance for days, if not weeks. His clothes hung on him as he looked fretfully between me and Kasian, and Lars.

"Niece?" he whispered, his gloved hands reaching for his sword.

"Uncle," I snarled at him, tears in my eyes as my true father tried to wrestle his steps towards me. But it was as if he didn't have full control over his own body. I turned to level the sabre at my flesh and blood: Havick. Behind us, I was aware of flame and light exploding in the fog as Crux and Danu attempted to fight off the Darkening. I was alone here, with my uncle already drawing his sword and my own foster-father a walking nightmare.

"Call it off!" I demanded of him, my fears turning into anger and hatred as I stalked forward, thinking only how I should kill him. It was all his fault. He was the one who had brought me to this. "Release my father from this!"

"You have come to kill me, haven't you, Lila? To take my

empire away." My uncle's eyes flashed from worry and confusion as he stepped behind Kasian, putting my undead father between us even as Lars started to laugh.

"*Lila?*" My father stopped and echoed the words that Havick had said.

"Yes!" Havick snapped. "That girl you stole. She's here – and she wants to kill you! Attack her!"

My father shook and trembled, raising his blade towards me – and I did not know how I would even be able to strike him down, even in such a state as he was in, until he lurched around in a circle, thrusting awkwardly not at me, but at Havick.

Yes!

"What! What are you doing?" Havick slid back in the churn of mud. "*There* is our enemy. The brat with the blade!"

"*Lila. Her name is Lila,*" my father croaked a little stronger, thrusting at my uncle again. *He had broken the spell that held him. He was still in there!* I readied my sword to help him kill my uncle.

"Bah!" Lars shouted from above us, and a wave of cold, ice-like power shivered over all of us. My father suddenly paused, falling to his knees, his flesh growing whiter and whiter.

"Always a problem with the newly dead," Lars growled. "Too fresh with memories." He clapped his hands, and that was it. My zombie father fell to the mud, half turning to me as he did so.

No! I jumped for the mound that Lars stood upon, but the Captain of the Dead was fast, already giving ground.

"Havick! Kill your pretender!" Lars snarled, and my uncle leapt forward, thrusting his broadsword at me in a wide sweep. It was an easy attack to meet, but the man's reach and his broadsword were far wider than my curving Raider's sabre, and I barely managed to deflect the blow as I staggered back.

"You never wanted Roskilde to be happy. You only ever wanted the dragons!" Havick shouted at me as he fought.

"Not true!" I said, giving ground and circling him. "I want the archipelago to be free! Freedom from tyrants!"

"By handing it over to Torvald instead?" My uncle lunged again, this time sweeping across and then turning to strike downwards. I parried the first, and as I turned to dodge the second, I saw Lars' eyes glittering at us both in obvious enthusiasm.

He was enjoying this, I suddenly saw. Lars Oldhorn was enjoying watching us kill each other, knowing that we would rise again and be his forever.

"DIE!" Havick said, his Darkening-confused mind making him see me as the answer to every wrong in his life. Consequently, his attack was obvious: a charging run-through that I could roll easily out of the way, before half-turning to kick him across the legs to make him fall on the floor.

"Stop," I commanded him, all the while wondering what I was doing. He had killed my birth parents! He was responsible for the deaths of so many of my people—of my foster-father.

"Ach!" Havick clamped a hand on his leg and swung his broadsword in a wide arc that I had to jump back from.

"Stop," I repeated. "This is what *he* wants. Lars Oldhorn. *He's* the one calling the shots, not you, uncle."

"Kill her!" Lars shouted furiously. "Kill the pretender!"

"This is *his* empire you're building, Uncle. An empire of the dead." I jumped back again from Havick's wild thrust, as my uncle staggered to his feet.

"If you don't kill her right now, Havick—" Lars raised his battleax and stalked down the hill towards both Havick and me.

"You'll what? Kill him? You were going to kill him anyway, weren't you? He's the only one who can reverse the spell, and that means that you cannot have him around for much longer…" I pulled the dark book from my back and threw it towards my uncle, where it thumped along the muddy floor.

"What are you talking about?" my uncle sneered. "Why would I reverse the spell?"

"Because Ohotto is dead. I killed her, and without her it's just you against Lars. Because Roskilde is an island of the walking dead. Because you haven't built *your* empire, you've built *his*," I burst out.

Lars let out a roar and leapt forward, swinging his battleax over his head to nearly cleave me in two. I jumped and raised my sabre to block the blow, but with juddering pain that went through my arms, my sabre snapped as the captain's fur-clad boots connected with my hip.

"Oof!" I sprawled backwards on the floor, winded. Somewhere behind me, Crux roared in anger. I rolled, raised my sabre – only now it was a broken stub of metal, and Lars Oldhorn was once again raising his battleax for another superhuman blow.

"Uncle!" I breathed. He was my only hope—my last living family—but it was too late. Lars had already reached the apex of his swing and was bringing the ax back down again.

It was just as the blade began its arc that the Captain of the Dead's eyes widened.

"*Hyurk.*" A strange, startled sound issued forth as Lars Oldhorn dropped his ax behind him, where it thudded heavily on the floor.

"What…?" I gasped as the captain hissed, turning—

There was my Uncle Havick, with the Dark Book of Enlil open and reciting the last few words. Something convulsed through the Darkening around me, a wave of power that emanated from the grimoire he was holding.

"What did you do?" Lars turned, his voice growing weaker and weaker as the spell unraveled. Oldhorn fell to his knees, and his aged skin frayed and powdered.

"You did it!" I said in amazement. "You really did it!"

Havick opened his mouth to respond to me, but before he could, Lars roared, and even with his fading, crumbling hands, he threw the battleax across the ground at my uncle.

"No!" I screamed, but the damage was already done. Lars Oldhorn's battleax hit my last remaining relative and he was thrown to the floor, dead.

"Uncle! Uncle!" I shouted, rushing to his side. All of these years I had hated him. I had despised him with a fury and passion reserved for the most evil, but now I realized that it had been a sort of hatred based on what he *represented* not what he was. Yes, my uncle had been a power-hungry and evil man, but he had mostly been a deeply misguided one. I had never met him, never even talked to him or seen him, and how can you hate or love someone you don't know? All of these thoughts flashed through my mind as I scrambled to my uncle and Lars Oldhorn crumbled into dust before us, the clouds of the Darkening wisping away and lifting from the battle. A great wind was rising, and the Army of the Dead were dissipating all around into the breeze, as if they had been built by nothing but dust in the first place.

"Lila...?" Havick coughed weakly. Even his form was now starting to crumble as the spell that he was tied into ate at him too.

"Why?" I asked softly.

"Because." His voice became a whisper-thin croak. "Sometimes you have to make what you do count. Not who you think you are." No sooner had he spoken the last word, then he evaporated in my arms.

EPILOGUE
LILA, COUNCILWOMAN

The Letters and Personal Records of Lila Roskilde-Malata, Ros, the Isle of Roskilde.

It has been a year since the events of the Battle of the Dead as they are now calling it. In that time, we have restored trade routes with Torvald, for one, and with the Southern Kingdoms – but the trade is slow as still the merchants are wary of coming out this far again.

It will take a long time for the wounds of the past to heal, I think. I know that for myself, that will certainly be the case.

After the Battle of the Dead, the coasts and the archipelago were thrown into disarray, and it was only the arrival of the island dragons that managed to bring calm and restore order. They set fires and protected the coasts from the Roskildean mega-galleons and guarded those displaced through the night. Such was the input from Queen Ysix and her island brood, that I think it went a long way to healing the rifts between the Western Archipelago and the mainland.

Despite my earliest of reservations, Torvald has remained a staunch ally – even if Lord Bower does still occasionally look at me as if I might steal his silverware! Once a Raider, always a Raider, I suppose.

The same can certainly be said of Costa – my father's quartermaster who abandoned us on the southland coasts and who has now formed his own alternate Raiding clan called 'The Sea Reavers' who are far worse than the Sea *Raiders* ever were.

As for Pela, and for the rest of us Raiders? I gave Pela rule over the Isle of Malata, though it hardly felt as if it were mine to give, and told her to choose for herself whatever life she would. She chose to be an independent state of the Free Islands, as many others did. I occasionally hear reports of sea-piracy in the near waters, and sometimes I wonder if my aging mother is behind it.

After the Battle of the Dead, I travelled with Crux and Danu, Rigar, Veen, and Halex for a little while. For a time, I just could not travel the islands without thinking of all that we had lost, and especially of my father Kasian. Any decision I made then (even though they were clamoring for me to do so) would have been based on misery and loss, and yes, I even saw that Danu was at least partially right. I needed to be a *wise* ruler. *The smartest person there,* as Pela would say. And I hadn't felt very smart after the Battle of the Dead. The old Riders took us to the distant Spice Coasts (which I had never seen) and even to the jungles beyond. It was at once a thrilling and eye-opening experience. By the time I returned, the Torvald Academy Dragons and Senga's Dragon Patrol (as she calls them) had managed to rout the last of the Havick-loyalists and restore order to Roskilde.

It is here, in the port-city of Ros, that I have called for a Council of All Islands, to discuss and decide upon the issues that affect us all. There is no King or Queen of the Islands because I am the last of the line of Roskilde, and I will not take the throne nor wear the Sea Crown. Far too much blood has been spilt in their name for my liking.

Instead, the Sea Crown sits in the Council Room, melted by Crux himself into a ring of gold on the floor, as a permanent reminder and symbol of the circle of islands. The Dark Book of Enlil, as much as I wanted to burn it, has instead been sent back to Torvald – where they claim that they will take better care of it this time. I think we can only hope on that issue, but we needed to maintain good faith with Torvald, and with the Western Witches gone, we did not have the facilities to hold it secure out here anymore.

Senga and Adair's Dragon Patrol protects the islands from the worst of the Reavers and the bandits, and the occasional warlord. They run testings every spring, where hopeful young boys and girls can try to persuade a young dragon to join with them. Watching their successes and failures reminds me of the person that I was, what feels like many years ago, and how I and Danu tried to unsuccessfully convince Sym's brood of hatchlings to bond with us.

As for Danu, he is well, and he is wise: a good husband. We got married last fall, when the summer warmth is still in the seas. Sometimes I catch his eyes drawn to the west, and I know he is thinking about the westward track that Afar, Chabon and the others took. Sometimes I fear if he will take it too, and sometimes, during the long and boring council sessions I fear that *I* will take it, just to be rid of their scrolls and paperwork!

But we are happy, and, since I am just a councilwoman and not a queen or a chieftain – we get plenty of time to sail the airs of the world, carried on Crux's wings.

END OF DRAGON PROPHECY
SEA DRAGONS TRILOGY BOOK THREE

Sea Dragons Series

Book One: Dragon Raider
(Published: March 28, 2018)

Book Two: Dragon Crown
(Published: May 30, 2018)

Book Three: Dragon Prophecy
(Published: July 25, 2018)

PS: Keep reading for an exclusive extract from **Dragon Trials.**

THANK YOU!

I hope you enjoyed **Dragon Prophecy**. Please don't forget to leave a review.

Receive free books, exclusive excerpts and be kept up to date on all of my new releases, when you sign up to my mailing list at AvaRichardsonBooks.com/mailing-list

Stay in touch! I'd also love to connect with you on:

Facebook: www.facebook.com/AvaRichardsonBooks

Goodreads:
www.goodreads.com/author/show/8167514.Ava_Richardson

RETURN OF THE DARKENING: BOOK ONE
Dragon Trials

AVA RICHARDSON

BLURB

High-born Agathea Flamma intends to bring honor to her family by following in her brothers' footsteps and taking her rightful place as a Dragon Rider. With her only other option being marriage, Thea will not accept failure. She's not thrilled at her awkward, scruffy partner, Seb, but their dragon has chosen, and now the unlikely duo must learn to work as a team.

Seventeen-year-old Sebastian has long been ashamed of his drunken father and poor upbringing, but then he's chosen to train as a Dragon Rider at the prestigious Dragon Academy. Thrust into a world where he doesn't fit in, Seb finds a connection with his dragon that is even more powerful than he imagined. Soon, he's doing all he can to succeed and not embarrass his new partner, Thea.

When Seb hears rumors that an old danger is re-emerging, he and Thea begin to investigate. Armed only with their determination and the dragon they both ride, Thea and Seb may be the only defence against the Darkening that threatens to sweep over the land. Together, they will have to learn to work together to save their kingdom…or die trying.

Get your copy of **Dragon Trials** at **AvaRichardsonBooks.com**

EXCERPT

Every fifth year, the skies over the city of Torvald darken as large shadows swoop over the city, dark wingbeats blowing open window shutters and their bird-like cries disturbing babes and sleeping animals alike.

The city folk of Torvald are prepared for this ritual however, as the great Dragon Horns—the long brass instruments stationed along the top towers of the dragon enclosure—are blown on those mornings. Farmers and market folk rush to guide their skittish cattle out of sight, whilst children flock to the narrow cobbled streets or crowd atop the flat rooftops.

Choosing Day is a time of great celebration, excitement and anticipation for Torvald. It is the time that the great enclosure is unbarred and the young dragonets are released into the sky to choose their riders from amongst the humans below. It is a day that could forever change your fortunes; if you are brave and lucky enough. It is a day that heroes are made, and the future of the realm is secured.

"Dobbett, no! Get down from there right now." Dobbett was a land-pig, although she looked somewhere between a short-snouted dog and a white fluffy cushion. She grunted nervously as she turned around and around atop the table, whimpering and grunting.

She always got like this. I wasn't very old the last time that Choosing Day came around; I must have been about thirteen or fourteen or so, but I remember how my little pet ran around my rooms, knocking everything off stands or dismantling shelves. I couldn't blame her: land-pigs are the natural food of dragons, and if she even caught a whiff of one, she went into a panic.

"No one's going to eat you, silly," I said to her in a stern voice, making sure I picked her up gently and set her down on the floor where her tiny claws immediately clacked on the tiles as she scampered under my bed.

Good Grief! I found myself smiling at her antics, despite myself. Dobbett was a welcome relief to the butterflies I was feeling in my stomach.

Today was Choosing Day, and that meant that today would be my last chance. If I wasn't picked now, then by the time another five years rolled by, Father would probably have married me off to some annoying, terribly fat merchant or nobleman.

Memories of the prince's last Winter Ball flashed through my mind, filling me at once with the most curious mixture of disgust and hopelessness. The prince, and all the royal family, had been there of course, and my older brothers too—Reynalt and Ryan—looking splendid in their dragon scale jerkins.

They managed to do it, I thought. *They got their own*

dragon. My two older brothers were chosen almost as soon as they were old enough to sit on the saddle—even though it is always the dragon itself that does the choosing.

"*As close as egg and mother, is a Flamma to a dragon,*" I mouthed the well-known Torvald saying desperately hoping it would prove true. I wanted to declare: I am Agathea Flamma, or more properly, *Lady* Agathea Flamma. Our household had sired Dragon Riders for the last hundred years, and the rooms of Flamma Hall were filled with the statues, busts and paintings of my great-uncles and grandfathers and great-great grandfathers who rode the mighty drakes into battle in defense of the city and the realm.

My brothers were chosen, why not me? Everyone had expected them to be chosen. No one expected me to be.

I am a girl. They say I am better suited to marrying well, running an estate, raising little Dragon Riders all of my own... "Ugh!" I snorted in disgust, throwing open the patio doors to the balcony of the tower and walking out into the fresh morning air.

The last of the Dragon Horns just finished their mournful cry. I could already hear cries and screams of excitement as the shapes flew out of Mount Hammal, the dragon enclosure far over the mountain from here. They looked so beautiful. Long, sinuous necks, powerful; each one a different colour. Today there are green, blue, black—even a red.

They swooped and soared over the city, skimming over its rooftops and around the many terraces to the cheers and cries of the people below. I saw some people trying to entice the dragons to choose them by waving colourful flags or roasting land-pigs right on their rooftops.

Not for these beasts, however. These great ones were reveling in their freedom: performing barrel rolls and turns in the air, one after another. Then some smell would catch their nose and they followed the scent like a lightning flash to their chosen rider.

No one really knows why or how the great wyrms chose their two riders. Some say it's magic, others say that dragons can read your soul, so they choose the ones that they know they can live and work with the best. You have to have two riders for every dragon though: a navigator and a protector. The navigator is like the pilot and the guide; some say they can almost sense their dragon's emotions. The protector is the one who gets to fire arrows, throw lances and use swords to defend both dragon and the navigator when they are on patrols.

Not that Torvald had gotten into any wars over the last hundred years. The fact that we had the dragons—or should that be the other way around?—meant our enemies rapidly sued for peace. We still have trouble with bandits and cattle rustlers of course—last summer all it took for my brothers to scare them off was one low fly-by. There has always been one threat, however—that of the Darkening returning.

My father swore the old stories were true, but my mother did not like to hear him speak of those tales. I have only heard the old legends once. My father's stories left me with such nightmares—where I dreamed of being claimed by darkness, where I was lost in a deep blackness—that it left me unable to do more than curl into a shivering ball and cry.

I have forgotten most of the old tales, but I still remember the fear they left in my bones. My brothers told me they are just stories to make children behave, but I wonder at times if they are right, for we still have Dragon Riders patrolling against the return of the Darkening.

What would Father think if I was actually chosen to be a rider? I scanned the horizon, searching for the dragons. *Where are they? Have all the riders already been chosen? Is my chance over?* It couldn't be. It just couldn't. I imagined the look on my father's face if he heard the news. He would be delighted, surely, that all his children had been chosen. It would make the Flamma House a force really to be reckoned with.

And I just want to make my father proud of me. I realize this, running to the balcony and turning around, hearing the telltale caw of the giant lizards; not being able to see them yet.

He wants me to get married, another part of my mind kept thinking. *He wants me to 'do the right thing' and bring some respectability to our family.*

"I can't do it," I whisper, shutting my eyes tight against tears threatening to spill over my lashes.

There was a breath of fresh air against my face and my hair lifted. A round of cheers and shouts rose up from the city below. I felt heartbroken. The last dragon must have made its choice—and it wasn't me.

Suddenly, it went dark. I opened my eyes—and almost fainted.

A red wyrm slowly descended to our tower. It was young, its forehead horns barely as big as my hand at the moment, but in fine shape. And a red, too. I knew they were fierce and rare. The wyrm made a twittering noise in the back of its throat. I could see its throat expanding and contracting like a bellows as it raised its wings to catch the thermals and hang in the air. Its eyes were a brilliant green-gold, a colour I had never seen before. It was holding me in its steady gaze. Now I could really understand why everyone thought they had the power to hypnotize.

Its great head with an elongated snout was still, almost calm, as it lowered its claws to grab onto the side of the tower, splintering rock and the wooden windowsill as it did so. Half of its bulk was atop the tower and the other half gently lowered onto the wide, semi-circular balcony beside me.

"Uh...h-hi?" I said, feeling a rush of panic as the beast slipped a forked tongue into the air, tasting its choice. All thought of the correct etiquette went out of my head as I stared into its great, golden-green eyes.

I got the incredible sensation this young beast was smirking at me as it tasted the air again and *huffed* gently into the space above my head. Breath smelling like wood-smoke mixed with something aromatic, like basil or pepper.

"Dear...dear dragon, my name is Agathea Flamma, of the H-House Flamma, and I th-thank you..." I tried to stammer through the traditional greeting that every child in Torvald learned by the time they were ten.

The beast nudged its head forward, slowly inclining it until it was just a foot away from me. I stretched out my hand, feeling a curious heat radiating from its scales. It was so shiny and new. The only other dragons I had seen were the ones that my brothers or the prince rode; they were much older, with scales that had lost some of their luster or become cracked, scratched and broken with time.

Incredibly, and I could hardly breathe, the creature bumped its head against my hand. Despite the heat radiating from its breath, the scales felt cool and smooth to my touch. Not cold, but not blistering hot either. Like a cool lake on a hot summer day.

"I-I," I tried to speak, finding myself unable to gather my thoughts or articulate just what I was feeling. *Me. A Dragon Rider. I'll be one of the very few women riders in the whole service.*

Before I could concentrate my thoughts, there was a buffet of strong air almost knocking me off of my feet and the dragon was in the air. *Am I wrong?* I thought for a moment the dragon must have made a mistake—maybe it had been sensing my older brothers and became confused.

But then the tower dropped away. I was yanked upward with a wail. The dragon had lightly clasped me in its two, warm-and-cool talons and I was being carried through the air like a precious prize, back to Mount Hammal and the dragon enclosure.

Get your copy of **Dragon Trials** at
AvaRichardsonBooks.com

Made in the USA
Lexington, KY
10 January 2019